"A *Circle of Stones* is a tender, intimate, and intriguing novel that reads between the lines of the well-inked Abraham narrative and tells the compelling story of Sarai—matriarch, healer, and teacher.

Betty Turcott has a great gift for being able to imaginatively climb into the skin of biblical women and faithfully reveal their humanity and agency. As a male reader I felt privileged and blessed to be invited into places unknown to me. As a person who carries a prayer stone, I felt a deep kinship with Sarai and her circle."

Rev. Dr. Larry Doyle. Faith United Church, Courtice ON

"This is a wonderful new book from renowned storyteller Betty Radford Turcott. She understands the stages of a woman's life and writes tenderly about love in one's senior years.

The ritual blessings alone are worth pondering. These beautiful and powerful words will affirm your own worth and value as you embrace them and offer them to others."

Rev. Shelley Roberts, Retired.

"Just as she brought biblical women to life in her book, *And She Said,* author Betty Radford Turcott has done it again with Sarai/Sarah whom we follow from her birth to her death. We are drawn into the amazing life of this great leader and healer of women, journeying with her as she gathers her special stones along the way.

Betty is a compelling storyteller and diligent researcher who immediately draws the reader into the book. I couldn't put it down."

Pat Gilmore, Director, Grand River Books, Paris, Ontario

"*The Circle of Stones* is a compelling narrative of the tale Sarah, ancestress of Israel. Betty Radford Turcott descriptively captures Sarah's story from an inquisitive young child to becoming Abraham's devoted and loyal wife, then the loving mother of Isaac, and to her very last breath.

This book beautifully seizes the genuine dynamism and strength of this true biblical matriarch!

Romance, suspense, drama! Biblical familiarity is not a prerequisite. Just immerse yourself and be enthralled by *The Circle of Stones*."

Stacey Tremblay, Child, Youth, Young Family Minister/ Leader

"A *Circle of Stones*, is an in-depth story of one woman's remarkable journey. Vivid descriptions offer an intimate look at the challenges and hardships that Sarah and other women of the Bible faced in a time when they were ignored, abused and discounted.

The commitment and support the women give each other is a testimony of their inner strength and faith, and an inspiration to modern women. Their rituals and ceremonies lift the human spirit and could serve as a model for women of any time to fearlessly celebrate who they are.

The author weaves tender stories between husband and wife, mother and child, and friend to friend, making A Circle of Stones a circle of love.

An uplifting read for any woman or man, and for anyone who has asked, 'What about the women of the Bible? What about their life adventures and their contributions?' I urge you to read this book for a wise and thought provoking view."

Gloria W Nye, Author of the Dragonfly novels.

Cover Design by Erin Samson

Cover Photo by shutterstock.com

Photo of Author by Jim Ellis

Published by
Kentisbeare Press
87 Waverley Rd.,
Bowmanville, O L1C 1L2

ISBN 978-0-9959905-1-7

Other books by Betty Radford Turcott

And She Said

A Circle of Stones

A Matriarch's Life Journey

Betty Radford Turcott

Author's Foreword

The stories of women throughout history have been a lifelong passion of mine. So much of the history of our foremothers has been lost. Some of it suppressed, much of it simply never recorded. It has been said that women were so busy doing, that they had little time for telling.

This is true for the women who are mentioned in the material collected in the writings we call the Bible. As I read the narrative I wondered about the story hidden behind or underneath the words. My imagination filled in that backstory.

This work of fiction is my crafting of one of those untold stories. Each of the stones Sarai/Sarah collects represents a turning point in her life. These events are part of the story recorded in the book of Genesis.

As I pictured the events, new characters entered the story, and their personalities became a part of the narrative. At the back of the book is a list of the main characters in the story, both the people named in scripture and the fictional ones created to flesh out the story.

Also at the back, there are some questions. They can be considered by the reader alone or provide a starting point for group discussion.

A Circle of Stones

A Matriarch's Life Journey

Betty Radford Turcott

Dedicated
In Loving Memory
to my husband

Gary E. Turcott
1935-2020
Married July 5, 1958

A perfect marriage is just
two imperfect people
who refuse to give up
on each other.

Prologue

Sarah made her way up the slope to a grove of tamarisk trees. Stooped with age, her steps were slow and tentative. She raised her eyes to the feathery pink blossoms beckoning their familiar welcome. She breathed in the sweet perfume and her shoulders relaxed as she opened her spirit to familiar calm feelings.

A curving branch hid the opening, and she lifted it to enter the sacred oval. At its centre rested her circle of stones. Precious stones which she had gathered over her lifetime. Hours spent here in meditation and prayer, made this a sacred place for her to come and rest. Her gaze settled on the rough blackened stone, the size of a man's fist. She had taken it from her mother's fire pit many years ago.

She lowered herself to a mossy stump, leaned over and touched the stone. Her thoughts drifted back to the stories of her life her mother told her. The day of her birth when her mother Binah stood on the birthing stones and life began for Sarai. The stories her mother revealed to her remained so sharp they felt more like a memory than a story. The many stories and memories carried her into long-ago times and faraway places.

Days of great joy.

Days of deep sorrow.

Days that shaped her spirit.

All held gently by the spirit of her circle of stones.

She sat on the cool grass and her reminiscence carried her back in time.

The City Of Ur

Chapter One

On a delightful summer evening, as the scent of blossoms and ripening grain filled the air, the house of women was a centre of activity. Called the moon house, it was a sanctuary for the women. A mystical place forbidden to men and boys.

Within its walls they practised the ancient rituals of the grandmothers whose names were lost in the mists of time. Here in seclusion, they spent the days when they were declared unclean because of their issue of blood.

When the moon was dark, most of the women gathered in this room to observe the birth of the tiny silver arc that meant a new moon cycle. Because the moon's rhythm and the bodily rhythms of the women were so connected, the legends and stories were forever joined and celebrated with delight.

In this room's confines, Binah stood on the bricks that formed the birthing stones. Her dark hair hung in damp strings and fell over her face as she squatted in labour. Her once pale blue dress was stained with sweat. The exertion and her tears, blurred her vision as she tried to keep her eyes focused on the sacred fire burning nearby.

From the fire comes my strength. From the fire comes my strength.

"What is she saying?" asked one of the midwives.

"Doesn't matter. It seems to be keeping her calm."

Her baby struggled to be born and the midwives supported Binah, as she strained to push the child out into the world. One on each side, they held her arms in support and gently rubbed her back to ease her pain. They gave her sips of strong camomile tea to sooth her. Anna, the primary midwife, sat on the bricks facing Binah. She was ready to catch the infant and place him on the pillow near her. She had warm water and salt to wash the infant and olive oil to soothe his skin.

The midwives glanced at each other and shook their heads.

"This is taking a long time. Even my back is getting sore."

"We've been here since late morning. It must end soon."

"She is losing her strength and the will to push anymore."

Anna spoke to Binah.

"Every child is a gift and a hope for the future," she crooned. "This infant is the means for our tribe to become a great nation. It is your duty, privilege and responsibility to have sons. You will be respected when this boy is born and bring great honour to the house of Terah. Now take a deep breath and push. Give this son of Terah life."

In the tree lined courtyard, Terah, Binah's husband remained at a respectful distance. With him were his sons, and four of his cronies. The boys sat on a bench, tired and sleepy, but full of curiosity. The men appeared to be unconcerned with the event taking place inside the nearby dwelling. They were talking and laughing in muted voices. But they became silent when a woman's piercing scream tore into the deepening darkness. The wails came with shorter periods of calm between them.

The males of the household were not permitted to be a part of this sacred time, for it continued to be the women who understood its pace and pattern. When it became quiet again, the chatter resumed, only to end at the next heart wrenching cry.

Inside, Binah heard the words of Anna and as the midwives gently wiped her tired body with warm water, she looked at this gentle, wise friend.

"I am strong. Irra the god of birth is with me."

With a great long moan and writhing force, Binah thrust the infant into the world. The women cried with relief that the ordeal was over.

"Well done, Binah."

"Soon you can rest."

"What a strong cry from your s—"

Then silence.

"All that work and it is just a girl."

"But she is strong and healthy."

"Never mind, next time you will have a son. Now rest."

After washing and rubbing the warm oil into the baby's skin Anna wrapped her in a blanket and went outside. The men were huddled near the door and Terah was holding tight to his son Abram's hand.

Anna carried the infant to her father. She opened the blanket, and they learned it was a girl. Terah's face fell. His friends pretended to be pleased, but the celebration was brief and they returned to their homes. Terah and the infant's half-brothers bent over to greet the child and welcome her. Abram was ten, Nahor eight and Haran six. Their mother had died giving birth to Haran. The two younger boys looked at her and nodded, they quickly walked to the house and disappeared into the semi-darkness. Terah reached out and laid his gnarled hand on the baby's head. She rested peacefully in the midwife's arms, her tiny mouth making sucking motions.

"Look father, she is hungry. She has her eyes wide open and is looking at me. I wonder what she is thinking."

Abram moved closer to her and held out a finger. She clutched it in her tiny hand and Abram and Terah smiled. It was a good sign. Her brother accepted her, and she had confirmed their relationship by holding his finger.

"She doesn't want to let go father. I'm glad I have a sister. I already have two brothers. A girl child will be new and interesting."

Anna tucked the blanket around the baby and walked back into the house cradling the mewing infant in her arms.

Once inside, the midwife gave the newborn to her mother and Binah cuddled her as she offered her breast. As she stared at the tiny bundle in her arms her heart overflowed with delight.

I know I should be sad that you are a girl, but I am so happy.

Binah looked at her daughter and gently opened the blanket and touched her perfect hands and toes. She stroked the dark, damp hair and wondered at its softness.

"Sarai. My little princess. How lovely you are. I promise you that I'll teach you well. You will be taught as you should be, according to our laws, but you'll also learn what it took me years of struggle to discover. We women are not cattle. We toil from dawn till dark, are traded and sold like beasts, but we are infinitely more than that. You will learn these truths as you grow into a woman."

She moved the baby to her other breast and stroked her cheek as she nursed.

"The goddesses that our grandmothers and mothers worshipped are still here to listen to our prayers. I'll teach you their names and how to offer our grain, and our bodily essence to them. They will guide you to be the woman that you should become."

The baby flourished, pampered and indulged by her loving mother. She was rarely out of Binah's sight and the doting mother rocked her and sang soothing songs when she was fretful.

As Sarai grew, Binah took delight in every new experience. Her first smile, a tiny white tooth, the first unsteady steps were celebrated with joy. Daily her mother talked to her, encouraging and teaching her, preparing her for her life as the daughter of the great clan leader Terah.

"Sarai, you are curious and adventuresome and that brings me such delight. Keep exploring, wondering and asking questions and you will grow to be a wise woman, a leader among the women."

Just as she said this, Sarai reached up and yanked a stack of dishes onto the floor.

"Not that curious. Now I have to buy more from the potter."

She picked Sarai, up and carried her to her little bed. Sarai grabbed her mother's shawl and pulled it to her. As Binah covered her for her nap, she thought about the future.

"I promise I will work toward an advantageous marriage for you. Your husband must be a special man to appreciate you; wise and thoughtful, kind and gentle, full of laughter and respect. I'll make sure that you know you are his wife, not his slave or concubine. Your skill and knowledge will bring him great honour, and so too the sons you bear."

Bending over, she stroked the soft hair and sang a lullaby to her sleepy child.

Chapter Two

Sarai was six years old and a happy, busy child. She was rarely still. Questions flowed from her in a continuous stream. Whenever she was outdoors, she ran from one interesting object to the next. Every flower, bird, tree, and animal needed to be named. If she found a colourful stone, she carried it with her until her mother insisted she throw it away. She imitated the sounds she heard in nature. One day she trilled like a bird, another buzzed like a bee, or hopped about pretending to be a frog. She begged to be allowed to see the moon each night. As she watched her mother, she copied her actions. She loved to rub sand over the dirty pots enjoying the sound and the feel of the warm soil. Sarai never tired of listening to her mother as she spun and wove, sewed and mended, cooked and cleaned.

On a cloudy day, in mid-afternoon, Sarai was sitting on a log near the river. She saw Binah walking toward her and with her was a tall girl. She was not smiling but looking very gloomy.

“Sarai, this is Eliana. She has come to live with us, and will be your friend. She will help you, teach you, and watch over you. She is not a servant or a slave, but part of our family. Eliana will be a big sister to you, so listen to her and learn from her as you have from me.”

“Hello, Eliana. Where do you live?”

"She lives with us now Sarai. Eliana needs a family, and you and I are going to be her family. Why don't you sit here too Eliana and you can get to know each other."

Eliana was quiet and gentle. Her hair was a soft brown, and her eyes matched them. There were dimples in her cheeks when she smiled and Sarai thought she was beautiful. As the weeks passed Sarai learned that Eliana had interesting games she taught Sarai and they became good friends. Eliana didn't talk much, but Sarai was so talkative she didn't notice.

While cleaning the lamps one morning Sarai spoke to Eliana about school.

"I wish I could go to school. I want to understand the marks they make on the clay. It is a mystery and I want to learn those strange marks that mean something. I want to be taught the secrets of the shapes. Why can't we go to school?"

"I don't know. I've never thought about it. I think you should ask your mother."

But when she asked her mother at their next meal, her father interrupted and said, "It is not for girls."

"You did not say it was forbidden to girls, father. Why can't I go if it is not forbidden?"

"Sarai, I said it is not for you. Don't ask me again. You will bring shame to yourself and to me if you keep on with this. It is finished. Not another word," and Terah walked away. Sarai was wise enough to understand that she should not ask again. But still she wondered why.

The questions never went away, and Sarai asked anyone who might be able to satisfy her curiosity.

Binah and the girls were sitting cross legged in the shade of an oak tree. They were cleaning wool, picking out burs, thorns and bits of bark and clumps of dirt. It was pleasant in the shade and Binah realized that Eliana was humming a tune as she worked. Binah smiled and nodded. Eliana was settling in and relaxing as she began to feel at home. Her mood was broken by Sarai's demanding voice.

"Mother, you said that before long I will be promised to someone in marriage."

"Yes, that will happen before you are much older. You are getting to be a big girl. You are nine years old now. It will be soon."

"But who will it be? One of the silly boys from our neighbour's houses?"

Binah put down her ball of wool and looked at her daughter.

"Why do you say the boys are silly?

"They wrestle, pushing and shoving and yelling. And they are lazy. They don't work as hard as I have to."

"Boys have their chores too, Sarai. But you do work hard and I am proud of you."

Binah straightened up and kneaded her aching back.

"But who will be my husband?"

"I don't know. Finding a husband for you is your father's responsibility. But I make suggestions when I can."

"I wish I could get answers to my questions. No school. Somebody for a husband but don't ask who."

"You have worked long enough. Both of you go and have fun."

Binah thought over the question of school. Usually boys were taught by their fathers, but Terah had no patience as a teacher, and so he traded wool for lessons. The three boys went to Obadiah, a learned man who lived nearby. His long white beard and stringy matted hair, gnarled hands and raspy voice, caused the boys to wonder how he long he had lived. His only answer was 'more rainy seasons than anyone could count'. She knew Abram loved to go and learn from Obadiah, but the other two had to be forced to learn from the wise old man

When Sarai could steal time from her duties, she liked to sit under the window in the room where the boys learned their lessons. She listened as Old Obie, as Abram called him, explained the law to them and taught them the letters that somehow became words. The more she heard, the deeper her longing became.

One morning her mother saw her and realized at once what she was doing.

She grabbed Sarai's hand and led her away.

"You mustn't do this. If Terah catches you, there will be trouble for you and me. I will keep quiet today, but don't you ever let me catch you here again. If I do, I will have to tell Terah, and that would mean great trouble for you."

Sarai cried as she realized her days of listening to the wonderful sounds of the letters and words was over.

As she did her chores and ran errands for her mother, she watched the boys. They never played with the girls and rarely spoke to them. Among the boys, she liked her half-brother Abram the best. Years older than she, he acted grown up. A leader among the boys, Abram often got them organized doing things that helped the village but on some days they created a mischievous prank. Sometimes Sarai thought him devious in the way he worked out his plans, but he did get things done.

"He is handsome," and she smiled. "And much more interesting than the other boys.

I would like it if you could be my husband Abram. Dare I ask mother? Probably not. It would likely get me a scolding or worse if father overheard.

Soon after she had been caught by the window, Abram came to her as she was in the garden weeding the garlic bed. She looked up at him and brushed the dirt from her hands. He sat beside her and gave her a small stick. He had one just the same in his hand. In the dirt he made two marks.

"Now you copy them."

Sarai looked at him in wonder.

"Go on. Try to make them just like mine."

After a few tries he was satisfied that they were done properly, and he smiled.

"But what do they mean?"

"It is your name, Sarai. Those marks mean Sarai. Samech and Resh. You must never tell anyone what I have shown you. And that means Eliana too. Not even she can know. Don't make the marks where anyone will see them. Never leave them in the dirt, always rub them away."

"I promise. Show me more marks and what they mean." Her heart was beating in her chest and a huge smile burst across her face.

"This is enough for now. I will teach you more, but it will not be often.

We can never be caught doing this. No one must ever find out."

"But I want to learn them all. I need to understand what they mean in the writings I see."

She grabbed his sleeve and tugged at it. Abram gently removed her hand.

"This has always been just for men, Sarai. I could be punished for what I have done. I think it is a shame that you want to learn and can't, while Haran just sits and fiddles with his stick when Obie teaches us. He has no interest in learning. When he makes a mess of his marks, we get punished. You should know by now that things are not always fair and you and I can't change that."

He groaned and snapped his writing stick into pieces. Sarai jumped, and he turned to her and looked into her eyes.

"I admire the way you want to learn, and I will help when I can. But we need to be very careful and this must always be our secret."

On a lovely spring morning when she was nine years old, Sarai was ready for her bath. She smelled a wonderful warm scent as the water was poured into a basin. Binah washed her back and rubbed her dry with a soft towel. Then she brushed her daughter's hair until it shone and rippled down her back. Binah left and Sarai turned to Eliana.

"This must be a special day today. I wonder what it might bring. What is going to happen?"

"Your bath water had the aroma of myrtle. Don't you know what that means?"

"No. What?"

"It means love and marriage. Now put this tunic on and hurry."

Sarai stroked the cloth as Eliana dressed her in a robe of soft, flowing, red linen. A matching ribbon tied back her hair, and combs with tiny shells on them added colour. She wiggled her fingers as her mother placed rings, with blue and green stones on her hands, and bracelets encircled her arms and her ankles. The ones on her feet had tiny bells in them and she laughed when they jingled as she walked.

"Why am I dressed up?"

"There is going to be a special dinner. The entire family will be here and the contract will be signed for the marriage of Abram."

Sarai plopped onto a cushion. Her heart plummeted. Abram was getting married. Tears filled her eyes and her breath failed her. Ever since she learned about marriage, she had dreamed she would be Abram's wife. Then remembering that she should be happy for him, she took a deep breath and scrubbed her eyes with her shaking hands.

"If this is a party, I am going to enjoy it."

The family gathered for the evening meal and everyone came, uncles, aunts, grandparents and the extended family. They feasted for hours, telling stories and laughing. Wine and beer flowed generously. There was much arguing back and forth between Terah and Abram. When Sarai asked why they were arguing, her mother explained.

"They are discussing the price that Abram must save before his marriage. It is for his bride as her security. It is meaningless as they are father and son, but it has to be done and so they play at a disagreement."

Sarai looked at him, dressed in a soft brown robe and a bright blue cloak. His beard was trimmed, and he wore rings on his fingers. Tears filled Sarai's eyes as she wondered who the girl could be.

"I don't care who she is, I am going to hate her, forever and ever." She scrubbed her eyes to wipe away the tears, and stuffed her fist in her mouth to silence her sobs.

Late into the evening, pieces of marked leather were exchanged between Terah and Abram and it was settled.

Immediately Sarai became the centre of attention among the women.

"You are so lovely tonight Sarai."

"And she can sew a straight seam every time."

"A bud ready to open."

"The bedding will come soon enough. She is still a child."

Sarai's eyes opened wide. She understood. She was the bride and Abram was her husband. She raced across the room to her mother, grabbed her hands, and spun her around.

"Mother, why didn't you tell me?"

"I thought you realized it. Why else were you bathed in myrtle and dressed up to look like the princess you are?" Binah curled Sarai's long dark hair around her fingers as she spoke.

"Are you tired? We can go home if you want to."

Sarai nodded and took her mother's hand.

They walked outside and the great golden moon smiled on them.

"Even the moon knows how important tonight is. Look how she glows and lights the path."

They walked silently to Binah's home. Inside, Sarai began to get ready for bed. Her mother took the lovely gown off, combed her hair and braided it for the night. Sarai saw Binah put the rings and jewels into a box; then the simple garment in which she slept was pulled over her head."I will tell you what has happened tonight. The marriage contract has been signed between Terah and Abram. This is very important for you."

Sarai lay on her mat, and Binah covered her with a soft blanket. She held Sarai's hand and spoke softly.

"The contract means that Abram must provide three things for you. He must be responsible for clothing, food, and marriage relations and he pledged that he will pay you money if he divorces you. This assures security and protection for you and your rights in the marriage. Your father has done well by you Sarai, but no better than you deserve." Her mother hugged her close and kissed her on both cheeks.

Sarai thought about marriage. Images flooded her mind, and she started to cry and pressed close to her mother.

"Do I have to leave mother? I can't be a wife. I am not ready."

"It is all right Sarai don't be afraid. Marriage can be wonderful and I still have years to prepare you. "

Her mother kissed her goodnight, covered her with a blanket, blew out the lamp and left her alone.

Laying in the dark she remembered the noises she heard in the corner of the room where her mother and father lay. Her mind flew to the images of the animals she had seen rutting, the males mounting the females, the noise and the pumping. It was the way animals got babies. Is that what people did? Is that what marriage meant? She began to whimper and then to weep. Her mother came to her and took her in her arms. While Binah stroked Sarai's hair she murmured soothing words and sang a soft, sweet song. Sarai looked at her mother though her eyes blurred with tears.

"Don't fret so my child. You will not be leaving yet. I will teach you, I will prepare you for what is to come. Don't be afraid. This is what life is. For now, drink this watered wine and go to sleep."

She lay on her mat but thoughts still whirled in her head.

The plan for my life is set. Someday I will have my own home. Eliana will come with me and I'll be happy about that. I am glad I am married to Abram but what will it be like? It won't happen soon. I have to start to bleed first and I hope that is many, many moons away.

She felt warm and uncomfortable. She threw the blanket off and curled up into a ball.

I listen sometimes, and what the older girls say is exciting, but also scary. I will learn from anyone I can. But for now things won't change. I will still have to work hard every day, while the boys play and go to school.

She turned onto her back and looked at the moonbeams making streaks of light across the floor. The tears stopped, her breathing slowed, and her eyes closed in sleep.

Chapter Three

Sarai awoke with a start. She sensed something wet between her legs. She jumped up and saw red stains on the sleeping mat. Her mother had told her this would happen soon for her breasts had started growing and soft hair now covered her private parts.

Sarai stood for a minute grasping the meaning of this. She was a woman. A woman! This change in her body meant that she was now ready for the consummation of her marriage. She remembered that night when she and Abram had been wed. It just four rainy seasons ago, but it seemed like yesterday and it seemed like forever. Terah and Abram signed the legal contract, and she belonged to Abram. Since her life carried on as it had before, it was easy to forget that they were married. At this moment it became real and the importance of this event left her breathless.

She went to find her mother. She stood just outside the tent talking to her friends. Sarai waited for her mother to notice her. When she did Sarai beckoned to her and walked inside the house.

Binah entered a moment later and Sarai ran to her and threw her arms around her. In a timid voice she said, “It happened last night.”

“What happened?”

“I became a woman mother.”

Binah hugged and kissed her and holding her hands, danced her around in a circle. Binah was laughing as she danced and Sarai soon caught her joyous mood and began to giggle along with her mother. As they twirled, their tunics flared around their ankles, a blur of beige and blue.

“Have you used the sheep wool, as I showed you?”

Sarai shook her head.

“Well, you look after that. I will tell the women to prepare the moon house to receive you tonight.”

Sarai fetched the little basket that her mother had given her when she explained how to care for herself at her moon time. She undid the string that tied it shut, and opened the lid. Inside were many balls of clean soft wool. She took a large one and placed it between her legs firmly pressing it into her body.

“When I am wearing this, I won’t be able to skip, or hop, or run. I’ll have to learn to walk slowly and hold it in place. I think I have really left the little girl Sarai behind and am becoming someone new. It will be easier in the moon room, for there, life is gentle and slow and calm.”

Sarai had walked by this house many times, but understood that she could not enter. She often stopped outside and listened. She delighted in the sound of the women’s rippling laughter; and smiled at the singing and the music she heard. The odours drifting on the breeze were a delight to her nose. There was no odour of sheep, or goat, or dirty sour smells, only the pleasant aroma of flowers, the scent of dates and figs and the warm, sweet fragrance of oil lamps.

Sarai was eager to enter this house where only women could gather. What happened inside was a mystery but she knew that her mother eagerly waited for the moon time. The women were also required by law and by custom to live in this space for the duration of their bleeding time. They rejoiced in this stage of their lives, but the law said that they were unclean. That meant that anyone who touched a woman when she was bleeding became unclean.

And so the women kept to themselves in this special place. Sarai had questions about this law and she wanted to understand all the rules. And so she asked Binah.

"Why am I not unclean when I cut my finger? That is my blood too. Why are men never unclean when they bleed?"

"Blood from a wound is not the same as the moon blood women shed. And the law is the law. It is how things are. Do not question the laws Sarai. Now go and wash and fix your hair, then put on a clean tunic."

She kissed Sarai and set off to tell the women to prepare for her daughter's celebration. When everything was ready, they walked hand in hand to the moon hut.

The evening, beginning to grow into the velvet darkness of night, was wonderfully mysterious. The twittering birds were silent, the small animals rested in their burrows, and the first stars peeped through the clouds. Somewhere in the darkness an own hooted from a tree top, and a dog mournfully howled at the moon. As they entered the room Sarai caught her breath.

She sensed the gentle breeze from the windows, covered with airy, lightly woven curtains to ensure the privacy of the women and still let in the fresh, clean air. The golden glow of the lamps flickered and animated the shadows, which were dancing on the walls and the floor and ceiling. Bright fabric hung in soft folds from pegs hammered into the mud walls and carvings of the moon in all her phases, hung around the room. Flowers and green twigs sprouted from jugs on the floor, and mats and brightly woven cushions covered the outer area of the room. The melodious voices of the women sitting around the room permeated her mind with songs of life and of women's stories.

Together they walked to a space where two exquisitely embroidered deep green cushions had been placed. Sarai sat and hugged her knees as she gazed around.

Binah whispered to her. "Here you will learn the answers to your questions."

I wonder who *will teach me. I hope it will be Moriya for she is old and wise and her name means teacher. I know that she is kind and patient. I hope she will tell me why things are as they are. Here each moon time I will learn from her. I will sing woman songs, laugh at their stories and enjoy this time away from work and animals and the rough ways of the men and boys.*

They sat together in this sacred circle of women. Sarai looked forward to the stories of the goddesses of their foremothers and stories of the beginnings of the moon time; to be told and re-told. The song floating on the pleasant air was a wordless one, just sound layered upon sound.

"It is wonderful mother. I've never heard music like it before."

Her mother didn't answer but gently squeezed her hand.

When the singing died away, Binah moved to the centre and called Sarai to come and stand beside her.

"Tonight my daughter Sarai joins us as a woman in this place. Let us welcome her to this new world opening up before her."

She took a slim circle of gold off her finger and gave it to Sarai.

"You will have to wear it on your biggest finger for now and move it as you grow. My mother received this ring when she first had her marriage blood. She gave it to me when I began to bleed. It is yours now and you will wear it until you pass it on to your daughter."

Sarai looked at it with wonder. Smooth and shiny, it gleamed in the light of the fire. She thought of the grandmother she never knew and realized the ring was very old and precious. She promised herself she would take care of it so she could pass it on to her daughter.

The room once again filled with the sounds of the women singing a welcoming song to Sarai and as they sang, Moriya came forward and put a crown of flowers in her hair, red, yellow, blue and white woven together with green leaves. Then she fastened a loop of braided copper wire around her ankle. Sarai had seen these bands on women and she was delighted that she was now part of the great circle and could share in the knowledge and wisdom of the women. Moriya spoke.

"The moon's cycle and a woman's cycle are nearly the same length. The mystery and wonder surrounding the two are special to us. They have endured since the moon made her first journey across the sky, and they carry the ancient beginnings of the legends and sacred stories repeated here. Look at the walls and you will see many moon shapes."

Sarai let her gaze flow around the room. Moons showing every phase hung from leather cords. They were silver crescents, large golden orbs, and half-moons in white or silver.

"The moon in all her phases is important to us and to our cycles of life. Like the moon we change; growing and receding, dark and hidden, or alive and glowing. Here in the company of other women, there is no stigma attached to our bleeding or to childbirth. We celebrate these events that belong to women alone. Here we enjoy a time of quiet reflection on our lives. It is a time to celebrate the things that women cherish. A time to enjoy the songs and stories of the grandmothers of days gone by."

Sarai gazed at the face of Moriya. Her blue eyes sparkled in the flickering light and the curve of her mouth held a smile of welcome. Pink cheeks, plump and round, softened her face, and the tightly bound braids of her ebony hair hung over each shoulder, touching her waist. They swung in rhythm to the words that flowed like a song from her moist lips. Her tunic, tinted a light red, draped softly around her ankles. On her dress were moon shapes and flowers of all colours.

Moriya is so beautiful.

Sarai was so enthralled by everything she saw and heard, she was barely breathing. But she could feel her heart pounding in her chest, beating a rhythm that was both exciting and reassuring. Her fingers were interlaced and her palms were sweaty.

"We honour the goddesses of our history but we worship El Shaddai too, the god of the mountain. We call her the breasted one. Look at the sacred mountain with its twin peaks and know she lives there. She is a god who nurtures us, feeds and supports us and leads us in peaceful ways. We venerate the gentle, healing ways of our foremothers that honoured life more than death. Here we make our burnt offerings of grain and bread and we return drops of blood to the earth as we wait for the new moon."

"The copper anklet you wear is a sign of maturity and it tells everyone that you are a woman ready for marriage. May it always bring you good fortune."

Jessica, the primary healer, came and took Sarai by the hand. They walked to the centre where a basin of water sat on a stool. Jessica swirled the water with her right hand.

"With this water, pure and fresh, I anoint you. You are as clean and pure as the stream where this water once flowed."

The drops fell from Jessica's hand onto her hair, her face and her hands. Sarai's tears joined the flow.

"This crown of flowers represents the gifts of mother earth. Wear it with delight."

The perfume was so heady, Sarai had a moment of dizziness as she drank in the scent.

"In this small bag is soil from our mother earth. Remember to honour her always and treat her with respect and care."

As she accepted the bag, she sensed the cool dampness of the living earth it contained.

"Tell us what you have chosen for your spirit symbol."

Sarai had a small smooth stone from the river in her hand.

"I have chosen a stone as my spirit symbol. I found it in the river, and it is smooth and round, shaped by the water and by time. I too will be shaped by time and by the waters of change. Stones are strong, and important, and they are very old and hold the wisdom of the past. This stone will always remind me of who I am, and who I am still becoming."

Jessica anointed Sarai with warm, sweet smelling oil and then kissed her in blessing. The women in the circle offered a silent welcoming cheer as they raised their hands and fluttered their fingers.

Sarai watched the flutter of all the fingers and it looked like a hundred butterflies. A circle of wings that welcomed her. Her knees felt weak, and she hoped she could sit on her cushion before she fell. She walked to her cushion and dropped onto its softness.

Moriya spoke in her quiet voice, but it carried to everyone in the room.

"It is time now to celebrate with foods that hold deep meaning for us."

As Moriya walked to a small table, Sarai noted three striking bowls on it. They were light brown but were painted in vivid colours. One had a loaf of bread, another, a clump of salt, and the third a vial of oil decorating its sides. And each had moon shapes painted in gold and silver.

"We share bread and salt and honey. Dip the bread in the honey, then into the salt. Bread means life; taste its richness. Savour the salt and honey, bitterness and sweetness."

Sarai tasted the bread, salt and honey and thought about the life that was before her.

She whispered to her mother. "I used to be afraid of my life, but now I feel that I will be okay. This has been a night to remember forever."

As the women left, many gave her a hug or a kiss. She was getting very sleepy. When they were alone, her mother sat beside her on the mat.

"You are my firstborn and my only daughter. Tonight we become sisters under the moon and best friends. But I will always be your mother. This is your first time to stay here. You are expected to share with the others, the work of cooking and cleaning. Enjoy this time, as it is restful and healing. Sleep well my child and come home when you aren't bleeding anymore."

She kissed Sarai, covered her with a soft blanket and blowing out the last lamp, picked up her own small light, and quietly walked out into the night.

As she lay in the near darkness waiting for sleep, she rolled the stone in her hand. Carefully opening the small bag of earth she added her stone. In the morning she planned to make a woven band and to wear this little bag around her neck. When sad or frightened she could touch it and it would help her be strong. Sarai watched where the moon made paths of light from the windows to the floor. Her mind was full of visions and thoughts as she relived the magical evening.

I am a woman. I will be strong and brave, and I will learn to be patient, kind and wise. And soon I will soon go to live with Abram as was pledged so long ago.

Imagining the ceremony, standing under the canopy with Abram, she drifted into a peaceful, restful sleep.

Chapter Four

During the next day, she thought of her night in the moon tent and the words that Moriya had said. Her active mind began to consider the different way that her husband worshipped El Shaddai. She was still thinking about it when Eliana walked to Sarai's fire. "How are you this morning? Feel any different?"

"I feel wonderful. Not really different, just feeling as if I am finding myself and liking who I am becoming."

"But your eyebrows are all scrunched down into your eyes. That usually means something is bothering you."

The water for the barley bubbled in the pot, and Sarai slowly added the grain as she stirred large circles around and around.

"Abram is changing, Eliana. He will have nothing to do with the idols that Terah makes. He is talking to the men and leading them away from the worship of the many gods of Ur and teaching them about the one great god. The one who is the god above all gods, El Shaddai of the fire mountain."

"Won't that mean trouble with the priests?"

"I hope not. Abram does what he believes to be right. He is strong enough to stand up to the priests."

Eliana sat on a stool, and held her chin in her hands as she rested her elbows on her knees.

"I have always been scared of the god who causes the earth to shake and the mountain to spit fire and ash. He is a god to be feared for he demands blood sacrifices. And when we have angered him, fire and ash rain down on us and the earth trembles."

"I have always been afraid of him too. But when I think about the god of the mountain, I liked what Moriya said." Sarai left the fire and sat beside Eliana.

"Moriya spoke of the god of the sacred mountain who is a mother to us. She called El Shaddai the breasted one. She said look at the mountain, it has two peaks. They remind us of the breasts of a woman."

"Are there two gods on the mountain?"

"I don't think so. I think it is one god. The men think of him as a mighty warrior. A god of blind obedience and vengeance. We see the twin peaks and we see the form of a nursing mother. A god who loves and teaches her children. And we call her the breasted one."

"So the mighty one and the breasted one are the same?"

"I think so. Women and men seem to understand and speak of the invisible god differently."

Eliana stood and stirred the pot, swirling the bubbling porridge in circles.

"Moriya said that the breasted one is the god of nurture and support. Wouldn't our lives be more pleasant if everyone worshiped a god of that nature rather than a god of flame and destruction?"

"So true, I think. I am glad I can talk to you Eliana. It was good to hear Moriya say what I have been thinking. I'd like to ask her a thousand questions."

While they worked, they each were deep in thought, and the time passed quickly.

Years went by while Sarai waited for the day she would become Abram's wife in every way. She felt ready to be his wife. There was nothing more she needed to learn.

"I hope it will happen soon. I know he needs to have the bride price, but how long does that take?"

And on a sunny day, when the rainy season ended, the long awaited morning dawned cloudless and fresh; the day she and Abram were to begin to live as wife and husband. She had been awake for a long time and it seemed as if she hadn't slept.

I am so excited. Today will be a day the village will remember forever. The floors of the house have been swept and cleaned. A new yellow curtain has been hung to make a small room in mother's large house for our wedding night. In it a feathery soft bed has been prepared; the room decorated with flowers, shells, candles and wine in the best goblets.

She rose from her mat, rolled it up and put in it the corner. With quick steps she went to bridal room.

Here Abram will come and take me as his wife. And then we go to father's house for a feast that will last for hours. I hope I can stay awake.

She and Abram were to have a modest home not far from her mother and it had been made ready for her. It was located on a rise of land, where cool, gentle breezes blew. The view from the roof was pleasant, especially in the dewy mornings. Sarai was sure that someday they would have an elegant home, for Abram would be a leader in the tribe and even richer than their father. Happy and excited as she was, she felt nervous as well. Her time in the house of women gave her an idea of what was going to happen. The women talked freely of what it meant, how it happened, what to do to please her husband and they told her that she needed to make sure that she was given pleasure too.

She reached around her neck and held her stone in her nervous hands.

"I'm not too sure about that. I can't imagine women telling their husbands such things.

"I know that it is my duty to please my husband in everything. It is frightening to realize that unless he is pleased, I can be divorced and turned out of the house. I don't want to think about it. Abram can say, 'I divorce you' three times, and I will no longer be his wife. I have no such an option."

As she yawned and stretched, she remembered the words she heard in the sacred space. The women said that some men are kind and gentle, other just interested in what they want or need.

"But what about what I want or need? It is so confusing. Maybe when we are married I can figure it all out. Sometimes I wish I could just accept whatever comes. Like Eliana."

"Did I hear my name? You are awake; that's good. We have a lot to do to make you beautiful."

Sarai made a face. Eliana had been with her as long as Sarai could remember. Playmate, friend, confidant, and now as young women they were like sisters, sharing secrets and dreams. Eliana was older than Sarai and assured her there was nothing to fear in marriage. She claimed that Rueben the stable boy was her lover, and they had great fun in the straw in the stable.

"Oh it hurts the first few times, but it gets better, trust me."

"But you aren't even betrothed to him!"

"What difference does that make? We love each other. Now stop talking and get ready for this wonderful day."

As she looked forward to the wedding, Sarai was thinking it had not been long since her first bleeding, and yet here she was preparing for her time to stand under the marriage canopy. Abram had the price agreed to in the contract at the marriage ceremony, and so the finalizing of the marriage could take place. Compared to the agreement, the marriage was uncomplicated. They just went to bed together and were fully married. Tonight she would learn what it meant to be a wife. Abram was ten years older, almost twenty-three. He had been a man for many years and she wondered if he had experienced the secrets of the bedroom. She hoped so, as it might make him more understanding. But she also hoped that this would be the first time for him too, so they could share the wonder of their marriage.

After she bathed and combed her hair, her mother came into the room carrying a garment.

"Here is the gown I have made for you. Let's slip in on and see how you look."

The soft white wool felt like a blanket of love as it slid over Sarai's naked body.

"I saw wool being prepared. It is so much work to make it white. I never imagined it was for me."

"You don't need to remind me that it is tedious, nasty work." Eliana tried to sound grumpy, but failed entirely.

"I spent hours stirring it in the vat of vinegar and urine; then washing it over and over till the stink was gone. Then I spread it on the bushes to dry, and I had to watch it every moment, so it didn't blow away, or worse, be stolen."

"It is so fine and soft, it must have taken days to spin and weave it. And finally to sew the golden thread all around the bottom and the neck and the sleeves. What a lot of work." Sarai threw her arms around her mother. "It is wonderful mother. Thank you."

"Your name means princess, and that is what you are to me. I decided that today you will wear a garment worthy of a princess."

Abram was getting ready as well. As he bathed and combed his hair and beard, he thought of the woman who was his wife, and of tonight when that contract was consummated and they would become lovers. He let her image fill his thoughts.

Eliezar, his servant stood nearby holding his clothes, which he had brushed until they were spotless.

"Have you noticed how tall she is, Eliezar? I can look into her eyes without stooping. I like that. And she is so delicate I can reach my hands around her waist and lift her easily."

"But she is strong Abram. She can carry the water so effortlessly it is almost a game for her."

"And her hair ripples to her waist, and there are bright golden spots in the warm brown curls. Her voice is soft and she never shrieks or yells."

"I am sure she will find a louder voice when she is displeased with you."

"I am moved when I hold her tiny hand in mine and feel her fingers curl around my palm."

"Enough of this nonsense. It is time to leave and go to her. Your friends are getting impatient."

"I am a lucky man and I will do my best to make a good husband to this one named Princess."

Sarai waited in the bridal room for Abram to come to her. She heard them coming, winding their way along the narrow street. Her husband and his friends, laughing, no doubt from the raucous stories they were telling each other. When the brief formalities ended, and the money was exchanged; the crowd was sent outside. Sarai held her breath. The flap to her bedroom opened and Abram came into the room.

She lay in the bed with the thin garment covering her young body. She took a long breathe and beckoned to him. Abram spoke her name in a hushed voice as he crossed the space to the bed. He stripped off his robe and was lying beside her in a moment. He kissed and stroked her, telling her not to be afraid. He caressed her face, outlined her ears, cupped and stroked her breast. She trembled at his touch.

Just as Sarai was drifting into blissful sleep, he jumped up.

"Come Sarai, it is time to go to our father's house for the feast."

Sarai stirred, stretched, yawned and dragged herself out of the memory of their time together. She wanted to bathe but knew that it was impossible. She cleaned herself with a ball of damp lamb's wool, smoothed her lovely white tunic, and covered herself with a blue cloak. They joined the noisy, boisterous procession to walk to Terah's house. The crowd was singing and dancing; some were making jokes and laughing. Virgins carrying lamps and wearing soft, blue tunics, were leading the way while others played pipes and tambourines.

Along the path people stood, wishing them well.

"Good luck to you both."

"May happiness always be a guest in your home."

"Lucky you Abram. She is a beauty."

"May you have many sons."

"And even a daughter," said a woman's tender voice. Sarai recognized Moriya, but couldn't find her in the press of bodies.

The feast was the best that Terah could offer, and even more elaborate than the one on the night of their marriage contract. They dined on roasted quail, and lamb in a mint sauce. A great fish, surrounded by lemon wedges, looked at her from the centre of the table. Fresh bread and honey cakes were in baskets with newly churned golden yellow butter and goat cheese in small wedges. Grapes, melons, dates and figs, spilled out of their baskets onto the table. Wine and beer flowed from the tall jars standing near the table.

Sarai ate little. She picked at the fruit and ate a little bread and cheese. Mostly she looked at her husband and sighed.

"Abram," she whispered. "I'm tired. When can we leave?"

"Soon, little one. Soon."

She just wanted to go to her new home and sleep. At last Abram winked at her and taking her hand led her out of their father's house to their home a few steps away. It surprised her when Abram made it obvious that this evening was just beginning. The sharing again of their bodies in an intimate embrace left Sarai breathless, and she knew for the first time, the hint of the pleasures yet to be discovered. Later as she waited for sleep, held tenderly in Abram's arms, she decided that marriage would be a journey of discovery and happiness. With no fears, only a sense of being loved and cared for, Sarai fell into a deep sleep with Abram breathing rhythmically beside her.

Chapter Five

Abram was still sleeping soundly. Sarai sat up and studied him. Her heart was beating a rapid pulse in her chest and her breath was as soft as a whisper. She stroked his hair, dark brown and curling where it was damp against his temple. His beard was full and surprisingly soft when she gently touched it. Strong bones outlined his cheeks and his chin was firm.

He is so handsome. And I am his wife. We will have strong and fine-looking sons.

She was glad his nose was straight and not too big. She remembered his eyes were brown with tiny gold flecks, and warm and kind. The strong arms were relaxed and his long legs straight and well-muscled. For a moment the temptation to move the light blanket drew her hand to uncover his male parts, but afraid he might awaken, she pulled her hand back.

She got up from the bed and threw on her everyday brown robe. Her white and gold dress lay draped over a stool, where she had dropped it the night before.

"I need to fold this and put it away in my chest. I'll do it later after we eat."

She walked to the water jars with her leather bucket, filled it and went to a secluded spot to wash away the evidence of the night just passed. Sarai thought about her new status as a wife. It was nothing to fear. Abram had been kind and gentle, and she wondered what other surprises marriage held. Drying herself she noticed a strange stone on the ground. She bent and picking it up; turned it over and over.

"I have never seen such a stone. Has my spirit stone sent you to me, and where have you come from?"

Rounded and smooth, it had been shaped by time and the winds and sands of the dry season. As she thought of her spirit symbol, she remembered last night with Abram. Her finger traced the wavy line that swirled on one side of the stone. A line that was the colour of dried blood.

This stone is the white sheet with the blood stains on it in my marriage bed. I will keep it as a reminder of last night. Stones are my spirit symbol and I think this is important. My life is changing and I want to keep alive the memory of important events.

Looking around, no one was watching, so she placed it under a bush and covered it with grass and leaves.

"I will come back and get you later and hide you in my room away from curious eyes."

She went back to the house and Abram was awake and getting his robe on. Her mother called that a meal was ready for them and they were to come when ready.

Abram beckoned, "Come here wife."

It was an unsettling command as she could not guess his mood from the tone of his voice. She approached him and he held out his arms. He drew her close and tenderly kissed her.

"I am sorry if I hurt you, but that is the way it is. As we grow together, your pleasure will be as great as mine, I promise you."

She remembered the words Eliana had said, and the secrets told in the tent of women. She hugged herself with happiness and taking Abram's hand in hers they turned and together walked to her mother's fire. There they squatted near the fire and shared bread, cheese and milk. Today they were going to move their few possessions to their very own house, not far from her mother. There, her life as Abram's wife would begin.

Days before when the location of their home had been determined, Abram and Terah shared a cool drink of goat's milk in the courtyard at Terah's home. Abram and his father began to argue in harsh voices and tempers flared. Sarai stood in the doorway listening to their intense conversation and it upset her.

"I will not be a priest father. I will not lead the people in false worship."

"It is your destiny. You are my first born, and you are expected to follow in my footsteps. It is your duty and your responsibility"

"I will not make wooden and clay idols. I won't sell false hope to our neighbours and friends, not even to innocent strangers. I will be a shepherd, my own boss, and true to what I believe."

Sarai held her breath as Binah joined her, drawn by the shouting.

"You would disobey the rules your grandfather and generations of our ancestors established? Not only defy me but even more shameful, discard the traditions of our people?"

Terah shook his finger at his rebellious son.

Abram stood and towered over his father. "I will not blindly follow a custom when it does not convey truth to me. If you insist on my becoming a priest, I will leave and go to the distant hills, living in caves and hunting for my food. My life is worth nothing to me if I cannot be who I need to be. I will live my life under the rule of El Shaddai and no other."

A leaden silence hung in the air. Sarai went into the house.

Binah's gentle voice broke the spell. "Terah, you have other sons who are more obedient than Abram. They will obey you and follow in your path."

The men turned and noticed Binah for the first time.

"My sons! My sons! Abram has rejected my life. Haran is useless. He is—"

Binah moved to stand beside Terah. "Nahor is a good man. He has been working with you for years in your workshop. He is the natural choice to take over your tasks." She laid her hand on Terah's arm. "Nahor loves to work with his hands. His creations are well made, and he respects the gods and the images the people want. Perhaps birth order is less important than shared values." Binah spoke softly but with sincerity.

Terah glowered at her, then at Abram. He turned as if to speak but spun away, turned his back to his first-born son and his deep groan filled the room. He spat a curse on the floor. "So be it. And the consequences will be on your head, Binah."

Sarai came back into the courtyard, carrying a tray. "Here is wine and a honey cake. Let us sit together and eat and drink as a family."

Terah stopped, frowned and pulled at his beard for a moment, shrugged and then sat on a stool, waiting to be served.

Abram and Sarai had been given sheep and goats, pottery and blankets, and tools to mark their marriage. Her mother had helped Sarai get her home ready. It belonged to Terah but had been empty for two seasons. They swept and cleaned and polished, and Binah gave her the items needed to start her household. Their small house was fitted with carpets, stools, and wooden chests. Sarai had the things she needed to cook meals, clean the house, and do the sewing and mending. Abram's and her sleeping mats lay side by side in an airy pleasant corner of the main room. In the heat of the dry season, they carried their mats to the roof where the breeze from the hills cooled the night air.

The herds were in a valley close to their home. Abram hired men to tend them day and night, but spent many hours out in the valley with the flocks. Sarai began to understand that life might not be what she had dreamed.

She sought out her mother and found her in her herb garden. She knelt beside her and began to pull weeds.

"I am happy mother, I really am, but I can't get used to the smell of Abram's clothes. I brush them, and wash them and hang them to dry in the breeze, but they still stink. And Abram has no interest in adding a room to our house. I would like more space for my treasures."

Binah looked at her only daughter and spoke calmly.

"Sarai, when a woman marries, she is no longer free to decide what happens. A wife is loyal to her husband, through bad or good, poor or rich, sick or well. I've known Abram for most of his life and he is a good man. He is kind, gentle and devoted to you. You will receive the best he has to offer."

"But he won't even talk about things I would like."

"Sarai, be thankful for what you have and don't waste your life pining for what will never be. You are more fortunate than most women. Remember, I only saw Terah once from a distance before he came to my marriage bed. You've known Abram all your life. And remember, I've been his mother too, and I've taught him and helped to shape who he is."

Sarai heard her mother's words and closed her eyes. She sat motionless for a long time. As she thought about what her mother had said, she promised herself she would live by those words each day. Touching Binah's arm, she spoke. "Mother, I will remember and I'll try to be grateful for what I have, and not long for what I do not have."

Chapter Six

As the seasons passed Sarai was heartbroken that each month her body shed its red flow. She continued to go to the moon house, but with a heavy heart.

Why am I not carrying Abram's child? What have I done that the gods closed my womb? How have I offended Innana, the goddess of fertility? I have offered my blood each month, pouring it into the earth as I prayed for a son.

As she reached the doorway to enter the house, she knew. Somehow she just knew.

I do not have an image of her; that must be what has angered her. I can't buy one. Abram would find out. I will make one of cloth, and hide it in my sleeping mat. Surely Innana will understand.

This thought sustained her hope as she entered the moon house with slow, measured steps. The whispered words she heard were sharp needles piercing her soul. The looks of pity were harder to bear than the sneers of disdain.

"Here she is again."

"Barren. No child from her virile husband."

"What has she done to offend the goddess?"

“She is not so high and mighty now. I used to be jealous of her, not anymore.”

“When he takes another wife, I’m first in line.”

This room had been a refuge, now it had become a source of shame and guilt. She wanted to stay away, but that would only cause her more grief, as the women would assume that she was pregnant. To be forced to tell the truth was an ordeal she could not endure and so she suffered her monthly time in the moon room in torment.

The rainy season had ended, and the land was turning brown and dry. As Sarai lay on her mat resting from the heat, she overheard Terah speaking with Abram. They were sitting in the shade of a tree in the courtyard, talking. Sarai could tell they were having a very serious discussion as they raised their voices from time to time. She overheard words: new grazing lands, evil neighbours, El Shaddai demands. These muttered phrases spoke to Sarai of their disgruntlement. Abram called to her to bring refreshments. She prepared fruit, bread, cheese, and wine. They took the food without any acknowledgement she existed.

When Terah left, Abram called her and said he had exciting news.

“I refuse to continue to live in this land where other gods are worshipped. When my brother Harron was buried in his tomb, there were people carrying idols of Nergal, the god of death. Our children see this idol worship and need to know they will grow up understanding that we worship only the god of the mountain,

El Shaddai. These other gods are not to be worshipped by our people."

Sarai muttered under her breath. "Father made a good living from those idols he now rejects."

Abram was pacing up and down the pathway in the courtyard. His face convulsed with disgust, his brown eyes flashing with anger.

"The god of the mountain has told me it is time to move. I have convinced father that our family is in danger of losing our faith if we stay here. And besides, the grass lands around the city are overused and not large enough for all the sheep and goats. I fear there will be conflict and that means danger for us. After much convincing father agrees with me and so, we will be moving."

Surprised, she asked, "Which valley are you moving the flocks to?"

"Sarai, didn't you hear what I said? We are moving to a new land. The mighty one has spoken. We must leave this place of false gods and human sacrifice. We will travel for many weeks, perhaps months. For the next phase of our lives we will be wanderers."

Sarai stood in Abram's path and forced him to stop pacing and look at her.

"Wanderers? Where will we sleep? How will we live?"

"We've purchased some small tents for us to live in as we travel, but we will need to make many more when we settle. On the trail we will sleep on the ground, covered with our cloaks. We will be able to see the stars and the moon, and the wind will sing us to sleep."

At his words her eyes grew wide, her mouth fell open, and there was a roaring sound in her head.

"Leave my home, my family, my friends? I don't want to be torn from everything that I appreciate and love."

Feelings seethed in her gut. Anger. Fear. Resentment. Her stomach churned, and she was sure she was going to spew her morning meal, like the mountain spewed fire. Taking long deep breaths, she managed to whisper, "Where are we going?"

"The way will be revealed to me."

"You mean you don't know where we are going."

"To the lands near the city of Haran, north and west from here."

"Are all the family coming?"

"No. Nahor is staying here. Lot, Haran's son, is coming with us and any who choose to join us are welcome. Your mother has decided to remain in Ur."

"Mother is not coming? We are leaving her behind! No! She must come, I need her. Why does she choose to stay behind alone?"

"Your mother has her reasons. We are leaving Ur very soon, Sarai. Start your preparations and give leadership to the women who will follow their husbands with us to our new lives."

Abram walked outside and sat in the shade of an ancient oak. Word was sent to the men to go to the town square at sunset to listen to a message from their patriarchs.

The day passed in a whirling blur of memories of the past and fantasies of the unknown future. She made a simple meal of bread and cheese. There was no energy to cook and no desire to please Abram.

The men and many women gathered in the central opening. They stood around in small groups, trying to guess the reason they had been summoned. Children stood woodenly near their parents.

"We are leaving Ur; Terah, Lot, me and our families."

The space was filled with the sound of many voices, all speaking at once. Abram held up his hands and waited for the noise to quiet down.

"We no longer wish to live among followers of false gods. As well, we need to seek new pastures for our flocks. It will be a long hard journey, but we are a strong and resilient people. You will have time to consider this, as it will take many days to prepare. No one will be forced to come, that includes servants and slaves. All who desire a new and better life are welcome."

The noise woke the sleeping dogs, and they added their howls to the cacophony.

Gradually the crowd dispersed in small groups. As they walked away, they were still debating what they had just been told.

Sarai found Eliana, and they walked to the river, and Sarai poured out her pain to her friend.

"I don't want to leave Ur. I want to be with mother when the babies come. I want to care for mother when she grows feeble, and I want to grow old and die here. I had always believed I would be buried beside mother and near my grandmothers. But that doesn't matter now. Abram is going and I must go too."

As they reached the river, Sarai picked up a stone and threw it into the water. She watched the circles grow wider and wider until they disappeared.

"Slaves and servants can decide their fate. I've no such choice. It doesn't matter how I suffer, how sad, lonely or afraid I will be. The god of the mountain said, 'Go,' So we must go."

"You won't be alone, Sarai. I am going. Reuben already told me. Lot has asked him to go, and he is eager for a new start. Naturally I am going with him and with you."

The two women sat, arms around each other, each quiet and reflective.

"I understand that I shouldn't be angry or hurt. But I am. It is my duty to obey Abram and follow him without questions. I am afraid. I am afraid because I don't understand and no one will answer my questions. And I am angry because what I need does not matter. I will never see my mother again. There will be no moon house. Even if it is painful for me to go there, it still fills a need deep within me."

A deep, tearing sob escaped from Sarai and she shuddered. Eliana rubbed Sarai's back and whispered, "Shhh, Shhhh, breathe Sarai, breathe."

Sarai took a deep slow breath. "How will we exist without a place to gather and tell stories, and offer sacrifices of blood and bread and grain? What will happen to the young girls as they become women with no place to be celebrated and honoured? How will we teach them the ways of the grandmothers? What will the old ones have to comfort them on their final journey? Why do our traditions mean nothing?"

"Sarai. women are wise and we will find a way to honour our traditions and patterns. You will find a way to help us live in our sacred ways. I know you will."

Many days passed and Sarai's deep anger and the resentment made no difference except to make her unhappy. She went through the motions of her daily chores like one without hope. She was listless and distracted. Her once glossy, black hair hung in greasy, messy braids down her back. Her soiled tunic had not been changed for days.

One day her mother came to her and sitting beside her spoke in her soft yet strong voice. "My dear daughter. I realize you are unhappy because of this need to move, and I understand. I am sad as well. But you are not a child who can pout and stamp her foot and have things change. They have decided and it will happen."

The two women, one still young, the other showing the lines that time had etched in her once flawless skin, sat together on a bench in the courtyard.

"Your attitude is having a harmful influence on the women who are going on this journey. You are the daughter of Terah and the wife of Abram. You are the one the women look to for guidance. You will be the matriarch; the wise woman in this new land and you must live up to the role."

Sarai opened her mouth to speak, but Binah held up her hand.

"The wisdom of the grandmothers will not abandon you. You know their strength and you know their stories. Draw on that. Draw on the wisdom of those who have gone before and be the woman you are called to be. You are wise, strong and brave and you can and you will lead the women into a new land, hopeful and ready for a new life. Consider what I have said my child."

Sarai looked into the dark pools of her mother's eyes. There was only darkness in them. "Mother, why are you staying here in Ur? Why are you not coming with us?"

"I have my reasons and we will talk later. But now I need to rest."

Binah kissed her daughter and left her by herself.

Sarai pondered her mother's words, and she knew that Binah was right. The women were becoming restless, angry and even rebellious.

No point asking why, or remaining resentful we are going. Leading the women is my role, and I have to do it. I didn't know what to expect when I married, but it certainly wasn't this.

She picked up a stick and made the marks in the dirt that spelled her name.

"I don't feel like a princess. I feel like a slave. But I am the wife of the clan leader. I must make Abram proud of me. I dare not make him angry or give him a reason to put me aside for another."

Sarai was talking to the wind as she did so often in times of unrest in her soul. She stood and kicked away the marks she had made. She walked to the communal space where many women had gathered to talk. She did not join them, but walked silently among them, listening to their subdued voices. She heard them name the same things she was feeling: pain, anger, fear, resentment. Dragging her feet, she walked home, oblivious to the golden moon that smiled on her from a velvet sky.

All during the long night, she wrestled with the demons that haunted her dreams. When she awoke, she took her spirit stone from its bag. Turning it over and over in her hand, she hoped to draw courage from its spirit.

“Am I strong? I always thought I was. Am I wise? Even Abram says I am. You have been tumbled about by water and sand, and I am battered by thoughts of change. You have survived and are more beautiful because of your journey. Can I be courageous like you?”

As she stood in the room, she became aware of a stale sour smell. She realized how untidy and grimy she was. “I stink. That is what I smell.” With a shiver she unbraided her hair, and heaving a deep sigh, walked to the river to bathe. When she had cleansed her body and washed her hair, she felt more like a person of importance.

Later, in a clean tunic, she walked to the well to meet the women. “Good morning. Isn’t the sun beautiful and warm? I just realized that this sun and the moon which we cherish will be there in our new land. That is comforting and full of hope, don’t you think?”

Sarai hoped her words sounded true, and that the women would take notice. She cleared her throat and sang a happy song about baking bread and one by one the women joined in. *I can do this, I know I can.*

Sarai smiled because it was true. If she tried to help the women to understand and accept, then surely she would come to a place of peaceful acceptance.

Day by day as Eliana and she worked to get ready for the journey, Eliana talked to Sarai about the changes. She hoped talking might help Sarai find some peace.

"I realize Lot has to come, but I wonder about him. He is a mystery to me. I sense he does not like the city. He seems to prefer the herds to people and is happiest out in fields tending the sheep and the goats. He only comes to the city when Terah or Abram summon him. But then he stays in the worst part of the city, drinking and gambling."

"Yes. Lot appears to have no interest in women or in marriage. He doesn't care that it is expected of him. He doesn't care about our customs or rules most of the time. There are times I envy his rebellious nature and his ability to go his own way. But he is a man, and I am a woman, and I will never have that freedom."

"We need to get more water, Sarai. Let's get the jars and sit by the river for a while."

They sat on a smooth rock and slipped off their sandals to dabble their feet in the refreshing water. Eliana threw a pebble into the river.

"I suppose Lot is coming to stay near Abram. Sometimes I think he is just a shadow of Abram. But he is our best herdsman. He knows when the sheep are ready to lamb, and he can always find an unblemished goat for the sacrifice. He knows the numbers of our herds and chooses their pastures and the time to move them. We can use his knowledge so it makes sense I suppose."

"But why is Melcah his sister staying behind? She would be good company and a friend on this wilderness journey. She says she is staying to look after mother, so I have to be grateful for that. I have so many feelings it is hard to deal with it."

"Like you Sarai, I dread what is ahead of us. The tents are always the women's responsibility. When we settle in whatever foreign land Abram finds, we women will be expected to make more tents and erect them. That means we gather every bit of goat hair and sheep wool we see on the shrubs and bushes, collecting it as we travel. Then we will have to clean it and wash it. If we want to dye the yarn, we pick berries and dig up roots. And we comb and spin the wool into threads.

As she spoke, Eliana mimed the actions. "Next come the endless hours of standing at the huge looms and weaving the threads into long lengths. And at last we sew these cumbersome pieces of heavy cloth into a tent. I am proud of us women and the work we do. We are strong and well muscled, but we will need all the strength and courage we can gather for this trip.

Nodding, Sarai spoke. "I wish this move wasn't necessary. Why must we go? Surely a solution can be found here in Ur, or at least a day or two's journey away."

Eliana replied as truthfully but as kindly as she could.

"Listen, Sarai, this will not help. You are leaving Ur. Get used to that idea and find something to look forward to. You have been convincing the women, and it is time you put aside these unhappy thoughts."

Sarai nodded, but her heart still was not ready to leave Ur and the life she loved. She was contended and happy in her home. The future was looming as a dark and foreboding unknown place, and her moods matched her vision. When she thought about what it meant for the women, her anger rose in her throat like bitter bile.

"For generations the women have lifted the heavy tent poles, stretched the great lengths of fabric to enclose them, and then they break their backs to stretch the roof and the sides taut. We still do that heavy work. Brace the poles, secure the tents with rocks we find and carry to the tent. And yet, we can't speak in the councils or even stand on the edge and listen to the arguments."

Sarai voiced her pain to Eliana and just saying it made Sarai furious, and as she stood, she banged the water jar against the rock in frustration. The clay shattered and Sarai ran to the tent to hide her tears of anger and frustration

As Sarai sat in the sacred moon space for her last moon time in Ur, she drank in the sights, sounds and smells of this place. Wrapped in her emotions, she felt as if she were watching from another space. A gentle hand on her shoulder brought her back to the present. Everyone was gone except Jessica, the principal healer. Jessica sat beside her and put her arm around Sarai's shoulders.

"A long time ago I saw the woman that was being born in the girl you were. Remember how I took you aside, and we sat by the river?"

"I remember. You told me that I was a strong and wise girl who could become a healer. I was thrilled when you offered to teach me and I loved the time you spent with me."

"It was a delight for me to see how eagerly you learned, how many, many questions you asked. And they were good questions, always leading you to understand more."

"But now that is going to end."

"In every ending, there is a beginning Sarai. You are ready to be named and set apart as a healer. It is time for the ceremony that will tell everyone that you are a healer. I can teach you nothing more."

“Am I really ready, Jessica? There is so much I don’t understand.”

“No one ever understands completely. Stay open; be ready to learn from anyone you can. But you are ready to take your place as the leader of the women in your new land. Focus on this new life and the opportunity it brings.”

They stood and Sarai looked deeply into Jessica’s warm brown eyes.

“In two days, we will gather here for the ceremony. Bath carefully, put on clean clothing and come at the setting of the sun. I will see you at our ceremony.”

Sarai looked around the room again and knew in her very soul that this was her new beginning. Her grief and anger had drained away like water from a pitcher. In its place was the hope for her new life. She touched her spirit stone and, smiling a genuine smile, left the room and walked to her home.

“At last, I think I am at peace. Only good dreams tonight

Chapter Seven

The day dawned with a sunrise that set the sky ablaze with red and orange flames. The mountain was quiet, El Shaddai, was pleased and Sarai took courage from that blessing. She opened her spirit bag and took out the stone. In her hand it was smooth and warm, reminding her of her strength and wisdom. Reverently she put the stone back in its bag and slipped the soft leather cord around her neck.

She did her chores that day and tried to keep her mind on the task of getting ready for the ceremony. The total change in her life did not seem so much of a burden now, and she was grateful to Jessica who had helped to heal her wounded spirit.

Eliana shared the simple evening meal with her and as they cleaned away the dishes, Sarai asked her to help her bathe and get ready. She chose a very pale sand coloured tunic and wore no jewelry except the copper ankle bracelet and the gold ring. Her hair fell to her waist, loose and free, held from her face by two shell combs.

Just as the sun slipped behind the hill and the sky turned pink and gold, Sarai walked to the moon house.

The room was crowded with the many women who had come to share in this extraordinary ceremony. They were singing a song of welcome and praise as Sarai entered. Gradually the song died away until only Jessica was singing a blessing for Sarai. Her voice faded into the mysterious shadows of twilight, and Sarai walked to the centre to the sacred fire.

Flame bearers walked around the room and lit lamps on the walls and the floor. The soft shadows began to dance in a mystical display, giving life to the space.

"During this sacred ceremony, I ask each of you to hold Sarai gently in your thoughts." Jessica's voice, soft yet vibrant, reached every corner of the room.

There was a time of soft, rustling sounds as the women settled comfortably on their mats and cushions. When they became still, the silence was broken only by the gentle wind that made the trees whisper and sing.

"Sarai, go to the basin and wash your hands as a symbol of your purification. When ready, come to me for the anointing."

Sarai dipped her hands in the cool water. It was scented with myrrh and cedar. She inhaled the perfume and felt its healing power course through her body. She moved in a dream like state to stand before Jessica.

"We are here to name Sarai a healer and to give her the symbols of her new status among us. You have studied well, and I know that you are wise and skillful. It is my honour and pleasure to pass this necklace on to you. It was given to me by my teacher, and I now hand it on to you. Wear it in pride and in humility. Keep it safe, and in time pass it on."

Jessica placed a necklace, made of rare white leather on Sarai's shoulders. Hanging from it, was an irregularly shaped stone, clear as pure water and held in a wire cage made of copper as fine as goat's hair.

"The necklace is too precious to be worn all the time, so this bracelet, with a smaller stone, is to be worn every day on your wrist. It tells everyone you are a healer."

As the bracelet was tied to Sarai's wrist, the women raised their hands and fluttered them in a silent salute and blessing.

Sarai was given a piece of bread and a sip of wine, and Jessica anointed her with oil and tucked a sprig of mint into her hair.

"You wear the badge of your work, and I anoint you with fragrant oil. You are now set apart for the task of healing hurts and sickness. Remember you are a daughter of El Shaddai and turn to her often for strength and wisdom."

Jessica placed her hand on Sarai's head and prayed.

"Blessed is El Shaddai
who brings grain from the earth for bread.
Blessed is El Shaddai
who creates the fruit of the vine for wine.
Blessed is El Shaddai
who causes healing herbs to grow
and flower and seed for medicines.
Bread and wine and healing herbs.
Gifts from El Shaddai.
Thanks be to the mother
god who lives on the holy mountain."

Once again hands fluttered in blessing and praise.

"What is your spirit symbol and what does it mean to you?"

"I have chosen a stone for my spirit symbol. Stones are old and wise. They are strong and important. This river stone has been shaped by water and by time. I hope to grow in wisdom and stand strong when faced with difficult choices. I too am shaped by the passage of time and by events, and I will learn to accept and even to appreciate change and growth."

The sound of the bird's wings as they settled for the night was echoed in the flutter of the hands of the women of Ur.

"And now it is time to enjoy bread and wine and honey cakes and to greet and welcome the new healer in our midst."

The celebration continued long into the night. They sang their songs of work, and hope, and healing. They danced in joy and happiness, threading and weaving around the sacred fire in the centre. The old and wise women sat on their cushions and re-told the stories of times past. As they tired the women left to go to their homes, greeting Sarai as they left. At the end, only Sarai, Binah and Jessica remained.

Jessica explained, "Tonight you sleep here alone, to consider your future. Think of the pain and sorrows you will carry, but also the joys and blessings. Sleep well, for your new life begins with the dawn."

Jessica held Sarai's hand in a warm, strong grasp. She kissed Sarai on both cheeks, nodded at Binah and left the room.

Binah came and she and Sarai sat on cushions near the fire.

"I am so proud of you Sarai. I always called you princess, as your name says. But you are much more than a pretty woman. You are strong, and wise, kind and gentle, smart and aware. Trust in the gods Sarai, follow the ways of the grandmothers. Trust

Abram, for he is your husband, and he is a good man. But trust yourself as well, for you know what is needed for your well-being and for the good of the women of the tribe. If the women are at peace, the tribe will be at peace. The future beckons. Take it in your open hands and dwell in harmony."

They looked deeply into each other's tear-filled eyes and smiled. Binah kissed her only daughter, then laid a hand on her in blessing. She walked serenely out into the night.

Sarai sat on the cushion deep in thought. A night bird called from the sky and Sarai decided to try to sleep. She walked to her mat lay on her back looking at the sky through the windows. She was at peace. Gone were the feelings of anger, confusion and fear.

"I am a healer, and I promise that like my stone, I will be strong, and wise, and I will honour our past, and remember the women who have helped me to grow."

Sleep came gently as Sarai looked around the room and thought about tomorrow and the future.

Chapter Eight

The sound of an orchestra of singing birds woke Sarai. Grabbing her clothes, she dressed and strolled outside into the courtyard to watch the sunrise. She sat, arms wrapped around her knees, embracing the radiant colours of the morning, and remembering the ceremony of the night before. On her wrist was the badge of her profession and as she twirled it, the light reflected from the stone in a brilliant rainbow of colour.

"I won't watch many more sunrises here in Ur. What will I do on my last few days? In the mornings I'll finish the packing and getting ready to move. In the afternoons, I'll visit friends and say my goodbyes. That will be difficult."

She went back to her house to wait for Eliana to begin the task ahead. She ate bread, and olives, and drank cool goat's milk.

Eliana appeared in the doorway and greeted Sarai with a warm hug.

"Where do we start?" asked Eliana

"Where we left off yesterday. Let's take the piles we are going to give away and put them in the main courtyard. Then we will take the junk to the central fire, and burn what we can."

"Reuben will come by later to bury the rest."

"Thank him for me, please. I hardly ever see him. Are you sure he has the time? He will be helping Lot, and you must need to sort your things too."

"It is fine Sarai. Reuben and I have little and we were finished sorting and packing days ago. You carry that pile and I'll take the other one."

The morning passed quickly and soon it was time for the break that came at the heat of the day. They walked to their favourite place by the river and Sarai gasped in surprise.

"You've planned a party. Oh, what a lovely idea Eliana."

She looked at the women gathered there. Her friends, many since childhood, smiled broadly as they enjoyed Sarai's response. They had a table covered with food and drink and another with its contents hidden under a white cloth. They shared the food, and the conversation was warm and genuine, as it is with good friends.

As the sun passed the highest point in its journey, Milcah stood and waited for quiet.

"We talked about gifts for you Sarai, but realize that you have little space to carry a lot of things. And so together we have just two gifts for you."

She lifted the white cloth from the table.

Sarai gasped and her eyes filled with tears. On the table was a white bowl decorated with the moon in all her phases floating around the rim of the bowl. The inside of the bowl had been painted azure blue, and Sarai couldn't decide if it was the sky or the sea. Beside it stood a white pitcher and painted on it was the holy mountain with its twin peaks.

Jessica spoke. "We know that you will need these for the future when there is a woman's space and you gather together for the moon times. Whenever you use them, remember your friends from the ancient city of Ur."

"It is time for us to go to our homes, and I suggest that we form a circle and Sarai can go around the circle and say goodbye to each of us."

Milcah moved to one side, and the women formed a circle from that point, with Sarai in the centre.

One by one, she hugged each of her friends and they said their fond goodbyes. Sarai wiped her tears and saw the there was only Milcah, Bilah and Jessica left.

"I have prepared a simple ceremony for us if you would like it." The melodious voice of Jessica invited them to share in a special farewell.

She pointed to a bench and indicated Sarai should sit. The other three gathered around her and each woman placed a hand on Sarai's head.

"Go in peace Sarai. Go with the love and blessing of the three of us." Sarai thought her heart might burst as she listened to the much loved sound of Jessica's voice.

"Never have I had such a pupil. It was a joy to watch you learn and grow. Those who will feel your healing touch are most fortunate. Go in good health to heal others." Jessica's voice had the same gentle power it always did.

Milcah's voice was strong and warm, with just a hint of tears. "I will miss you Sarai, but be assured that I will care for your mother with the same love that you would. Go in peace."

Bilah, stood beside her daughter. She had thought carefully about what she was going to say, but her throat closed in grief.

"I love you, daughter. Go with my blessing."

The women held each other close, and parted with one last hug. The ones staying in Ur walked back to their homes. Sarai sat for a long time holding these precious moments close. Then she picked up her gifts, wrapped them in the white cloth and walked home.

After she ate the evening meal, she tidied her house and wrapping a shawl around her shoulders, climbed the steps to the roof. The sun was a huge orange ball, sitting on the mountain top, reluctant to end the day.

Sarai looked south over the forest which stretched between the city wall and the harbour. The sailing ships from a faraway world, rocked in the harbour, creaking and groaning at the ropes that tethered them to the dock.

She breathed deeply and revelled in the scent of the sea and the aromatic cedar trees.

"Someday I'd like to go to distant places and see the world. But I don't suppose that will ever happen. My world is Abram's world."

Turning to her right, warm flush spread in her belly as she scanned the city. Many houses were in darkness, but here and there a candle still glimmered from a roof top. The moon shed enough light for her to make out the crooked streets, meandering up and down the little hills. At the centre a large dark square looked ominous.

"Nothing to fear in that darkness. It is the market place, quiet and at rest tonight. In the morning it will come to life and I will take a final walk through its wonders."

She jumped as the hoot of an owl in a nearby tree startled her. She sat on a stool near the edge of the roof and tried to imagine her world for the next few months. No matter how hard she tried, she could only envision what she had known all her life.

"I have questions, many, many questions. No answers. Time alone with bring me what I want to know. But good or bad, in a day or two my new life begins. Enough talking to that wise old owl. Even he can't settle my uncertainties. Time to sleep, maybe to dream of the future."

Sarai turned in a complete circle, arms stretched wide to try and hold it all. She breathed deeply and let her mind and her heart drink in her beloved home.

"I will never forget, but I want to remember everything in its enchantment and delight. The smell of the sea, the whisper of the pines, the hum of the market, even the noises of the night."

She pulled her shawl tightly around her, against the chill of the night and with measured steps descended the stairs to the main living area.

At her bedside, she folded her hands, looked at her home and prayed.

"For the joy of this home, for the mystery of this world, for my family, friends and for Abram, I am grateful. El Shaddai, accept my thanks and gratitude. Remember me even when I am far away from your holy mountain. Do not forget me, and hear again my plea for a son. Perhaps a new land with be filled with new possibilities."

She reached under her mat, and freed the small rag idol from its hiding place under her bed, and holding her tightly, lay down to a peaceful sleep.

The morning dawned; warm and still, promising a hot day. Sarai could sense the heat, and the sun was just peeking over the mountain. She prepared gruel and fruit and was ready to eat, when Abram arrived at her fire.

"May I eat with you, this morning?"

Sarai grinned at him and gave him a bowl and spoon. Together they sat by the small fire and ate their meal. They were silent, but the lack of words did not stop their eyes from carrying their desires. The meal finished, Sarai stood, and so did Abram.

"I need you Sarai."

He cupped a breast with one hand and ran his thumb across her lips. His eyes held hers and she looked deeply into his. They turned and walked back into their home.

The sun, a golden globe of light, rode high in the sky. Its rays bathed the streets in molten gold, and heat waves shimmered from the polished stones of the temples. Sarai walked out of the courtyard and into the street with Abram.

"What are you doing today, Abram?"

"Once more I am going to check the plans for our march toward our new home. I have gone over it many times, but I need to have its lines burned into my memory. And you?"

"I am going to take a last walk around the market and say my goodbyes to the merchants."

"Don't buy anything. You will have to find a way to carry it if you do."

"I'll be careful. If I take no coins, I can buy nothing."

They smiled warmly at each other and turned to follow the street—Abram to the house of Lot and Sarai to the market.

Eliana joined her and hand in hand they entered the maze of little lanes, short streets and the jumble of shops.

"Eliana, don't you love the way the flags, red, blue, yellow, green and purple look as if they are waving a welcome to us."

The brightly coloured canvas safeguarding the goods had been rolled back and tied to the roof of each stall.

"I like the flags, but the smell of the market sometimes is just too overpowering."

"I find it exciting. Floating in the air, is the aroma of plants and flowers, earthy smells—the rich soil of the farms and fields. Perfumes and oils from everywhere tickle my nose and my imagination. Spices and cheese make my tummy gurgle.

"But the meat hanging there on hooks. It makes my stomach turn."

"Oh, Eliana. Just enjoy the sights and sounds, smells and odours. The market is such a place of life, I will miss it terribly."

As they walked, Sarai tried to notice everything. She wanted so much to remember.

At a crossroads, Eliana left to buy a drink and Sarai stood and took in the scene

At this corner a small altar to one of the gods had been built. Someone had placed flowers around the base, and oil had recently been poured over the stones.

How many people have stood here and prayed? I fully don't understand it, but surely the devotion of the faithful has meaning and brings hope to those who believe.

The noise of many voices caught her attention. At the next corner a group had gathered. They were arguing about something. As she drew closer, she saw men huddled in a group, waving fists, pointing fingers, and making important faces.

I know it is politics, religion, weather or the prices at the stalls. How father loved to come here and argue with friends and strangers. What will we do without a market?

She continued to stroll among the stalls, speaking with the merchants she knew, nodding and smiling and saying no to temptations that called to her to buy. As she walked along a narrow path, the grass tramped into brown dust by many feet, she heard her name.

"Sarai."

"Eli, good morning. I'm taking a last walk around the market."

"Wc will miss you Sarai, your smile and your friendly words."

"And I will miss you too, Eli."

"You have never bought an idol from me, and I understand that. You and Abram don't believe in the many gods that the people worship. I have watched you these many years, Sarai, and now I see a woman, charming and beautiful. I'm an old man, and I understand much. I have a small gift for you. Please don't be offended."

"How could I be offended at a gift? But you don't need to give me a gift."

"I know that you do not yet have a child, and I'm sure your arms long to hold a wee one. I have wrapped in this fine piece of linen a small carving of the goddess Innana. Please accept her and with her, my prayer that a child will be born to you soon."

He reached under his table and drew out a small package which he handed to her.

"It is carved from the best ivory and the work is well done. Take her and may she bring you joy."

Sarai could not refuse. She took the package and tucked it into her sleeve.

"Thank you Eli, for the goddess and for your kindness. May you live in peace in this time of growing older."

She bowed to the white haired old man, and he returned her bow.

The market lost its fascination. Sarai walked back the way she came and entered her room. She sat on a stool and held the gift gently in her hand.

Dare I keep it? Where can I hide her? I will keep her tucked away in my wicker basket of clothes. Abram never goes there. I don't worship this goddess, but if she hears my prayers to El Shaddai, that is no fault of mine. And I kept my promise. I didn't buy anything.

She buried the bundle at the bottom of her basket, wrapped in a scarf that she seldom wore. The other clothes were placed on top, and Sarai closed the lid with a sigh.

She was going to have the evening meal with Abram and Lot and got ready to go to the central room of the house. Eliezar and Eliana had prepared the meal, and they sat together, to share the food.

As the stars peeked out of their blanket of sleep, she and Abram sat in the courtyard.

"Abram, how are you going to get the animals and people organized for us to leave?"

"I have been planning it with Lot and a few of the elders. It is all set out."

Sarai sat closer to Abram and enjoyed the warmth of his body next to hers.

"Reuben and Lot have been training strong, young men to use spears and bows and arrows. They will march at the front and at the back and keep watch. Others, who can run fast will act as scouts and find the best path for us, and look out for dangers."

"Will they carry weapons?

"Yes. But most will be hidden in the ox carts that carry our heavy goods. They will be scattered throughout the long line of travellers. Every man will be expected to defend us, if there is trouble."

"Where will the women be?"

"The animals, women and children will travel in the centre of the line. They will be surrounded and protected by carts and by the men."

Sarai shifted around so that she could see Abram's face as he explained.

"There will be donkey carts, to carry food and water, and our possessions. At the very back will be a pair of oxen and fastened to their yoke will be the tent poles. The small ends will be tied to the yoke and the strong bigger ends will ride on a leather dish, dragging on the ground."

She leaned into his strength, and was assured that everything was in good hands, Abram's hands.

"Look the golden arc of the moon, Sarai. It is time to rest. Tomorrow will be busy again."

Arm in arm, they moved indoors and settled on their beds for the night.

The Journey

Chapter Nine

The day to leave arrived. There was no turning back. Sarai knew the move would change everything. It was difficult to tell how she was feeling. There was excitement and hope but there was also regret and fear. She arose at dawn and prepared the last meal in this place that had been home for so many years. Then she stood by her doorway with Eliana, who was frowning.

"This will be chaos. How will we get in line in order to move? People will just be milling about and what about all the animals?"

"Abram has it all planned, and he has made charts and maps to show how we are to line up. Lot knows and so do the head herdsmen and shepherds. Abram can do this, trust him Eliana."

Sarai watched the sky turn pink and gold as she worked. Taking in every tree and bush, house and garden, she burned the images into her mind, spirit and heart. She would always remember, but needed to drink in this picture to carry the memory in the dry and barren days ahead.

Abram came and stood beside her. They spoke little, for there was nothing left to be said. Many evenings they had talked long into the night sharing regrets, hopes and questions.

As they watched, people who were staying in Ur came to greet Sarai and Abram. They came to say good-by and to bring gifts of wine, beer, figs, grapes, and grain. Some presented oils and herbs for cooking and for healing. Others brought a gift of salt, spices or olives. Abram had left one cart empty and this generous sharing of love was packed into it.

While Eliana cleared away the breakfast remains and covered the fire with sand, Sarai went for the last time to her mother's house. Binah sat on a stool waiting for her. When she noticed Sarai, she stood tall and rigid; her face a mask. Her eyes were deep, dark pools and her lips a thin hard line. Only laboured breathing and the tears gathering in her eyes, gave a hint to the depth of her feelings. As Sarai looked at her mother, she felt great love for this woman, who appeared as if any movement would cause her to shatter. When Sarai came close, they embraced and wept. There were no words. Binah stroked her daughter's hair, and Sarai gazed into her mother's eyes, seeing the pain. Sarai did not know how she could leave her. She had to know why her mother was not coming on the journey with Terah and her.

"Mother, please, please tell me why you are staying here in Ur?"

Her voice breaking, Binah spoke.

"I cannot go and nothing will change my mind. Your place is with Abram. My place is here. Go with no regrets. Our love and memories will sustain us. Sarai, I have not been well for many moons. I know that I have dropsy and there is no cure, only humiliation as my abilities decline. I won't be a worry or a burden to you on the journey. I will stay here and Melcha will care for me. You know that if I went, the responsibility would be on your shoulders and yours alone."

Trembling with emotion, Binah sat on the bench at her door, and Sarai dropped down beside her. "Terah really cares little about me and my problems. Ever since my sons were born, he spends little time or attention on me. He will not care and I will not grieve that he is gone. Do not worry about me. Do not waste time or energy wondering about me; just remember me as I am now; your loving mother and still able to look after myself. You will have enough to fret about, you won't need me adding to your worries. Look after yourself and your good and fine husband. Think of your new life and your role as the leader of the women. You are wise and strong, and I raised you to think for yourself. Now it is time to think of yourself as you begin this great journey."

Breathing deeply, at last Sarai spoke. "I will not argue mother, for you taught me that regret or anger will not change anything. And you can make your own decisions. I will grieve for you and my heart will ache with your absence. But I will endure, if only to honour all that you have taught me."

They stood, holding each other for a long time until Sarai broke the heavy silence.

"Mother, I have a request. I would like to take one stone from your cooking fire. I know I will never forget you, but a stone will remind me of you and everything you taught me and your great love for me. Every time I am working or sitting by my fire I will feel you with me."

Binah's eyes widened in surprise. "Come." She picked up a container of water and they moved to the fire. Sarai looked at the stones and pointed to one. Binah poured water to cool it, picked the stone up and cleaned it on the sand and the grass near the fire. Handing it to Sarai, she hugged and kissed her, and once more stroked her hair. Then she turned and ran into her house sobbing. Tears streaming down her cheeks, Sarai stood and looked for the last time at the place where she had been born, had grown up, married and lived all of her life.

Filled with emotion she spoke to the empty space.

"Here at mother's side I first walked and talked. By that tree I realized Abram was a possible husband, and at Terah's house I watched him become a man. In mother's home in the bridal room we discovered the joy that could be had in each other's body. Over there, at the house of women, I heard the secrets of a woman's body and learned that the bleeding was a wonderful part of being a woman. And in that sacred space, each moon I grieved when my womb shed its red flood and each time I cried as my heart broke."

Faintly she heard her name, and she was back in the present. Hiding her stone in her sleeve and wiping her tear-stained face she turned and walked to the cart that carried her belongings. She tucked the stone under a bundle and with a heavy heart, steeled herself to take the first step to a new life.

Abram came and held her close. "Are you all right?" He lifted her chin and looked into her eyes. Her face was streaked with tears. He gently wiped the tears away.

"I know that this is hard, dear wife, but when the Holy One speaks, we must listen. This place is no longer a good place to live. The children are being led away from God and are learning to revere idols of false gods. In the new land we will teach them again the greatness of El Shaddai. You are now a grown woman, wise and experienced, and you shall be the one that leads the women. In our new home you will take your rightful place as the matriarch. Father can no longer lead, your mother remains here in Ur, and Terah's children, you and I, will be the authority in Canaan. I am counting on you Sarai to be my helper and advisor. There is much that I can learn from you and together we will build a great nation."

He hugged her close for a minute then turned and walked forward to get the caravan started.

Sarai thought about what he had said, and it was true. She walked to where Eliana was standing.

"All this is beginning to make sense, Eliana. Terah is no longer a good example for the people. He spends too much time with his wine flask, and drinks until he falls asleep where ever he sits. He no longer works making the idols, partly because he no longer approves, but mostly because his eyes are dim and his hands shake. Abram is the true leader of this clan and as his wife, I have stature and standing."

Together they tied the canvas over Sarai's cart.

"He has asked me to be his companion in this difficult task and I will do it. I will think about what the clan needs, what will be helpful, especially for the women and the children, and will share my ideas with Abram as he asks, and even when he doesn't. What an amazing thing! My husband recognizing that I have wisdom and experience and my words are of value. I will hold my head high and live up to my name, Sarai, princess."

"That sounds a lot more like the voice of a wise woman."

Noise was all around them. People calling out goodbye and safe journey. Animals stamping their feet and bleating. Wagons straining to move, creaking and groaning under their heavy loads. The sound of whips cracking over the heads of the donkeys pierced the air like sharp needles.

With no fanfare, no announcement, no speeches, the great line of the tribe of Terah groaned into motion. When they started, on that first morning, Terah, wearing a bright red cloak, was at the front of the long caravan. He carried a great staff, much taller than he was. It was the staff of a chief, a warrior, and the symbol of leadership. He swaggered and strutted and with a great sweep of his arm signalled the march was to begin. Waving the staff, he took the first steps on their journey.

"What a phoney," said Sarai. "He couldn't lead a thirsty donkey to water. He can never lead us to better pastures. Terah can hardly find his tent some days, how will he find water and food and the way to our new home?"

"Don't trouble yourself. Everyone knows Abram is our leader. Terah is all bluff and bluster. Before our sandals get dirty, he will be in a wagon drinking beer."

"You are right, Eliana. I will not let him make me unhappy. Look ahead of us, this trail is intriguing. See how it twists between the hills. It disappears into the valley and appears again on the next hill. It is as if it was beckoning us to follow."

"Yes, Sarai there are interesting things to see. Look at those distant hills, what wonderful colours. They are green and grey and blue all at the same time. Notice how the clouds make shadows on the grass in the meadow ahead of us and with the breeze the long grass seems to be dancing. The picture changes every moment," encouraged Eliana.

"It is beautiful." answered Sarai. "I like to watch our caravan too. Away ahead are the archers, so small I can hardly see them, but I know they are there. I can't see Abram but he is there somewhere and I trust him and his God. I have to. I have to."

She spoke firmly, but there was a catch in her voice. Eliana heard it, and said, "What can we sing? That will help to pass the time."

She ran to Sarai's cart and grabbed their tambourines. Shaking them and laughing she ran back to Sarai. Together they danced to the music of the tambourines, the steady plodding beat of the animal's hooves, and the grumble of the wagon wheels in the dirt.

When tired of the dance, Sarai ran toward the front of the long procession where she could spot Abram walking with the archers, and pride washed over her. He was the leader, the chief of this huge band. She felt a moment of happiness for he looked regal as he walked; striding on his strong legs, arms swinging and his eyes always on the horizon. He was not carrying his staff; his presence signified he was the leader. A staff was not necessary to validate his place at the head of this great company of nomads.

She stood still until Eliana caught up and the two friends walked along and talked about many things, remembering the good times at Ur.

Immediately over a small rise Abram was standing by the path. He was greeting everyone as they went by. A cheery word, a smile and a nod, a bit of teasing for one of the young men and a quick hug and kiss for Sarai. She realized he planned to stay there and talk to each group as they filed past him. He would have to run to catch up, but he could do that and not even be out of breath, he was so strong and virile.

"Now that is a leader," said Eliana.

Sarai smiled.

Moment by moment step by step, hour by hour, she walked. In the morning coolness and the evening shadows, she walked. In the swirling dust and the blistering heat she walked. As she put one foot in front of the other each step was taking her away from her home and moving her toward a new life

Many hours and many hills and valleys later, they stopped for the night. Near a clump of bushes they made a large circle in the flat area at the bottom of a ring of hills. Fires soon burned, and the women were getting the food ready, calling to each other as they worked. A hearty meal was prepared for they had not eaten since their early morning meal. This would be the pattern for the duration of their journey.

The men carried water from a stream. Abram had commanded it and the men grumbled about doing women's work.

Abram said, "Carry water or cook lentils," and the men understood he meant it, so they carried water. Once again Sarai's heart swelled with love and pride. When she had talked to him concerning the place of women; that they were just a little more important than the cattle and how that felt to her and to all the women, he must have been listening.

Sarah spoke to Eliana, "If only water wasn't so precious I would take this bucket and pour it all over my head. I would love to feel the water run down my body and drip off the end of my nose. It would help to wash away the remaining feelings I carry as a heavy burden."

Gritting her teeth, and tasting sand, she took a small drink then smiled a broad smile.

"I'm hungry. Come on, let's get this meal ready and enjoy our first meal on our journey."

Abram smiled at her and she sensed he was pleased with their first day.

Eliana served the stew to Abram and Sarai, and filled her own bowl. They ate silently, resting after the long march. When he had eaten, with a wave Abram walked away to check the camp and make sure all was done to be ready for the night.

Sarai started to think out loud as she cleaned up. "So many tasks are women's work. Cleaning, cooking, washing, sewing, planting, weeding, gathering the harvest, picking wild berries, finding edible roots and tending the children. The women share the tasks, and that makes the work lighter for each one. As we work, we sing songs and talk about our work, our worries and our joys and blessings. We are strong and can feel pride in what we accomplish."

But the job every woman and child hated was collecting animal dung for fuel. It had to be done or there would be no fires, no hot stew to eat. They carried sticks and paddles to pick it up and put it in baskets. When dry it made a good hot, small fire for cooking. Wood was always scarce and to find any on the journey was not practical, and so they did what had to be done.

"Picking up and drying dung is the worst job of all. We do it, but we don't have to like it. And now we have to do it while we keep on the move. I can't understand why we are like beasts who work from dawn to dusk. As we travel, that seems to be all that the men do, walk. We walk just as far and then have to get meals and sleeping places prepared for everyone."

Eliana gave a fake groan. "At least Abram made the men carry water for us. It seemed like a big thing for the men to do, but it made the women's task easier. Maybe he should watch his back after today. They sure grumbled a lot. We must remember to thank him for his kindness."

By the time the stars were twinkling in the sky and the moon was rising over the far hills, the camp was settling for the night. Abram instructed the men to erect the goat hair canvas to create simple shelters which provided some cover for the very young and for the old ones. Most slept in the open, covered by their cloaks. The night was cool, with just a gentle breeze and to sleep under the stars was new and exciting. A few small fires were burning, and the watchmen took turns circling the camp, alert to any danger. Abram and Sarai crept under a cart and curling up together slept the deep sleep of the exhausted.

Chapter Ten

The way to Canaan, followed the Euphrates River which wound north and west. If the journey went well, with no major delays, they expected to arrive in Harran in two months. Harran was a major trading centre, and Abram planned to stop there until the rainy season passed. They would rest until they continued the trip south. Canaan was another month or two of hard travel, and he decided a time to rebuild a solid family community would be wise.

After the first day of travel they camped in a large circle for safety, with a central fire in the centre. The complete silence during the night indicated the exhaustion of those resting beneath the stars.

The morning routine took longer than Abram had hoped. Getting into the line of travel was not as simple as he anticipated. The day they had left Ur, the wagons had been previously lined up, and that simplified the task. Abram decided he needed to make a plan before the next morning. He thought about it as they walked. Each cart would be given a symbol and a flag on the cart which determined its place in line. A cart was assigned to each family, and they were to walk together with their cart.

"Sarai, I need you and the women to make coloured flags to hang on the wagons. Lot and I will mark them with charcoal to show the order. It will make the morning routine go more quickly."

She gathered some women and they tore up cloth to make the squares and then the men put the marks on them. The charcoal wouldn't last many days, but by then the order would be known. It took time to explain the colourful flags attached to each wagon. The woman head of each family was given a small matching piece to help identify her cart. The first morning there was confusion, but when everyone figured it out, it would help to get the caravan lined up ready to leave.

Sarai congratulated herself. She was learning this new role of being the leader among the women. As she forced herself to be cheerful, it was becoming easier. She thought to herself, *maybe, just maybe, I am becoming the woman I need to be as a leader.* And she smiled a real smile of satisfaction and promise.

As they walked, Sarai and Eliana noted the plants that they saw, always looking for medicinal herbs. Sarai carried a bag which she used to keep any plants she collected. They looked for daisies, myrrh, willow and cinnamon bark. Sarai hung the plants to dry on her cart and later pounded the dried leaves or berries into a fine powder.

Abram came by once every day to visit Sarai. On the fourth day in the early afternoon, he took her by the hand, and beckoned Eliana to follow. He went to a partly empty cart and lifting Sarai he placed her on the cart and then did the same with Eliana.

"You will ride till we stop for the night. No arguments. I know others are tired as well, but you are limping Sarai. You need to rest as I think you have twisted your ankle. We will take care of it when we stop."

Turning to Eliana he said, "You are responsible to keep her here. Do whatever you have to do." Then he was gone, back to the task of keeping everything running smoothly.

Sarai had to admit her ankle hurt, and she gladly rode for the rest of the day. She never planned to mention it and was deeply touched that Abram noticed. He must be watching her carefully to detect such a small thing, and her heart was warmed, and she smiled as she lay down.

That night when they stopped, Abram stood on a tree stump in the central meeting place and everyone gathered around to listen. His tall figure was comforting as he spoke in his strong yet warm voice.

"We are making good time. I am pleased with our progress and your strength and courage. I ask the women to do something special and cook honey cakes. We will celebrate tonight and rest here tomorrow. There is clean water in the stream and we can bathe in the large quiet pools and fill our water jars."

He selected two men to follow him. When they returned they carried two large water jars. When Abram poured out the first cup, a cheer rose into the air. The casks were filled with wine. Abram had hidden them in one of the carts, ready for a time such as this. Once again, Sarai's heart swelled with pride. "He thinks of everything, and yet he has called me wise."

After the families had eaten, the cakes were shared, and wine poured for everyone. Abram called the children to him, and he helped each of them to honey he had found in a comb. He and the children laughed as they sucked the honey and it dribbled down Abram's chin into his beard. People brought their lyres, tambourines and drums and there was singing and dancing.

It was a wonderful evening, and precisely what everyone needed after so many days of plodding along, weary and footsore. As Sarai watched Abram with the children, laughing and enjoying their company, she thought what a wonderful father he would be. And once more her gut twisted into a knot and she choked back her tears.

The journey resumed, and each day was unerringly like the day before. The sun beat down and heat waves shimmered from the hills. The river wound through low-lying valleys and they had to climb over steep hills. Everyone walked up these inclines and strong hands and backs were needed to push the wagons. On the other side of the river they caught glimpses of the caravan trail.

"Why don't we follow the caravan roads?" Sarai asked Abram as they walked together.

"It was difficult to cross the river near Ur. It is wide and deep and flowing rapidly to the sea. We will cross it further along where it is narrow and shallow."

"But we could meet traders and—"

"Yes we could. But robbers stalk the trade routes. They won't be bothered to cross the river to rob a band of ragged wanderers. We are safer on this side of the river."

The travellers plodded in quiet boredom. The wail of an infant, the sobs of a child, the grunt of an ox and braying of a donkey occasionally broke the stillness.

Eliana and Sarai were walking together as they did every day.

"I am so tired, Sarai. The same thing day after day: sand, rocks, trees, sky and heat."

"Maybe you would like some robbers to attack, or a donkey cart run away."

Eliana laughed, "You are right my friend, as you always are."

Abram came to Sarai that evening after he had walked around the camp as was his custom. Taking her hand, he walked away from her fire to a place beside the river, where they could not be heard.

"Our father is dying. I think he will live until we reach our new home, but not much longer. Spend time with him Sarai. Listen to him complain, and sing to him."

"I will Abram. Whatever else he may be he is my father."

Sarai sat in the evening shadows and thought of her mother. And soon she was going to lose her father too.

I know that is life. Birth and growth and death. But lately I seem to experience only loss and grief.

The days came and went; the monotony grinding away any attempts at cheerfulness. The litters that carried their precious tents raised a great cloud of dust. It swirled around the oxen then rose into the air to disappear. A few people had complained at the outset because Abram put them at the very back of the line, near the rear guards.

"They will be stolen."

" The poles will crack and no one will be aware of it."

"We will lose them, every one."

"What will we do if we have neither tents nor poles to hold them up?"

The complaining voices droned on but Abram appeared not to hear. Seeing the rolling clouds of dust raised by the wagon, the doubters understood now why the ox cart was at the rear, but no one admitted Abram was right.

As the journey crawled at its steady mind numbing pace, a few people began to grumble that they should have stayed in Ur.

"There we had plenty to eat and drink."

"We could pick fruit and berries from the trees and vines in our gardens."

"We slept in our safe and comfortable houses."

Abram listened for two days then once again he climbed on a cart where he could be seen and heard.

"Each of you came of your own free will. You were not forced; you chose to join Terah and me in this journey. You do not have to stay. You can return to Ur, anytime."

Long looks passed between the travellers and some shuffled their feet in the dirt and looked down at the dust.

"Come to me and I will give you two days rations and then you are free to leave. You will not be permitted to take sheep or goats. You will be able to find food and water on the way back, as we have on our journey to this place. If you choose to continue, there will be no more talk of Ur. The reasons you decided to join this move are the reasons we continue. Remember them and look to the hills for strength."

Then he got off the cart and walked away and sat apart under a small tree. Sarai went and sat beside him. They sat in silence, each deep in their own thoughts. Hearing Abram heave a deep and mournful sigh, Sarai said, “I know Abram. I know.” She reached out and held his big strong hand in her small one. They sat together till it was time to settle for the night.

Not one person decided to return to Ur, and the complaining stopped, at least when Abram could hear. In the morning they continued the journey, and no further mention was made of the past.

Chapter Eleven

Day after day, week after week they endured the same drudgery; walking westward toward an unknown future. Sarai and Eliana talked as they walked, trying to guess what they might find when Abram finally called a halt to their trek.

“Do you suppose there will be a city where we can live?”

“I don’t think we should hope for that, Eliana. We are herders and farmers. We can’t afford to live in a city.”

“But Ur was a city.”

“I know. But our family had craftsmen and traders, weavers and bakers. Don’t forget Terah carved idols. Without the money they earned we could not have had a place in the city.”

“I was hoping to sleep under a roof and shop at a market again.”

“There will have to be at least a prosperous village nearby. At worst, we may settle on a trade route and be able to sell our animals, cheese, carvings and woven goods to them.”

“Reuben and I talked about that, and he said we could make more money selling directly to the people. The traders have to make a living off our goods too, and it drives the cost up and we don’t get its full value.”

"I suspect he is right. I don't know much about trading. But whatever we find, we will settle in a good place, and stop wandering for a while."

The simplest of things became a momentous event for the weary wanderers. One evening as they started to set camp, the scouts ran back and told Abram there was a large covey of quail just ahead.

"Hunters with bows are to follow the scouts. The older boys are to go as well. If you are skillful, there will be fresh meat to roast on our fires tonight."

The hunting party crept stealthily along the trail. The birds fed on the ground and were unaware. As the men neared, the huge flock rose into the air, blacking out the setting sun.

The arrows of the warriors soared into the sky and birds were falling. The youth ran to find the birds and any arrows that cut the air and had fallen to the ground. Their shouts of success resounded at the camp. On long poles carried between their shoulders the youth were bringing dozens of birds to the camp site. Hanging over the poles were enough birds to feed everyone with freshly cooked meat. Once again Abram called a day's halt and everyone feasted and sang late into the night.

Miriam came to Sarai and asked to speak with her. They withdrew to a quiet spot under a cedar tree.

"This is my daughter, Leah. Today she had her first moon blood. Is there anything we can do to welcome her to the world of women?"

"Let me think it over. We will do something to honour her tonight."

Sarai sought out Abram and explained what she wanted. In a short time men cut branches to make poles. They carefully sharpened the butt end into a point. These were driven into the ground to fill in open spaces in a small stand of trees. Women brought the tent coverings used for the elderly to sleep under. They also brought blankets and rugs. With thorn needles and strong twine they fastened the fabric to the trees and the poles that filled in the gaps. When finished, a circle had been made, large enough to hold the women of the caravan.

Sarai went to her wagon and found the bowl, the pitcher and the moon banner. She fastened the banner over the doorway panel and placed the bowl and pitcher on a stool she had carried to the circle.

Eliana had been busy creating a circle of leather to make a band for Leah's ankle. It would have to do until a proper copper one could be made. She spoke to Miriam, and she had her gold ring, ready to pass on to Leah. They walked to the river and filled the pitcher with water. On the way back they gathered flowers to make a crown for Leah. Sarai laid a sacred fire in the centre of the circle.

At sunset the women gathered with cushions to sit on and formed a joyous ring around the inner edge of their sacred space.

When Miriam and Leah arrived, musicians welcomed them with the songs of the grandmothers, and Sarai led them in the ritual. The crown was placed on Leah's head and her mother slipped the ring on Leah's finger. Then Sarai fastened the woven leather circle around her ankle. Sarai did her best to remember the words and said them with a great sense of awe. At each special moment in the ceremony they raised their hands and fluttered their fingers in a silent salute.

Wine and bread were shared and the stories of their foremothers told. Laughter and music filled the space. When it ended, Leah was hugged and given a warm welcome to the woman's space they had created.

As they left the women quietly took down the canvas sheets and the blankets. The poles stood in silent tribute to what had taken place.

They had been following the river every day since they left Ur. It was getting smaller each day, and Abram felt that it could be crossed in a day or two. He sent scouts to find a safe place for the crossing. At the signal that a place had been found the long procession cheered.

From a stump near the edge of the river, Abram explained the crossing.

"It seems to be safe here, but I want the warriors to have bows ready and to stand guard, half on each side of the river."

In no time, the strong warriors and hunters spread out along the banks of the river and watched from either side.

"The herders and shepherds will go across next. Tall boys can carry the smallest kids and lambs. We don't want to lose any in the river. Just a few men will stay on the other side to guard the flock. The rest will return to help move the carts and wagons."

The herders led the animals into the gently flowing river and began their walk to the other side. The little lambs and kids on the shoulders of the boys or in their arms were carried to the other side. Everyone looked on from the shore. The crossing passed without incident and a cheer rose in a salute. With a lot of calling, bleating and baaing, mothers found their babies and the young ones suckled eagerly.

“Carts and wagons next. Men, be ready to help if wheels get stuck, or animals are spooked. Some men should stay on the other side, but most will return to help the women and children cross.”

It proved to be an excellent place to cross, the bottom felt firm and with just a few small rocks to navigate. The wagons made slow but steady progress. Men walked by the draught animals and kept them calm while they plodded in the clear water. The wagon pulling the tent poles and canvas went last, and strong men lifted the ends of the poles out of the water to keep them dry and safe.

“Now the children and the rest of us can cross.”

The children splashed and played in the water, squealing in delight as they jumped up and then collapsed in the stream. Their parents smiled as they heard the music of children laughing and shouting in happy play. Standing near their children, they were soon being splashed and the adults too began to laugh and splash the children, and soon both old and young cupped their hands and threw water at everyone and anyone. Sarai decided to join the fun and getting a bowl; she filled it with water and carried it carefully to where Abram stood watching. She came up behind him and threw the water. The camp became silent. Abram turned around, shaking water from his hair and beard. His face was the picture of anger, and those nearby took a few steps back. But Sarai noted the familiar sparkle in his eyes and the hint of a smile.

“I am going to pay for this, but how?”

In one motion Abram swept her off her feet, carried her into the stream and dropped her into a deep, quiet pool. She disappeared from sight for one moment. When she surfaced, and stood up, she shook her head and sprayed water all over Abram. He laughed a great hearty laugh, and they splashed each other until weak from laughter they waded to the shore. A joyous cheer went up from the people, and everyone waded in the water playing, laughing and calling out to each other in carefree abandon.

When the crossing was completed, the laughter ceased, everyone sat on the bank to dry in the warmth of the hot sun. In that moment, Abram stood on a rock.

"Our scouts, herders and warriors stood in the hot sun, watching us play and refresh ourselves. They guarded us and our safety. We will now become the guardians of the caravan and the weary, hot men will have time to refresh themselves."

With a great shout, armour and weapons were thrown aside and these strong, brave men of Ur left their responsibilities and played in the water like happy, carefree children.

That evening the camp, still playful and full of laughter, joined in singing and dancing. The beat of drums and the tinkling of tambourines replaced the music of splashing water.

Once more Abram knew exactly what to do. What a magnificent man he is. Full of dignity and authority when needed but capable of mischief as well.

When the moon sailed on her journey across the sky, and the camp slept, happy dreams filled each heart.

During the next days the mood remained happy, and travel easy and pleasant. Abram walked beside Sarai.

"I think we are getting close to Haran. When the wind was right, I smelt the faint odour of smoke. And at night as I walk the camp in the darkness, I can see a faint glow on the clouds. The glow of fires I think."

Sarai hugged Abram with joy to think that they neared the end of their long trek.

After another two nights and days passed, a scout arrived shouting as he ran into the camp.

"We have found Haran. It is over the next few hills. The road is smooth and easy. We are home."

A grand cheer echoed from the hills. Sarai found Abram and wept in his arms. Abram lifted Terah from his bed and helped him put on his red cloak. Terah stood as straight as he could beside the cart, leaning heavily on it.

"I have brought you to a new land and a new home. Blessed be the Holy One who has led me here and blessed are you who have followed." His servants lifted him back into his cart where he lay on his mat and fell asleep.

For just a moment Sarai felt a wave of deep resentment as Terah took the credit for what Abram had accomplished, but she reminded herself that their father was a dying old man.

Just before they entered the city, Sarai searched the ground until she found a stone the colour of the sand they had wearily walked on for so many days. She added it to the bag that held her other memory stones. When she felt discontented with life, she would touch the stone and remember how much they had sacrificed to be here.

Two babies had died on the journey, one scarcely a day old, the other just learning to walk. Everyone had paused in their march, and laid the small bodies in foreign soil beneath the scrub bushes that grew beside the road, carefully covering the small mounds with as many stones as they could find. The mothers gathered to mourn near Sarai's canopy. During the days that followed, women walked with the grieving mothers. Not one adult or youth had perished on the journey. Abram always found water and food when they needed it. Their supply of flour and lentils was nearly gone, but there had been enough. Terah continued to be very ill, but he lived to see their new homeland and rejoice in the hope he had held for so long.

The leaders came to the top of a small hill. Below stretched a scenic valley, green with grass, and dotted with colourful flowers. The Balikh River meandered along the valley floor and glittered in the sunlight. The excitement bubbled over in shouts of happiness.

"Look at the trees, how lovely they are."

"That means we will have wood for our fires."

"The river is a blue and silver ribbon twisting through the valley."

"Each hill is a green feast for our flocks."

The men who had been leading, lined up along the road winding down into the valley. They formed an honour guard, and the people held their heads high as they walked toward their new location.

When they reached the valley, Abram called everyone to gather and asked for silence.

"What now?"

"He needs to hear himself speak. He likes the sound of his voice."

"Be quiet. I want to hear him."

They stood and watched as Abram built a very small, crude altar of stones, poured oil on it, and offered prayers of thanksgiving to the Holy One of the mountain. The mountain was far, far away but its

peaks could be seen, rising toward the sky, piercing the clouds, and pointing the way to the dwelling place of the gods. Today it spewed red sparks into the sky; smoke and ash churned out of its top and the thunder growled softly in their new valley. It looked as if El Shaddai was reminding the people that he was still their God.

"Thanks be to the giver of life, for our safety." Abram's strong voice echoed in the valley.

"Blessed be the holy name." The voices of the people answered, and the echo rang in the hills.

The great city of Haran lay nearby, close enough to see tall buildings and smell the pungent smoke of its fires. As the sky darkened from blue to black, they lit their fires, cooked their simple meal, and prepared for one more night to sleep under the stars. With the sun rise their new life would begin.

Chapter Twelve

Sarai woke with the sun. She could see Eliana busy making the morning meal. It smelled wonderful. She stretched her legs and reached to the sky. Grabbing the tunic she had worn yesterday and the day before and before that, she pulled on it over her head. She wrinkled her nose as the stale smell struck her.

"It will be wonderful when I can wear clean clothes again, and bathe and wash my hair. I hope the river is quiet running and not too cold."

Abram walked toward her, bringing fresh bread and milk. The three of them sat together on the ground and shared their first meal in the valley that was to be home.

"It looks perfect Abram. I see plenty of green lush grass, and the river is so blue it resembles a jewel running along the valley floor."

"And look at the hills, they are strong protection." Eliana spoke with trepidation in her voice.

"Why do you think of protection on such a grand morning?"

"Storms come, there are bandits. Such things happen. A few guard houses on the hills and we will have plenty of warning."

Abram chuckled. “Sarai, I think Eliana spends too much time with Reuben. She is starting to think like a general.”

The three of them laughed together in comfortable companionship. The rest of the clan was stirring in the valley. Fires were sending gentle curls of smoke to the sky, and happy voices echoed from the hills.

The weeks ahead were going to be very busy. The tents they had hauled for so many miles needed to be set up. It was heavy work, usually done by the women.

“I know what you are thinking Sari.” Abram spoke into the silence. “The men will be helping with the tents. We need to get them up as quickly as we can, so it becomes everyone’s task.”

Sarai’s eyes met Abram’s and her gaze told him how grateful she was.

The decision about who would sleep in the tents they brought from Ur was the talk of the day. There were many opinions.

“The old people should be the first housed.”

“But the babies need protection from flies and the chill of the night.”

“The ones who have the most sheep and goats should have them. They provide the things we need, so they deserve their rest.”

“Abram and Sarai should have the first one. They brought us here safely.”

The chatter went on and on as they worked.

At sunset a delegation came to Abram and asked for an audience. They sat in a circle and talked for a long time. Sarai took them food and drink, but they became silent when she was near. She heard nothing. They talked till the moon sailed high in the sky, but their voices were quiet and serious. When they left, Abram extinguished his lamp and Sarai knew she would be in the dark till morning.

The day dawned and Sarai couldn't wait to ask Abram what had been decided. He came, carrying water to fill her water jars. He took a long time filling them and setting them just right so they couldn't tip over. She wasn't able to contain her curiosity and blurted out, "What was the meeting about?"

"We made decisions concerning the tents and who should have the first ones. The old and the youngest will be housed first. The rest will wait until we make or buy more. But the biggest discussion concerned you and me. They insisted that because I was such a great leader—" He winked as he puffed out his chest as he spoke in a deep important tone. "Because of my position and stature, I should have a large tent to hold meetings, listen to complaints and give my judgments and rulings. They stated that as my first wife you must have your own place. You will need it to tend to the affairs of the women."

"But Abram, I—"

"It is no use Sarai. I argued, but they were insistent. They said it was needed as you should not be present when the men talk. Also when I take another wife; she will need her own tent as well. And the pattern should be set now."

Sarai spluttered and nearly choked.

Abram grinned at her.

"You need not worry. I have no plans to take another wife."

His warm eyes sparkled with laughter as he added, "yet"

Sarai threw her crust of bread at him and laughed as well. But in her heart she felt a stab of doubt.

"Very soon I will need to go to the city and establish contact with our neighbours. The main gates face us and are just a short walk away. I will go as soon as things are a little more settled here."

The days passed with many groans in response to orders barked aloud. Abram drew a plan in the sand for the location of the tents, and everyone came to study it. The tents formed a circle on the south side of the river. The centre would be left open, a large, sweeping space for communal gatherings. Pastures and garden areas were in the valley to the east and also on the low hills that circled the area where they planned to erect tents.

Late that evening, as people milled around in the open space, Abram came and climbed onto a wagon. The crowd sat on the ground around him and settled into silence.

"We have made good progress here. Look near the river. The pens for the animals are standing ready. It was a brilliant idea to fence these areas with thorn bushes. It has saved many trees, and a living fence needs little care. Our fields have been tilled for crops, and shelters are being built of brush for the shepherds and herdsmen. Soon we can begin planting our seeds and vines. Life will become settled once again."

Sarai moved closer and stood beside him on his makeshift platform.

"We have wool that we carried with us, and it is time to get the looms set up and begin weaving new tent fabric. That will be started tomorrow. And here is my order for this work. Everyone will be involved. The men who are not assigned to other work, and that will include archers and spearmen, will help set up the looms. They will carry the heavy baskets of thread and help in any way the women ask. Getting them water, fruit or wine."

A great rustling and muttering spread around the seated crowd like an autumn wind. Abram held up his hand for silence.

"Things change. We no longer live in a city where people have their own tasks and there are enough hands to do the work. Here, if we are to survive, we need to work together to accomplish all that needs to be done. In the morning, the young folks and children are to go searching for stones that will be used to build a permanent altar. Part of our meagre stores of grain will be used and a perfect lamb and kid will be sacrificed. El Shaddai needs to smell the smoke from our sacred place and know that we have not forgotten him. Now go to your rest. Sleep well, for you have earned it."

He shocked everyone by being the first one at the wagons next morning. He helped carry the wooden frames and he oversaw the work to set them up. He carried the heavy skeins of thread they had bought and threw the shuttle for the first half-day. The men realized at that moment they were going to be doing what they saw as women's work. They grumbled amongst themselves, but not too loudly, and they worked alongside their wives. As time passed, it began to be accepted, and everyone was pleased at the speed at which the thread became long pieces of strong, sturdy fabric.

As Sarai and Eliana worked side by side, they spoke quietly.

"Will this change last or is it a temporary thing?"

"I suspect, that once we are settled, it will return to the way it has always been. But, Eliana, I am going to enjoy this while it happens. Tomorrow can take care of tomorrow."

As this work carried on, Sarai remembered the space in the house of Jessica, the healer. She pictured the large room where the women gathered for the new moon ceremony and for their time of exclusion when they had their moon time each month. Where might there be such a place for them here?

For many days she pondered what to do. As the leader of the women she knew it was her responsibility. At the end of a long day, she sought out Abram and confided in him.

"You know the importance of an altar where you go to make your offerings to the Holy One of the mountain?"

He nodded.

"And you know about the room in mother's home that was forbidden to the men."

Again he nodded.

"In that room, we women make our offerings and we worship. We have ceremonies that honour the presence of the holy and that mark special times in women's lives. In that place the girls learned how to be women, how to care for their bodily needs and to honour the grandmothers of the past."

Abram stirred and shifted his position.

Am I making him uncomfortable? But I need to say this to him.

"Mother's house is not here and we have no place to gather. We need private space. What can we do? Enlarge my tent? Build a shelter of trees? But there are few trees. Tell me what to do Abram."

He stroked his beard and thought.

"I know that this is important. To you, to the women and to the people. I remember the circle we made out on the trail and how significant it was. I had planned to purchase a large tent for our soldiers and warriors for their training, but at the present this is much more important, I think. When we go the city, we'll search for a suitable tent and canopy to meet your needs."

Clapping her hands, she squealed, "Oh, Abram. That is more than I dared to hope for. You do understand. I believe that if we women are happy, everyone will be more cheerful." She threw her arms around him and promised he would have his favourite lentil stew to eat with his beer at the meal tomorrow. As she went to her tent, her happy feet skipped with joy.

"Eliana, he never stops surprising me. I told him that we needed a place that we could go for our moon times. I expected some help from him, maybe enlarging my tent and adding a canopy, but this is wonderful. He has promised me we will have our own large and spacious tent. What a fascinating man he is. I once thought I would need to be careful around him and protective of myself and all the women. Perhaps I misjudged him."

Every member of the tribe, able to do so, was working. Many tended the newly planted seeds and vines they had brought all the way from Ur. The men with skill at building continued to construct pens to hold the milk goats. The herders had scouted out the hills and valleys and the goats and sheep were led to pastures with plenty of grass and water. Temporary brush shelters had been erected for the herders to sleep in at night, who took turns staying awake to stand guard. They were well equipped for their work. The sturdy wooden staff they carried had a sharp piece of slate imbedded in the end. It served as a spear and was useful for dealing with snakes. The herders also carried a knife, a sling, and something to hold water. Those with skill to play had a flute which helped to pass the time and calm the sheep. The clothing the herders wore consisted of a sheepskin mantle or cape worn over their tunics to shield them from the elements. Sturdy sandals protected their feet from the rough terrain. Along with the water bag, they carried another for bread, olives, cheese and dried fruit. They stayed out in the pasture for a number of days. When they returned to the camp, other herders relieved them.

Everywhere in the camp, people worked energetically. They shook and brushed the dust from their tents, rugs and blankets. Food containers and dishes had to be rinsed to get rid of the soil from their long march. Clothes washed in the stream, hung anywhere they would dry and children told to watch that they didn't blow away. Abram knew he needed to visit the city and invite their elders to a meal. The residents of Haran walked outside the walls, eyeing the newcomers with curious stares. Everything must be ready when they met the people of the city. Abram's tribe was a proud nation, and they wanted to show that they were not pitiable nomads who might be a threat to the city. They came not as beggars or robbers, but as allies. Sarai stood by her tent on the small rise of land where it sat and Eliana stood with her arm around Sarai's shoulders.

"It hasn't been two moons yet and we have a camp we can be proud of."

"The black tents look comforting as they stand around the great communal fire pit."

"Tomorrow, Abram, Lot, and others are going to the city to meet with the elders there."

"I hope it goes well Sarai. So much depends on that first contact."

"They have ignored us so far, and that is a good sign. They are not threatened or worried about our sudden appearance."

"Wouldn't it be wonderful if we could stay here forever?"

"Hmmm. It would be, but remember we are a people who wander. It is in our blood to move with the need for new grazing lands."

Eliana groaned and started to walk to her place to sleep.

"Do you have to be so sensible? Just let me have my illusions for one night."

The delegation walked to Haran the next morning and stayed most of the day. After his return at dusk, Abram asked Sarai to walk with him to the riverbank. Sitting close to each other Abram shared with Sarai his trip to the city.

"We took them gifts and assured them we intended to be good neighbours. I said we had many trained fighters who would help them if trouble threatened. We gave blankets, and beaded bags, wine and honey cakes, and our fine woven cloth to them. I told them we had many things to offer in trade. I invited the officials and their families to a feast, where we will entertain them and exchange symbolic gifts."

Sarai sat on her favourite rock and invited Abram to move closer to her. He put his arm around her waist and hugged her.

"Tell me everything you saw. How do the people live? Is it a pleasing city to look at?"

"Whoa Sarai. Give me a chance to explain. The Balikh River runs just outside the walls on its way to the Euphrates River. And Sarai, those walls are strong and they are so long it would take more than a whole day to walk all around the city. The houses are buildings such as you have never seen. The base is mud brick and there are smooth walls that are shoulder high and straight and square. At that height there is a flat shelf that makes a small platform and then a cone rises in a curved arc above the flat platform to enclose the space. Inside the house it is tall enough for even me to stand erect. The top has gaps to let smoke out, with a small mud flap to keep out the rain. Small spaces in the walls of the cone let light enter the room. These dwellings of various sizes, stretched as far as we could see. The houses reminded me of the nests of the weaver bird."

"I think they must be very strange. Who would want to live in a house that looked like the nest of a bird? I can't imagine such a house. I hope to visit them for myself one day."

"You will, Sarai, you will. We walked through the market square where traders came from far away centres, Damascus, Tyre, and Carchemish. The leaders of Harran spoke of the wonderful items that could be bought and sold at the many stalls that lined the square. Against the north wall of the city is another large open square, paved with flat stones." Abram chased a fly from his face. "From it arises a great ziggurat, going up in tiers, each one smaller than the one beneath it, perfectly square and made of baked bricks. Steps lead to the top, where a shrine to Sin, the moon god, sits. We will still be living near people who worship other gods. But at least they are not our near neighbours and friends."

"Did you understand their talk?"

"Most of the time. Our tongues are similar, but there are many words that are somewhat different. But it will be no cause for trouble. I think they are our brothers from long ago."

The women were informed that the town elders had been invited to a festive dinner, and they began to make preparations. They cooked lentils and beans, roasted sheep and goats, made fresh cheeses, and ventured into the city to the market to buy figs and dates. One large vessel of the finest wine had been carefully carried with them and kept in anticipation of such an occasion. Singers and musicians practised their music, and a play that told the story of this great people was repeated over and over again, until it sounded perfect. The children learned a new game of ball that they hoped to play for the visitors. The leaders, Abram and Lot, had prepared speeches of welcome and had gifts of cloth and pottery for their guests.

In Abram's large tent, the best rugs lay spread on the ground and curtains of fine wool divided the main part of the tent from the space where the women would work and serve the food and wine to the male guests. Lamps hung from the tent poles and pieces of the best pottery showed their colours in the lamp light. Everyone cleaned and shined their rings, bangles, and hair ornaments. It was planned to be the most elaborate celebration that the tribe had seen for a long, long time and everyone wanted to impress the officials from Haran. In spite of all the work and worry, the people were anticipating the food and the entertainment after their long hard trek to this new home.

The day of the feast dawned as perfect as anyone could wish. The winds blew gently and carried the odours of the animals away from the tents. The sun shone in an azure blue cloudless sky, an omen of peace and prosperity. The children scrubbed their grubby hands and feet, and their hair gleamed from the enthusiastic brushing. The older ones were made to wear clothes, but allowed to go barefoot. The last preparations had been done when cheerful music floated across the valley.

"They are coming," excited voices called from tent to tent and the children ran to the edge of the camp to enjoy the procession as it came near.

Sarai sat on the grass beside Miriam, an old woman who was nearly blind.

"I can see them Miriam. Musicians are leading the way, wearing bright blue cloaks. Behind them are slaves carrying large trays of food and gifts. They are partly naked, wearing just a loin cloth."

"I never thought I'd be grateful to be blind," joked Miriam.

"Next are the elders, dressed in robes of every colour, decorated with shells and feathers. Their chief is riding high above the heads of the people, carried on a litter and sitting on a carved wooden throne. He has a huge hat on his head with a long feather on it. He is smiling and waving and as he nods and turns his head, the feather is swaying a greeting. They are at Abram's tent, and the litter is down on the grass, and the chief is bowing to Abram. Not a real bow, just a nod of his head. Abram bowed in return, but just a small bow not a deep one."

"Thank you Sarai, for helping me to visualize the parade. You are like a daughter to me."

With a quick hug, Sarai left Miriam and ran to Abram's tent to help the women.

Abram welcomed the people of Ur to his humble camp. From behind every tent, tree and rock, curious eyes watched as these richly garbed men entered Abram's tent. The women stood outside in anticipation of the evening festivities. Just inside the door, seated on a low stool, completely enveloped in cushions and blankets, sat Terah.

Abram introduced him to the guests.

"This is my father, Terah, the head of the clan, an ancient wise man. He has lived for many rainy seasons, many more than the turtle has seen. Our chief has seen the most wonderful things and tells us amazing stories. He led us here, through deserts, wilderness and many dangers. And he greets you and offers you gifts from our people."

With great ceremony and long speeches gifts were exchanged between the two groups of leaders. Terah as the elder statesman of the tribe was presented with a stunning cloak, decorated with shells and feathers. He grinned his toothless grin and tried to rise, but was not able. In return his servant brought a large and impressive carved walking stick, with the symbol of the moon god at the top. It was an elegantly carved bull, smoothed and polished until it gleamed and it was presented to the chief from Haran.

Behind the curtain, the women watched all that was going on and whispered to each other behind their hands.

"The chief is so fat. He won't be any good in a battle."

"Or in a bed."

"Sh. He will hear you. Don't spoil this for everyone."

Stifled laughter filled the air.

Hours later, when everyone had enjoyed the food and wine and could eat and drink no more, the entertainment began. The women, hidden behind a soft curtain, sang a welcome song, and they were applauded and praised. The men sang songs of herding sheep, building roads and fighting battles. Each song was greeting with cheering and words of thanks. The older children were brought to the front of the tent, and the men went outside to watch as they played their game of ball to amuse the guests. There was laughter and clapping and everyone was having a wonderful time. The little drama captured the attention of everyone, and received much praise. Terah was snoring in the corner, propped up by his cushions.

Long after the full moon had climbed out of her sleeping place, the party continued. The children were put to bed, the old ones retired on their own. Women and children from Haran began the walk back to the town to settle for the night. The men had one more beer, told one more story and with the great orb of the moon high in the sky they said their goodbyes. Both groups felt it was an auspicious beginning to their living in peace and harmony in this great valley.

Abram and Sarai stood before his tent.

"Look Sarai, far to the east I can see the towering peak of the holy mountain."

"El Shaddai is pleased. See the gentle shower of sparks and smoke."

"I must get a proper altar built for our sacrifices. And we must see that your tent for the women is erected soon."

"Goodnight Abram. I will rest now. It has been a very busy day."

Abram took a relaxing walk around the camp site. He looked at the tents, the animal pens, the newly planted vines and trees, the gardens that held the promise of onions, lentils, wheat and herbs. What he saw pleased him and he turned his eyes to the mountain.

"Mighty One. Hear my pledge. We will serve only you, El Shaddai, great god of the mountain. In the morning I will build an altar in the foothills of these mountains, beneath the dwelling place of the most high. I have delayed too long. We will make a sacrifice of a fine sheep. A thank offering for our safety and for this new land where we will live in peace."

With plans for the morning on his mind he retired to his tent and was asleep at once.

Chapter Thirteen

Abram was up early to fulfill his sacred duty. Over the past few days, the children had gathered stones and taken them to Abram for approval. There was a large supply to load into a cart for the donkey to pull. With three servants he gathered the needed tools and clay and straw to cement stones in place. When all was ready, Abram asked for the blessing of El Shaddai on this day's work and they set out to walk toward the great rock formation. He climbed a short distance up its side, past the grassy hills, and into the beginning of the rocky outcroppings that indicated the base of the mountain. He stopped and with great care built the altar and offered the sacrifice of an unblemished lamb.

"El Shaddai, Almighty One of the mountain.

Blessed be your sacred name.

In safety we have come to this land of plenty.

Blessed be your sacred name

In safety we have built our homes.

Blessed be your sacred name.

In safety we will till our fields and raise our crops.

Blessed be your sacred name.

In honour of you,

we have raised an altar to your holy name.

Blessed be your name."

He took a small bag from around his neck. It held soil from the land of Ur. He sprinkled it all around the new altar to make El Shaddai feel at home in this new land. Abram was sure the god could smell the odour of the rich soil he had carried so far from Ur to Haran and trusted that as the aroma wafted upward, El Shaddai would remember and would welcome this familiar smell.

Sarai awoke and looked to her husband's tent. All seemed quiet. Only Eliezer was there, sweeping the rugs and tidying the tent after the party. Sarai had lain awake for much of the night. She was feverish and restless. Longing filled her heart and her body. At first she thought it was for home, but as she lay attentive to her feelings, she recognized the yearning. She wanted her husband. They had not been together for the long march; too tired, too little time, too little privacy. Abram's days and nights had been so filled with the arduous task of getting his people safely to Haran, that there had been no energy or time to think of personal needs. Sarai lay and thought and made a decision. When the evening came she would go to Abram. It was risky. It went against custom. It was bold, but it was what she needed to do.

The routines of the camp were in place and people went about their work singing and laughing as they had when they lived in Ur. Sarai felt good. Good about this new land, good about their life, and good about their decision. She went to her storage box and from it she took the white linen and gold tunic she had not used since her wedding night. As she brushed it carefully and hung it in the tent to air she thought.

I would like to hang it out in the sun, that would be best, but it would draw stares and questions. And I don't want to answer them or bear the taunts and the laughter.

When Eliana saw it, she raised her eyebrows, then smiled but said nothing. After the evening meal, she suggested that Sarai might like to have her hair washed. The two women shared a smile and a hug and began to get Sarai ready. With her hair washed and dried Sarai gave Eliana two combs decorated with tiny shells.

"Abram bought these from a trader and I have never used them. Fasten my hair with them and let it hang loosely down my back."

Eliana took them and held Sarai's hair, drawn back from her face, with the combs. She picked up the dress and gave it to Sarai. As the cool linen slid over her naked body Sarah shivered, not with the cold, but with anticipation.

Knowing that he had done his best to make this a good home for his people, Abram decided to talk a walk around the camp while the last rays of the sun shone upon his fields. Deeply satisfied by what he saw he was ready to retire to his tent. As he approached, he could see a small lamp burning and a shadow on the wall.

"I put out all the lamps, who dares enter my tent uninvited?"

He approached the tent cautiously, prepared to fight off the intruder with his staff. But the shadow stood motionless by his bed. As he lifted the door flap, he saw it was a woman's form.

A gentle voice whispered, “Husband, I have come to you. I know I have come unbidden, but I hope I can be forgiven. For too long we have not held each other’s body close in intimacy. We have had no pleasure in each other as the task of the march has weighed heavily on you. Do not send me away I beg you. Let me come to your bed on this night of new beginnings and new life. Perhaps tonight new life may start in me as well.”

Abram’s eyes adjusted to the dim light, and he saw his beautiful bride beside the bed; dressed in her wedding tunic and wearing nothing else. As his eyes drank in her beauty, his body responded and the heat gathered in his loins, and his male member throbbed in anticipation. In one stride Abram was beside her and swept her into his arms and carried her to his bed, already groaning with his need of her.

Chapter Fourteen

The morning was sunny and warm. Sarai looked at her store of herbs and medicines and knew that she needed to replenish them. As she lifted her basket down, her thoughts were of the healer who remained in Ur. Sarai remembered the wise, gentle, capable woman whom she loved and respected.

Eliana stood just outside the tent doorway. She heard Sarai's voice and didn't wish to intrude, but Sarai noticed her and invited her to enter.

"I know I am talking to myself again but I am thinking of Jessica, whose name means one who can foresee."

"You speak of her often. Tell me about her please."

"She saw something in me as she watched me growing up. She said I was thoughtful, kind and smart, and she chose me to be her pupil and to become a healer. I spent hours walking with Jessica, learning about plants. She taught me their names, how to prepare them, what we used them for." Sarai took a deep breath and let it out slowly. "I miss her. From her I learned how to make the healing teas from leaves and roots, with a bit of honey. I was a clumsy pupil sometimes. How embarrassed I felt when the fat caught fire as I heated it to make ointments and salves. But Jessica always understood."

Sarai sat on a plump cushion and Eliana plopped down beside her.

"I remember so well, the night Jessica named me as a healer."

"Tell me about your ceremony, please Sarai. Unless it is a secret."

"It isn't a secret. All the women join in the ceremony. Jessica anointed me and gave me symbols of my trade. There were flowers, and oil lamps, dancing and singing. On the day we left Ur; I was standing near her tent, she beckoned me to sit beside her.

"I tried to thank her for all she had done for me and I remember her words. 'Oh Sarai—I need no thanks. I saw something in you waiting to be born and I was honoured to be the midwife to your birth as a healer. You have a quick and agile mind and teaching you was a pleasure. To watch your brow crease as you listened to my words, and then to see your eyes light up with your dazzling smile as you understood, is a gift I shall always treasure. If she is fortunate once in a life-time, a pupil such as you comes to sit at the feet of a teacher.'"

Sarai paused for a moment and wiped a tear from her cheek. Eliana took her hand.

"Jessica's voice trembled as she spoke and I know she was as moved as I was. I told her I would miss her. I told her there was so much I still want to learn. So much I needed to know. I wondered who would teach me. She assured me I didn't need to worry, that I was ready to be the healer for our people. With a hug and a farewell kiss, she told me to go in peace."

Shaking her head to clear away the memory, Sarai picked up her basket, and they set out to see what this new land offered.

They searched for marjoram, aloe, anise, mint, mustard, and mandrakes. Many of these could be added to the oil of the olives to make them effective. They treated burns, cuts, poor digestion, stomach and head aches and much time and attention went to care for pregnant and nursing women. Sarai wondered about the wise woman in the city and hoped that they could meet and share their knowledge. She hoped the market would yield other roots and plants which she used that did not grow locally.

They searched until the sun was high in the sky and then stopped by the stream to rest. As she and Eliana sat side by side, Sarai looked at this companion of a lifetime, remembering, speculating and wondering led her to speak.

"Eliana we've been friends for as long as I can remember. I can hardly recall a day without you by my side. Yet, I know you were not always part of our family. Can you tell me how you came to be with us?"

Eliana stayed quiet for a long time.

"Have I offended you? If so I am sorry, but if you can tell me, I would like to know where you came from and how you came to live with us."

"I am not offended Sarai. It happened so long ago, I have to remember, and it is hard. I've not forgotten, but I was just a child. I often feel that my life really began when I joined your mother in her tent."

Cupping her hands, she dipped them into the water and let it run through her fingers, watching it sparkle as it ran back into the source of its life and energy. Eliana took water and washed her face. As Sarai watched, Eliana appeared to be cleansing the pain from her story to free her to tell it.

“We lived in Erech, a day’s journey north of Ur. My mother’s name was Gia and my father was Eli. He was not a big man, but in my eyes he was the most important person in the world. He often held me on his knee and told me stories of his family who lived in Ur. Mother was beautiful; her dark shiny hair fell in waves down her back when she left it free from the braids she wore most of the time. Her eyes were brown and warm and sparkled when she laughed. She gave her smile freely and when it spread across her face, I felt warmed by it. She made honey cakes for me and was teaching me how to make them. I loved to help her mix the flour and spices and then blend in the sweet honey. It was wonderful to sit with her and wait while they baked in the clay oven, and oh the aroma. I can still smell it and remember its taste as we shared the first warm slice.”

For a long moment she stared into the river and Sarai wondered if she had forgotten her story. She sat still and waited for Eliana to continue.

“We were making a trip to Ur to visit our family and to show them my new little brother. We were on our way to the temple to present him to the gods and to seek their blessing.”

She reached over with her hand, still cool from the river, and took Sarai’s hand in hers.

“Our small cart carried our clothing, food and gifts for the family. The trip was a wonderful adventure for me, and mother and I were pointing out the wonders we saw along the road. My father spoke to my mother.”

“Don’t look back; we have trouble. Wrap a blanket around Eliana’s shoulders, but leave her legs free. Give her some bread, cheese and figs, and a skin of water.”

"This puzzled me, as my father guided the donkey off the road toward the grassy edge of a field of wheat. Mother gave me the food and water and told me to do as I was told. 'When you are on the ground, run into the field as far as you can, and hide like a little rabbit. If you are hungry or thirsty, you have what you need. As night comes, roll up in the blanket and sleep. Do not leave the field until the sun is high in the sky,' father spoke in his calm but serious voice."

"Father slowed the cart to a stop, picked me up and set me on the grass but I fell and my hands and knees were dirty and they hurt. He said, 'Run at once, hide in the wheat and stay quiet as a mouse."

"I ran into the field and listened as the cart clattered down the road. I ran until I was out of breath and then sat on the ground. From the direction of the road, I heard shouting, and the noise of breaking wood, then cries of fear and shouts of glee. Then I heard horses galloping off into the distance and I thought I could smell smoke."

Great tears were streaming down Eliana's cheeks. Sarai squeezed her hand and said that she could stop; she didn't need to remember any more. Eliana wiped her tears and in a few minutes began to speak again.

"I ate and drank and sat and wondered about this strange game. But I was not afraid. I was sure my parents would come and find me. As the darkness overtook the sky, and the stars twinkled above me, I lay on the blanket on my back and tried to count them. When I looked up next, the stars were gone, the sky was blue. I had slept the whole night, and it was morning. I sat up and listened, but all was still. For a long time I sat there, I don't know how long, but at last went to find my parents. I thought maybe they were hiding nearby waiting for me to find them. As I walked between the rows, I remembered father said to be quiet and so I did not call for them. I walked until I had drunk all the water and still carried the empty leather skin. Hot and tired, I just kept walking and walking."

Again Eliana paused and took a deep, slow breath.

"Suddenly the wheat ended, but there I saw no road I had gone the wrong way and wondered how I would ever find my family. Right there, at the edge of the field, I sat and began to cry. How long I sat there, I don't know, but I felt someone near me. A boy, much bigger that I was sitting beside me. He gave me a drink of water and some bread."

"He asked if I was tired and if I had come a long way. I nodded yes and almost started to cry again. He gently took my hand and said, 'I'll bet you are hungry. Come with me and at our house you can get food and anything else you need. Why don't you climb on my back and pretend I am your donkey? I'll run and you can whip me to make me go faster'."

"I didn't want to whip him, but being carried sounded nice. He helped me onto his back and I held on. His hair smelled clean, and I thought how dirty I was and that I must smell like mud and dirt. He never said a word, but just ran to a large house on the edge of the city of Ur, where a woman with a kind smile and soft eyes looked at me. She reached out and took my hand."

"Over the next few hours, she bathed me, fed me, rubbed salve on my hands and knees and brushed and braided my hair. No one had ever done that but my mother. It felt strange, but she was gentle and hummed a pretty song while she worked. She told me that Abram had explained where he found me and asked if I could tell her what had happened. I did, between sobs. She sat me on her lap and said that my father and mother loved me very much. In her soft gentle voice she went on, 'They were not playing a game of hide and seek Eliana, they did that to save your life. It was a group of robbers that your father saw, and I am so sorry, but our herders, found your family. They had been killed, and the wagon burned. The donkey was gone and I expect they stole everything that they could carry'."

"She held me while I cried and rocked me in her arms. When I stopped she said that they had buried my family under a lovely cedar tree and whenever I wanted she would take me there to say goodbye. I said I wanted to go right then. We walked together to the place and holding my hand she showed the three mounds of earth, my brother's tiny mound was between my parents. She gave me a handful of earth mixed with myrrh and told me I could sprinkle it on the earth. I did and then she said a few words but I don't remember them. We walked back to the house of women and went in. Your mother said that at a time like this, it was good to be with others who had buried family. The women were singing songs of lament and I listened and they made me feel better. I must have fallen asleep for I woke up later in your mother's house."

Sarai put her arm around Eliana. "I am sorry. You have suffered so much, and I ask you to relive it."

Eliana gave a weak smile.

"She asked if I knew the names of the relatives we would visit, but all I could tell her was grandma and grandpa. She promised me they would try to find them. I know they sent messengers all over Ur, but no one could help and so I stayed and your mother cared for me and I became your friend, companion and helper. Binah could have made me a slave, but she never did. I felt more like your older sister than a servant or slave. I have been happy Sarai and I love my new family as much as my former one."

"And we loved you, and I think of you as my sister."

They sat holding hands looking into the distance for a long time.

"I have another question my friend. Eliana, are you and Reuben still meeting each other?"

"Yes, whenever we can. I just wonder what the future holds for us. I see nothing encouraging."

"What do you want if you could have the future of your dreams?"

"We love each other and want to be together. But you know that Reuben is a slave and he cannot marry a free woman. Sometimes I wish that your mother had made me a slave then we could be together."

"Oh, Eliana. You don't want to be a slave! Do you? Do you love him that much?"

"With all my heart. Neither of us sees any future for our love. I don't want a child without a husband, that doesn't seem a good situation for my future."

"I often wonder why you have not become pregnant. Here I wish I could, and you hope you don't."

"Sarai. Don't you know anything? If we simply hoped, I would be carrying two or three babies in my arms by now. Reuben spills his seed on the ground, not into me."

"I never heard of such a thing."

They sat silently for a time while Sarai thought about what she has just learned.

"Life is so unfair. I yearn for what I can't have and so do you. But our longings are different. What is to become of us?"

"My dear, sweet, innocent friend. We are women. We carry on. We do what we can. We grab whatever joy and happiness life offers us, and we live in the present. I have to leave the future in the hands of the gods and be content with my life. It is good compared to many women. We are two fortunate women, loved by exceptional men. No one beats or abuses us. We are well fed and clothed. What more can any woman expect of life?"

They sat, each deep in her own thoughts. Sarai's head was resting on Eliana's shoulder and her arm was around Sarai.

"Look, Sarai, the sun is getting low in the sky. We must go back to the village and get your cooking fire ready. I'll carry the basket and race you."

Laughing like young girls, they ran to their tents and their responsibilities.

Sarai sat outside her tent thinking about all she had been told by Eliana. She noticed Lot and Reuben walking by and called to Lot.

"Come and sit awhile with me Lot. I need to talk to you."

Reuben continued on the path and Lot squatted beside Sarai.

"Lot I have a question. Will you please tell me how Reuben came into your possession?"

"It was a long time ago in Ur. I was walking near the slave market and saw a family standing on the platform, a woman, a man and a thin, sickly lad. I guessed he was just a little younger than me, but he looked much younger. I walked over to watch. As I came closer, I could hear them speaking to each other and realized they were Hebrews. The couple had just been sold and were taken away. The boy stood there, and I don't think he understood that he was now alone and going to be sold. I felt so sorry for him, and being one of us, I bought him and he has been with me ever since."

"Lot! What were you thinking? We Hebrews do not keep our brothers as slaves. He should have been free from the day you brought him to your tent. Why didn't you?"

"You know I pay little attention to our laws. There are too many for a simple man like me. I just go about my business. I took care of him and he grew strong and he is clever. I raised him like a son and I just never thought of the law."

"Have you taught him our laws and customs?"

"I am no teacher. He watches me and learns I guess, and I try to answer his questions. Sometimes I send him to Abram for answers and they get along well. They both like to talk about things that I care little for. It is a good arrangement."

"Maybe, but it is not right. I will have to think about this. Thank you, Lot. And you have done a good job of raising him. He is a fine man and you can be proud. Goodnight and thanks again."

Sarai sat with her chin in her hands. *I will have to talk to Abram, but do I dare go to him uninvited?*

He had never turned her away, but he had been so busy and he carried such responsibility. Did he need this problem today? Just as she entered her tent, she saw Abram put a small lamp outside his door. It was their signal. With delight she started to run to him and then stopped and slowed her pace to a walk and slowed her breathing as well.

She entered the tent and was in his arms at once. He held her close, and covered her hair, her face, her hands and arms with warm demanding kisses. She slipped out of her cloak and her tunic and looked around to see Abram standing by the bed, his tunic lay crumpled at his feet. Together they lay, locked in each other's arms, their legs entwined.

Later when they were spent, they lay gently breathing and savouring the delight their bodies brought and Sarai wondered if she dare ask what she had been thinking. Yes, she dared. What better time?

And so she told him that she had learned how Eliana came to live with them and how grateful she was for his kindness.

"It costs nothing to be kind," murmured Abram. He turned to look at Sarai and smiled his broad and teasing smile.

"All right wife, what are you thinking? You are planning something, I can tell by the look on your face."

Before she lost her courage, she told him. "Eliana and Reuben have loved each other for a long time and they wanted to marry and have children."

"Sarai, you know a free woman cannot marry a slave, and what they do is wrong and against all we believe in," Abram said patiently, as if explaining something to a child.

"But you can change that. You can make it so they can marry."

"You want me to make her a slave, after all these years?" Abrams eyebrows went way up and he looked shocked.

"No. No. That's not it. Give Reuben his freedom. Lot bought him at a slave market and he knew Rueben was a Hebrew and he should have been free from the time he came to live with Lot. He has served well for many years. He has caused no trouble, nor has he caused you a moment of disappointment. Reward him for his loyalty and recognize that he is of our race."

"I did not know that he was Hebrew. We have done him a great wrong and I need to correct it. If I freed Reuben, they could marry. But he has no bride price unless he has been stealing from me."

Sarai slapped him with the end of the blanket. "You know he hasn't. Think Abram, there is no one to demand a bride price, there is no one to pay it to. She has no father, no brother, no one, and neither does he. They have only each other. And it is time they married as they have been together many times."

"They have been doing wrong, and you know the punishment for their sin."

"They have harmed no one. All they have done is love each other. Can love be such a great sin?"

Abram said, "Hmm. I will have to think about this my wife. We have treated him as a faithful servant to Lot, not as a slave. He seems to not know his errors, and perhaps this has been my failing, and it has brought us to this regrettable place."

Abram sat up and covering himself with his loin cloth, put his hand under his chin and muttered under his breath. Then he stood and paced up and down still muttering.

"Abram. What are you thinking? Tell me, will you do it? For them?" And she smiled her most beguiling smile. "For me?"

Abram stopped pacing and looking at her said, "Tell them to come to my tent after they have eaten tomorrow morning. They need to answer some questions, so have them here ready for me to talk to them. Now it is time for sleep. Return to your tent, and I shall see you in the morning."

Surprised because she usually stayed after they had made love, but she left as he had asked. As she walked away, Sarai didn't know if he was angry or just needed to be alone to decide. It will be a long night for me she thought.

Abram turned as she left and smiled a big wide smile. "I am going to enjoy this," he said to the night sky.

Chapter Fifteen

As she prepared their meal, Sarai told Eliana what she had done and they must present themselves to Abram. Eliana froze. In an icy voice she spoke. "Abram could have us stoned for fornication. He can dismiss Reuben and banish him to the desert. I should never have talked so freely to you. How could you betray my trust?" She ran from the tent.

Sarai is such an innocent, so naïve. She would never think of the consequences, only a happy ending. What have I done? She stumbled along the path. "Reuben. Reuben."

He came running to meet her. "What is wrong? Are you hurt?"

"I have told Sarai about us, and she has told Abram. He demands we go to him."

"Why? Why would you do that? Now we are in danger Eliana, great danger. Grab what you can and we will run away. It is the only thing to do. Hurry."

"Reuben. We cannot run. Where would we go? How would we live? You would be a runaway slave. We would be running for the rest of our lives, always looking around corners, wondering who would recognize us as runaways. I will not live like a criminal. I am staying to face whatever comes to me. You can stay or you can leave. I will not change my mind. This is my home, Sarai is my family. I stay here."

Reuben stared at her. His anger melted away as he saw her determination. "If you stay, I stay. May the gods protect us, and may Abram be merciful."

Abram was waiting for them as they walked hand in hand to his tent. Lot was there and so was Sarai.

Abram lifted the tent flap. "We will go inside away from curious eyes".

Inside, the couple stood close together, holding tightly to each other. Sarai smiled and tried to look reassuring, but she did not know what Abram planned. He would not speak of it when she asked.

Abram stood before them; his face unreadable. He held his staff, the sign of his absolute authority over this frightened couple. Frozen in place, they were barely breathing.

"What have I done?" Sarai moaned.

Abram cleared his throat. "I have learned that you have broken our laws and commandments. You have lain together in secret. That is forbidden." Eliana trembled and Reuben hugged her closer. "I understand that you talk of marriage. You know that can't be. A slave cannot marry a free woman. Never." His cold glare studied Reuben. "Reuben kneel before me."

Sarai gasped. Abram never asked that of his slaves. Rueben stepped forward and knelt. His body was tense, waiting for the worst. His face, set and resigned. he looked up at Abram. Sarai sensed that Lot had moved to stand beside her. As Eliana fell to her knees wailing in anguish, Sarai touched her companion's shoulder, but Eliana shook it off, refusing the comfort it offered

Abram thumped his staff on the ground. "Be quiet woman. Stop this noise."

Sarai watched Rueben. *How can he be so calm? He looks to be in control of his feelings. Even on his knees he is strong. What courage he shows to look up to Abram and meet his eyes. His head is held proudly, his shoulders square and his back straight. He is not flinching or cowering. He is not ashamed and not afraid.*

Abram raised his right hand and held his staff over Reuben. He paused, and dropped the staff. His deep imposing voice filled the tent.

"I have recently learned that you are Hebrew, Reuben, and should have been free the moment Lot claimed you. This has been a grave wrong." Abram put his hand on Reuben's shoulder. He looked at Sarai with just a hint of a smile. "Rise Reuben, you are a free man of the tribe of Terah, Abram and Lot."

Somewhere a hawk called. A dog howled. No one moved. There was silence. Then Sarai squealed in delight and grabbed Abram and kissed him. Reuben rose as Eliana touched him and they clung to each other and with tears and laughter began to dance around the tent. Sarai and Abram joined them in the dance, and Lot stood like a statue, completely speechless.

When they became calmer, Reuben and Eliana started to express their thanks, but Abram held up his hand. "Forgive me for my little drama, but I couldn't resist teasing you. However this is not finished. You need to symbolically rid yourself of your past. Reuben, you must prepare yourself with a ritual bath, cleansing your body, mind and spirit. We have no house where we can do this, so we will build a booth of branches to stop prying eyes. There, you and I and Lot will perform the ritual washing. We don't need others to watch and it will be done just after the sun sets. Wear a simple loin cloth and come to the river alone.

The next morning Abram called the couple to come to his tent and asked them what they intended to do now. They had not thought beyond the day's events.

"If you agree I have made some arrangements. Eliana, you have no mother that you can go to for a bridal chamber. No friends are ready to walk you through the steps of the marriage ceremony. This is a most unusual situation. Therefore Eliana, Sarai and I will walk you to a tent prepared for your bridal chamber and we will leave you there. Reuben will come to you. When you are ready, come together to my tent, where a meal will be ready. The unused tent at the back of Sarai's is yours from today onward for your home. Lot has paid you for three years of service, since you are now a free man. A chest is in the tent with your payment in it. And you will continue to be paid as a free man working for Lot. This evening, meet here as the sun sets and you will be married."

When they were alone, Sarai told Abram she wanted to prepare a festive meal for them.

"Yes, let us do that. I will slaughter a lamb and we will also have pigeons. Eliazer will help."

Sarai was unable to think of a way to express her thanks to her husband. She quietly told him so. He smiled that teasing smile he had and said, "Perhaps I can find a way," and he gently patted her bottom.

Sarai found Eliazar. “We have a wedding feast to prepare. I need your help.”

“Who is getting married?”

“Eliana. She and Reuben will marry at sunset. Lot is to bring us a lamb and some pigeons. We’ll serve the lamb with mint, the pigeons with have a ginger and honey sauce, served with lentils. We will need almond cakes and sweet bread, grapes, dates, almonds and cheese. Lot is making pomegranate juice to drink along with the wine. I need you to keep the cooking fires burning.”

Abram watched as they began their work. Feeling contented he entered his tent to offer prayers of thanks to which ever god had brought this happy day.

Chapter Sixteen

Terah and his followers settled in their new land. The river flowing past their camp provided the fish and fresh water they needed. The pastures were lush with grass and shrubs for the goats and the sheep. With the rich land and plenty of water their flocks grew in numbers. Fig and olive orchards flourished in the valley and Abram bought the large piece of land on which they grew. The children grew fat and ran around on sturdy, plump legs. As the women ate the good grain and mutton, they grew healthy again and the woman's tent was busy as they shared the joys and the aches and worries of bellies that grew round.

They had built a more elaborate altar on the lower slopes of the mountain and the people climbed the hill to sacrifice their lambs and goats to El Shaddai. He looked upon his people and their burnt offerings with favour and blessing and the faraway mountain slept peacefully. The people understood the agreement made with their god. If they made the proper sacrifices and obeyed the rules, then El Shaddai, appeased, withheld the angry fire and floods or droughts. The rains came when needed and the sun shone to ripen the grain. Trade at the markets in Haran proved to be profitable; this was the life they had been seeking.

In a quiet moment as they sat and watched the sunset, Sarai spoke with Abram about something that troubled her.

"We have not reached Canaan; we have been here for many rainy seasons. I enjoy this settled feeling and the people do too, but I wonder why have we stopped? You were told to go to Canaan."

"Terah can travel no further. I do not want to bury him in the wilderness. We will bury him here and his tomb will be marked as he deserves. We will stay until we bury our father. I have found a dry cave that will be his tomb. A stone worker is making a marker for it."

As each day passed, Terah grew feebler and the strong voice no longer ordered wine or cheese or olives. He asked for porridge and broth. One morning when Abram entered his father's tent, he came out in a few minutes, beating his breast in grief. The old man had drawn his last breath. Abram made the arrangements and they laid Terah to rest in the cave on the slopes leading to the mountain, looking down on the tents below.

The tribe followed the family to the grave and everyone remembered Terah as a great man.

"He made us a great people and a great nation."

"He made the best carvings in all of Ur."

"He led us here to this land of plenty and we are safe in this valley."

"I seem to remember Abram making most of the decisions."

"Hush. This is to honour Terah. Abram is still with us."

The bearers placed his body in the cave and Abram offered praise to his father and prayers for the soul of this ancient leader.

The grave marker, with his name chiseled into the stone, showed the place where Terah, the great sheik of Ur, lay in peace.

Sarai and Abram stayed at the grave after others had left and planted an almond tree.

“Father loved the flowers of the almond tree, didn’t he?” Abram spoke with quiet dignity.

“Yes, he was always happy when they bloomed, and he liked the nuts also.”

“I remember mother baking almond cakes for him, and how he ate them eagerly.”

As the sky turned red and gold, they walked back to their tents content that they had seen their father laid to rest in this good land.

Abram was now the official leader of this great and growing nation. Those he led loved and respected him, but there were the inevitable grumblers. Abram kept the army training in the hills and valleys.

“I hate training in this hot sun.”

“We are good warriors. Why do we need to keep shooting arrows and throwing spears?”

“There are no enemies; we are safe here.”

“Abram says we never know. Things can change in a moment.”

“I just wish he would change his mind and let us rest.”

Abram kept his ears open when in the city and he heard the talk of the travellers in the caravans. No land was ever safe from ambitious kings and rulers and Aram knew they had sufficient wealth to attract a greedy aggressor. If anyone raided them, Abram wanted to make the invaders pay for their attack. While the men trained, the women tore strips of cloth and kept it clean, wrapped in goatskin, ready to bandage the wounded if a battle came to their peaceful valley.

Weeks later under the silver stars Sarai and Abram sat by his tent. As she looked at her husband his furrowed brow and tightly clenched hands showed his concern. “Sarai. This is a good valley, food, water and good grass land, everything we need to grow and prosper is here in abundance. But I dislike living so close to such evil deeds. We have seen what happens in Haran, and we are once again living with people who do not worship El Shaddai. That was the reason we had to leave Ur.”

“We are doing well here, Abram. Are you getting restless again?”

“I have not seen it, and I do not want to, but I believe that human sacrifice is offered to the god Sin. As you reminded me, we stopped here on the way, because of the health of Terah. He would have died on the trail with no marker or ceremony. But he died here, contented, and he felt he was at home. I think it is time we moved on and travelled to the land God has given us in Canaan.”

“But Abram, we—

“Sarai. While we stay here, we are in disobedience to the command of the mighty one. There is also much talk of invaders coming this way. I do not want to see our families slaughtered, or sold into slavery. I know there will be discontent and unhappiness, but Sarai, as you reminded me, it is what El Shaddai commanded and it will be best for us."

And so, Abram ordered that the tents be struck and packed. From the back of a cart as he had done so often in the past, he stood and explained his reasons to his clan. "Anyone who wishes to remain here may take what he owns and continue to live in the valley or move to the city to live amid wickedness and evil."

Two families stayed, and Abram wished them well and gave them each two goats and three sheep from his own flock as a parting gift. The ones who remained with their chief muttered quietly to each other, but they began once again to get ready to travel to the land that Abram said God had promised them. They would travel south to Canaan, through rich grass lands with plenty of water and game to hunt. Many remembered the former journey and understood the tasks they had to do. They worked together and in a short time were ready once more to undertake a long journey.

The morning when they were getting ready to go, Sarai and Eliana took a last walk around the valley.

"I want to remember this place. We've spent pleasant, peaceful days here. Many happy times. Babies born, and children are growing tall and strong."

"Reuben and I were married here and we've been so happy."

"I've been happy too. But it is also where I have said goodbye to my father and he sleeps on the hill. Here, I am the leader of the women. They still disparage me because I am barren. I hear them whisper and snicker behind their hands. I am sure they pity Abram and there are those who put themselves in his way, hoping he is looking for a second wife."

"You have to ignore them. They are just envious of your place as Abram's wife."

"I can disregard the remarks, but those who shun me, as if my empty womb would taint them, are harder to forget. I've endured this for a long time, but it gets harder as the years pass me by, and each time my moon time comes, I am shamed once again."

Eliana took Sarai's hand as she spoke. "But there is great respect and affection for your skill as a healer, a friend and a wise woman."

"I try to keep that in my mind and pay no attention to the insults. But it gets more painful as the years are passing by."

Together they walked around the camp, enjoying the comforting smell of smoke and meat being roasted.

"Look Sarai. The mountain sleeps tonight. I hate the fire and smoke when it comes. It makes me afraid and angry. All the noise and danger, dirt and death, and what does it accomplish? Nothing it seems to me. Since the mountain is quiet, I wonder if El Shaddai cares that we did not go on to Canaan?"

"As is our custom, Abram says we go, and so we move, again. This time I will find it easier to lead the way and set the example."

"Once more, we pack up our lives and walk into the unknown."

As they reached Sarai's tent she stepped inside and grabbed two shawls for them. They sat on the ground and wrapped the soft fabric around their shoulders against the chill of the evening.

"Eliana, just once I'd like to hear El Shaddai speak and tell me what to do. I know it's not possible as I am only a woman. But I have dreams and hopes, fears and expectations. Why are my prayers of no account? Why do we women do the hard labour but can't do the things that the almighty one demands? Maybe if we offered the blood sacrifices he demands, our voices would be heard and then we might hear that voice speaking from clouds and on the wind."

"But I don't want to worship a god that sends fire and destruction when I make a mistake. If a small blemish on a goat makes this god so angry he can destroy whole villages, what kind of god is he?"

Sarai yawned and stretched. "I can find no answers to these questions and they give me a headache. I will make my grain offerings to the breasted one of the mountain and carry on in my own way. Perhaps there is only one god on the holy mountain, we just know that god differently. Men see him as all powerful, because that is what they want to be. Women who try to live gentler, calmer lives, see a god who loves and nurtures. Perhaps someday women will have our voices heard in the dwellings of the gods. But until then, things are as they are."

The two friends said goodnight and went to their sleeping mats for the night. Tomorrow will bring its own challenges.

Before the camp was fully awake, Sarai sat outside her tent as the first streaks of colour touched the clouds. Sarai looked at her feet and there was a very unusual stone. It was very black, and it appeared to be smooth to touch even though the surface was rippled. It looked like waves as if the top was covered in overlapping curls of black stone. She picked it up and was surprised at how light it was. She expected it be as heavy as her fire stones, but it was much lighter. *Did the mountain fire make you? I think you've come to me from the sacred mountain, for you look as if you'vein the holy fire. But you survived and I too have survived. The strong spirit of endurance is in both of us.*

She added this stone to the others she had collected. She kept them in a wicker basket which was in the chest where she kept her blankets and cloaks. Eliana called to her.

"Sarai, come and join Reuben and me for our morning meal. It is ready and you've just been dreaming, not cooking."

When they finished and cleaned up their dishes, Reuben put out the fire and left to find Lot. The moment to leave arrived. She joined the long line of people, carts and animals. They had lined up as they had before, without many directions from the elders, for they remembered the order of their march. Abram stood at the front with his staff and he called out the order to get ready to move.

They began the trek in the cool weather just after the rainy season, but before the hot summer sun baked everything to a dry dull brown. There were good trails to follow, and they travelled many miles each day. It was so unlike the desert travels to Haran. The grass grew green and tall, and clumps of flowers grew in the open spaces; anemone, lilies, daisies and roses. Their scent filled the air with sweet perfume. Bees hummed as they flew from one flower to another. Birds flitted among the trees and their chirping cheered the travellers. Rabbits and deer fed in the meadows or by the streams. It was a land that promised life. The land El Shaddai promised to Abram.

After many weeks, they came to a broad valley where Abram called a halt. Speaking from the back of a cart, he pointed to a magnificent tree.

"That tree is the sacred oak of Moreh. Traders often rest here in its shade. We too will rest, while I await a word from the mighty one of the mountain."

As days passed, Abram paced around the camp. When the children tried to follow him, he chased them away. He had no time for the trivial games of children. He had little time for meals or sleep or Sarai. The men were restless; the women uneasy. They were no longer moving, but neither were they settled. After many long, frustrating days, word came to Abram.

Once more he stood before the gathered crowd and spoke. "See this great land to the south. We have been travelling to this land for many days. We are here in the land God promised to show me. This great valley will be our home. We go further into it, and then we will once again erect our great tent city. This is the final stage of our long journey."

A cheer arose from the crowd. A cheer that meant relief from their arduous travelling. A cheer that meant hope for a new and prosperous life. A cheer of thanksgiving for safe arrival.

Continuing south, they moved deep into the land of Canaan. As they travelled, each time they stopped for a rest, Abram constructed a simple altar to the Holy One of the mountain and offered a burnt offering of grain or corn. This not only honoured the god of their journey but marked the territory of Abram and his people. After days of travel Abram came to a wide and picturesque valley, with trees and flowers growing along the river banks. It was between Bethel on the East and Ai on the West. Here he called a halt to the journey and declared this was to be their new home. Then the laborious work of re-building their settlement began. Everyone had a task to do, and since they had done it before, the transition from nomads to a settled people went smoothly. One of the first things Abram did was to build a permanent altar on the highest hill. The sacred mountain was visible but far away and often shrouded in clouds.

The familiar patterns emerged and life slowed. Some complained that they missed the markets of the city, but they sought new markets. The traders passed nearby, and a market grew up beside the road. Contentment settled on their tent city.

While cooking the evening meal, Sarai and Eliana were chatting together as they did every day.

"Sarai, do you think we will stay here?"

"We can only hope. But this is the place that Abram says El Shaddai led us to, so I like to believe we will stay."

"Then why don't we build sturdy houses in which to live? Why do we still dwell in tents like wanderers?"

"I don't know. All I know is that I live each day, in trust that this will be my dwelling place for the rest of my life."

"It feels as if our roles have changed. I am the one with questions and you are the accepting one. What has happened to us?"

"I think we may be growing older and wiser. Older for sure. Wiser, maybe."

They laughed together and sat to eat their meal, as Abram and Reuben joined them.

After three rainy seasons, just when the vines and trees were well established, the gardens planted and producing, and all was peaceful and in order; the rains failed. The streams dried up and famine stalked them. They wondered what they had forgotten to do to honour their god. Abram tried to think of reasons El Shaddai had forsaken them. At night he talked to Sarai.

“Have I made a mistake in forsaking the other gods? Perhaps Tammuz the god of vegetation is angry, or Adad the rain god, or Ninurta the god of crops and harvest. Are they withholding their gifts because they are no longer worshipped? I have rejected Dagon and the sacrifices he demanded. What if I am wrong, Sarai? Is it my fault we are starving?”

“I do not know Abram. I have never understood the gods and their need to be appeased with sacrifices. If you don’t know, who will find the answer for us? I simply know you are a good and faithful follower of El Shaddai.”

Sarai threw another log on the fire and they watched the shower of sparks float away into the gathering darkness.

“But I wonder have we moved too far away from the holy mountain? Can he no longer smell the odour of our offerings? But he told me we have to move. I don’t know, I just don’t know.”

Sarai reached out and took Abram’s big strong hand in her small one. “I don’t know either, Abram. But I trust you and your faith and wisdom. You will find the way to save our people. Do not doubt yourself. Follow your heart.”

They sat together until the moon found her resting place for the day. Silently, each deep in their own thoughts, they went to their sleeping mats to rest.

Egypt

Chapter Seventeen

After days of talk and questioning among the elders, they made a decision. Abram and Sarai, with a small party of servants and guards, would go to Egypt where food was plentiful. If the tribe did not survive, at least the small band might and they could return when the famine ended. Before he left, Abram took much of his gold and silver to bury in a cave in the rocky outcroppings on the hill side. Sarai realized what he was doing, and she asked him to hide a heavy basket that she said was very important to her. Abram looked puzzled, but he asked no questions and took it along with his own things, to the cave. He planted thorn bushes in front of the opening and carried rocks to help to hide the entrance to the cave.

After careful preparations the small group and their few flocks began their travel. They stayed near the coast of the great sea to avoid the desert and departed south. In Egypt Abram hoped to buy food from the Pharaoh and return with enough to keep his family alive.

Eliana stayed with Reuben, and Rivkah joined Sarai as her servant and companion. Sarai talked to her as they walked, struggling with feelings of loss once more. *Rivkah tries her best, but she isn't Eliana. I must be patient and give her a chance. It will be better when we get to know and trust each other.*

At the end of the first day Sarai sighed. "Here we are again. Sleeping under the stars. The nights are cool, much cooler than I had expected. We live on bread, fruit and cheese, until it runs out. Then what?"

"I don't know Sarai. I have never lived in the desert. What will it be like in Egypt?"

"Hot, dry, and tiresome. The date palm we found yesterday was a treat, even if the dates were drying up. Water is what we need to look for."

"Are there wells along the way?"

Sarai snorted. "Not in the desert. We hope to find a stream or even better an oasis. There we can fill our water skins, bathe and wash our clothes. Sing with me, to pass the time."

The further south they went, the drier it became. When there was water in stale pools it was flat and tasteless, but it was water. They rested in the shade of scrawny trees during the heat of the day. When evening came, Sarai sat with her husband.

"Abram, I hear that Egypt has a mighty river that never goes dry."

"Yes. That is why they always have food for their people and to share. I hope to buy grain and cattle."

"I'm glad we stop in the hottest part of the day. I feel like a cake set out on a rock to bake in the sun. The heat drains my energy, my hope, and my confidence."

"It never shows Sarai. I am proud of your courage and your strength and trust."

Even as they lay beside each other to sleep, Sarai found it hard to be generous in her thoughts toward Abram. *Why do we have to travel again? I hate smelling like a donkey. The new moon is in the sky, but there is no tent to welcome the silver arc. Will I ever again share that time of wonder and joy with women? I think I should have married Judah the carpenter and stayed in Ur.*

One boiling hot morning after a long, arduous climb, they crested a hill. Abram signalled a rest and everyone just dropped to the hot sand where they stood. Something drew Sarai to look ahead below the hill. She cried with joy as she saw a great river flowing through the valley. Along its banks, trees with graceful branches waved a welcome. She could see the gigantic, pointed stone structures they had been told were the tombs of the Pharaohs. They were so tall their tips appeared to touch the sky. Covered in smooth stone, they gleamed and sparkled in the sun.

"How great and powerful these men must have been to build such tombs."

Rivkah came and stood beside her. "I am afraid, Sarai. I don't want to go the city."

"Then stay on this hill and die." There was no pity in her voice, only despair.

Abram announced that they would rest until morning and prepare. They should brush the dirt of their travels from their clothes and hair and clean themselves to prepare to meet these powerful and wealthy people.

It was a busy afternoon and evening, and when all were resting and it was quiet, Abram spoke to Sarai. "I will tell the Pharaoh that you are my sister. It is safer to do that."

"That is a true statement Abram, but I am also your wife, and I don't understand what you mean by safer."

"Sarai, leave these diplomatic matters to me. Just do as I say. Good night."

With that he rolled over and started snoring. Sarai lay awake for a long time wondering about the morning, as she drifted into sleep.

Maybe I'll stay on the hill with Rivkah and die in peace. But I can't. I am Abram's wife and that means I follow him wherever he goes, to the ends of the earth if that is his will. I feel as if I am at the ends of the earth and perhaps the end of my days.

As she tried to imagine what they would find in this strange city, her breathing slowed, her eyes closed, and Sarai slept in the land of the great Pharaoh.

Chapter Eighteen

It felt as if she had hardly closed her eyes when Abram stirred and ordered her to get up and feed him. Rubbing her eyes, she called Rivkah, and they prepared the last meal of bread, olives, and dates. The cheese had been eaten days ago. There was no wine, and no time to make tea, so everyone drank the brackish water they had carried from the last oasis. No one was in a pleasant mood as they started down the hill to the river.

In spite of the gloomy start to the day, Sarai could not contain her excitement. From what she had noticed from the hilltop the evening before, this city contained marvels such as she had never seen. She had many questions, but as she asked Rivkah, she knew that neither had any answers.

"I wonder what the people are like? Will they understand us? Will I understand them? What do the women wear, and how do they fix their hair? What will we eat? I have so many questions I can't wait to see and to experience this great city."

"I wonder just as you do, but I am not so eager to find out. I don't mind being your slave but I will die before I will serve these foreign masters."

"Keep your fears to yourself. I am going to keep alert and learn everything I can from these people. They have such wonderful buildings, we can learn much from them."

Descending the sandy hill was treacherous. The sand slid from beneath their feet and poured down the slope, threatening to carry them with it. Feet scurried to keep up with the shifting world, and arms whirled in circles to maintain balance.

Oh, I hope no one is watching.

At the bottom, breathless and humiliated, Sarai caught her breath and touched her flaming cheeks. She looked toward the city and spotted guards bearing crossed lances standing at the huge stone gate. They acted oblivious to the sand hill and were talking together. The small group formed a line and began the walk to the gate. As they came near the city Sarai couldn't believe the wonders before her.

"Look at those pillars, Abram. They are taller than a tamarisk tree. And they have paintings covering them. They stretch along the road as far as I can see."

"I see them Sarai. These are a powerful and cultured people. They are ancient and their sculptures and statues are the talk of the traders. Try not to look like a child who has seen nothing of the world. We need to impress their leaders."

The guards noticed them as they approached and stood tall as they formed a barrier with their spears. They spoke, and strange sounds poured from their lips. Abram replied. "We come in peace and wish to speak with your leaders."

The guards barked out orders and a young man ran along the avenue that stretched before them leading into the city. There was no other sound or movement. Sarai stood as still as she could, but she kept fidgeting from one foot to the other. After a long time, four men strode toward them.

"I believe I speak your language and will carry your messages."

"Yes. I understand you. We come in peace and wish to talk to officials of this great and splendid city, in the land of the magnificent Pharaoh."

Sarai's attention wandered as she stared at the messengers. Three wore short girdles and their chests and legs were bare, they carried weapons and their stern and foreboding faces did not carry a welcome. The other man wore a robe that touched the ground. His breast plate shone blue and gold and a large circular head dress was the same colour. He carried a dagger in a sheath at his waist. The conversation went back and forth but she didn't follow it. She was entranced by the appearance of these men and stared in silence.

They turned and Abram stepped toward them. He poked Sarai, and she followed behind him. The others walked behind Sarai, staring at everything that they saw. The guards parted their lances, and the group walked between the pillars and onto a long broad avenue.

"We will soon meet the grand vizier, second in command to Pharaoh. Try to act as the wife of an important official, here on business.

They walked along the road, lined with graceful palms and huge statues. Sarai whispered to Rivkah. "All these statues along the street are bigger than life. They are large enough to sit on and rest. But surely no one would dare."

"These statues are frightening. The body is a lion, the head is a man. What can they mean? Are there these creatures in this city? I am scared Sarai. I want to go back."

For one moment Sarai wondered if she should have stayed on the hill as Rivkah wanted, but she kept walking. *If I had, I'd never have seen these wonders. I enjoy the sound of the wind in the trees. It is a welcome song. I hope the people are as gentle as the breeze. Even the sand isn't as hot as it was out in the open. The river and the breeze must keep it cooler. And we walk in the shadow of these wonderful buildings and statues.*

At the end of this long avenue the palace stood in its splendid magnificence. The building was made of stunning golden stone and there were statues and gardens with fountains surrounding it. The buildings around the palace, made of mud bricks, appeared well -shaped and smooth. At the gates they stopped and Abram bowed to the official waiting there.

Sarai stopped paying attention to the flattering words Abram was droning on to the translator. She watched the river flowing lazily past them and she fixed her eyes on the city where there were more houses than she had seen in her lifetime. People were moving about and the clothing they wore was unlike anything she had ever seen. The headdresses appeared strange to Sarai, and she stared wide-eyed. A boy standing near the vizier was bald except for a lock of hair that grew from one side of his head. She startled when she heard Abram speaking about her.

"Yes, the beautiful one, standing there is my sister," she heard Abram say and started to add and my wife, but Abram spat out, "Silence."

Sarai remained quiet. What happened next caused her palms to sweat and her guts to churn. The translator told her to go with two of the armed men. They came and stood on each side of her and shoved her ahead of them. She tried to look back at Abram but the burly guard pushed her through a gate which slammed shut behind her. A delightful garden courtyard opened before her. The stone walkway lined with beds of white jasmine, purple anemone and red poppies, caught her eye. The scent filled the air, borne on a gentle breeze. Her heart skipped a beat when she recognized her beloved tamarisk tree near the door of a building. A large fat man greeted her with a nod and beckoned her to follow. She walked along the stone path to the open doorway and entered the building. It surrounded her with deliciously cool air and she walked into a large room with only women present.

Their white dresses made of soft fabric flowed when they walked and had an interesting weave. The women wore jewelled bracelets on their arms and ankles. Their eyes painted black all around them, were friendly. Black hair held by jewelled bands fell freely down their backs. Their cheeks and lips were as red as the pomegranate. Sarai stood speechless. No one greeted her, only the wide-eyed stares of these elegant women met her astonished glance. Sarai felt awkward and embarrassed at her simple, travel stained clothing.

How can I feel and act important when I look worse than a slave?

After a long time, a woman approached and spoke in Hebrew.

"My name is Hagar. I am Egyptian now, but am Hebrew born and I speak your language. I will be your maid and translator while you are here in the harem."

"What is this harem?"

"It is the part of the palace where the women live together, and no man can enter. Pharaoh treats the women in his household with kindness. In the harem are wives, concubines, servants and slaves, and the Queen of Egypt, Pharaoh's first wife. We have everything we need and you will soon learn our ways. Come. You need a bath," replied Hagar in a pleasant musical voice.

At the word bath, Sarai's trepidation vanished, and she followed Hagar into a bright cheerful room with a large pool in the centre. It was open to the sky, and flowering trees and bushes nested around the walls.

A pool! I am going to bathe in a pool made of stone. The water flows through it, like a river. How can that be? The perfume of the flowers in the room, sweet and lemony, yet spicy and earthy, made her head spin, and she swooned. *I am a princess of Ur and I will not disgrace my ancestors before these strangers. I will not faint.*

Women surrounded her and took off her clothes and sandals. Hagar said that they'd be burned. Sarai stamped her foot and said, "No. They will be washed and cleaned and returned to me. They are mine and I will keep them." *I don't know why this is important to me, but it is. They are not aware that I am a princess from Ur, but I remember how to give orders and how to get what I need.*

Hagar spoke to the women and Sarai hoped she told them what she had said. The women looked aghast, shrugged, and using sticks they carried Sarai's things away.

The next few hours were a dream. Sarai bathed in the fresh flowing water. She lay back and relaxed as the aches and pains floated away. Women came and washed her with soft sponges using a paste that foamed and left a delicious scent on her skin. They washed her hair, rinsed and then washed and rinsed again, with the same foamy paste. The women pointed to a table, covered with a soft sheet. Sarai climbed onto the cool slab, and slaves oiled and massaged her weary body. The remaining aches and pains vanished as firm but gentle hands kneaded her sore and tender muscles.

As she relaxed, she hummed a song, but stopped when she realized everyone was staring. Hagar gave her a tunic, white and luxurious, the same as the others wore. It lay soft and cool against her perfumed skin. Then they showed her to a seat and a young woman brushed her hair until it shone and placed a band decorated with bits of coloured material around her head to keep her hair in place. Sarai knew she smelled just wonderful and the stink of donkey was forgotten. *I can't wait to show Abram.* Then it hit her. They will never allow Abram in this room, and she suspected she couldn't leave. *When can I see him again? I have no control over this or what happens to me. If I will live or die, I don't know. But I will try to appreciate this time here and if it is to be my end, at least I die surrounded by beauty.*

Hagar walked with her around the palace rooms and showed her where the women slept, ate, and amused themselves with music, needlework, mosaics, and paints. The immense rooms overwhelmed her, and when she looked up, the ceilings were far above her head. They were covered with paintings, and so were the walls. Vivid scenes of battles, gods, and ordinary people all in rich colours, swam before her eyes. The floor was an intricate pattern made with coloured stone and marble. It left Sarai breathless with its splendour and charm. They went to eat their evening meal and Sarai wondered what they would serve.

"You sit here, on this cushion. I can't stay as I am not a kitchen slave. Just follow what the others do and you will be fine."

She recognized many of the foods, but there were things she did not know and she tried them with delight. A leafy green vegetable tasted crisp and refreshing. The strange orange fruit was thirst quenching and sweet. They sat at a round table and hot food arrived in a large bowl placed in the centre and everyone took from it, picking the stew up on bread and bringing it to their mouths. Bowls were provided to wash hands between the courses. Sarai learned what to do by watching, and stuffed herself until her stomach hurt, but she didn't care. *This will be an adventure, so I might as well enjoy it. And I will learn as much as I can. Perhaps Hagar will talk to me about medicines and treatments for diseases.*

After an evening of music and dancing, Hagar took her to her place to sleep. A stone platform with legs and a raised ledge for her head was in the room.

"Is this where I sleep? How do I rest on a table with short fat legs?"

Hagar laughed. "Just lie down and put your head on the raised end."

"This isn't so bad. The mattress is soft."

"It is made of cotton and so is this sheet. They have been perfumed with lavender. It will help you to have a restful sleep."

Sarai wasn't sure she could sleep on this strange platform, but to her surprise, it was comfortable and she drifted into a deep dreamless sleep.

Chapter Nineteen

Sarai woke to the sound of people walking in a hallway. Muffled footsteps shuffled by her room. Confusion overcame her. Then memories flooded her mind.

I am in the palace of the Pharaoh.

She stood and slipped off the cotton robe she was wearing and reached for the gown she had taken off at bedtime. It had disappeared. In its place was a very similar one, but it had blue stitches around the collar and hem. She shrugged her shoulders as she slipped it over her head.

"Sarai, are you awake?" For a minute she couldn't place the voice and then remembered Hagar.

"Yes, I am getting dressed.Come in."

"Good morning. I hope you slept well."

"I did. I think I was exhausted from all the walking I did. What happened to the dress I wore yesterday?"

"Don't you like this one?"

"Oh yes, it is fine. But where is the other one?"

"You will receive a clean one each morning. Here in the heat, things get soiled quickly. We change our clothes each day."

"That is a lot of washing."

"The slaves do it, and they don't mind. It is easy work. Come, we will brush your hair and then eat our morning meal."

They ate together, with a few other women, in a small courtyard just outside the hall that ran by Sarai's room. The garden was serene and peaceful. A fountain sent cooling spray into the air and the sound of running water soothed the tiny fears that nibbled at Sarai's gut. She enjoyed the fresh fruit, cheese and buns made from barley flour and sweetened with dates.

I wonder what each day will bring. I am both excited and nervous to experience this new life.

The days passed swiftly as there was so much to see and learn. Sarai watched the women and tried to copy their dainty way of eating, laughing and speaking. She watched how they walked with tiny steps, so different from the strong confident strides she was used to making. When she tried to move her feet in the same manner, she almost fell.

This is so silly and awkward. If I had walked like this in the dessert, I would still be out there, hungry, hot and thirsty. But it is graceful compared to my strong strides. I'll keep trying.

She had no chores to do. Servants took care of every detail. She and Hagar had time to talk, and they shared with each other the things that women talk about, clothes, family, food, entertainment, and the uncertainty of their lives.

"You speak Hebrew Hagar, yet you are here in Egypt."

"As a small child, bandits stole me from my parents when they raided our caravan. They sold me to an Egyptian family that Pharaoh enslaved for debts owed to the palace. I've lived here most of my life. They tell me I was a beautiful child, and they placed me here to be groomed for Pharaoh. There are several Hebrews here, and we talk when we can and that has kept my mother's language alive in my memory."

"All your life? Here? A slave?"

"It isn't a bad life, Sarai. There is plenty to eat, lovely clothes to wear, and the work is easy. No one beats me, or rapes me, and there are good friends among the women here. While some are free and some are slaves, we treat each other with respect. I've no wish to marry and belong to a man who might abuse me and then turn me out with just a few words. No thank you. My life is pleasant and easy."

They finished their meal and went for a walk around the courtyard. The sun was a ball of red fire in the sky, but there were palm trees, grass, flowers, and fountains and the air was cooler than Sarai expected it to be.

"Marriage can be good Hagar. Abram is kind and has never raised his hand to me. He has not divorced me, even though he has reason to, for I am childless. He has not taken another wife, or a concubine. My husband loves me and I am the matriarch of our tribe and—"

Hagar put up a hand to stop Sarai.

"Sarai, stop and think. You are here in this harem room and your husband is alive because he said you were his sister."

"I am his sister. We have different mothers, but the same father."

"You speak as if you were his wife. Are you his wife or sister?"

"I am both. It may be hard to understand, but it is true," Sarai replied with a touch of exasperation.

"Pharaoh does not know you are his wife. Abram lied to Pharaoh and for his own purpose. Your husband knows, I am sure, that as his wife, if Pharaoh desires you, Abram is as good as dead. Pharaoh would never lie with another man's wife, but a widow is no problem. If you are Abram's sister, Pharaoh will pay him a goodly price for you, if he decided to keep you as a concubine."

Sarai dropped onto a bench, dumbfounded, speechless. The pretty dresses, good food and pleasant days, became a sour lump in her belly. A concubine! Pharaoh's concubine! What had Abram done? Did he understand? But he knew because he concealed their marriage. As the truth became real to her, the shock turned into a deep rage.

"He denied me as his wife. How dare he deny me! I am not a thing to be bartered and sold, not even for his life. I am his wife, leader of the women, wise and learned. I am the primary healer. He turns to me for advice."

She stood and paced up and down the path, waving her arms and stamping her feet in utter frustration.

"He has given me to Pharaoh for his own security. Am I so easily dismissed? Pharaoh will use me and then toss me aside. Eventually turned back to Abram? Stoning is the end for a woman who has been a sexual partner to a man other than her husband. The reasons wouldn't matter. Guilty. Sinful. Disgraced. No! I won't do it."

She looked at Hagar, her eyes flashed, her hands trembled and her voice filled with disgust.

"Hagar, no man, not even the great Pharaoh can use me in this way. I will tell the truth that I am Abram's wife."

"Sarai, take a long breath and think. Forget everything that came before and relax and enjoy this life you have. You have beautiful clothing, more than enough food, friends and music and art. I decided long ago that I could live a life of misery longing for what I had lost, but I embraced the future and its possibilities."

"You made your choice and I will make mine. I won't be sold like a sheep, not even for Abram's life."

"What can you do about it now?"

Sarai flopped down on the floor and wept. "I will think about what to do but I won't be Pharaoh's plaything."

The day dragged on for her. The music didn't soothe her mind, her fingers wouldn't make the tiny stitches, and she kept poking herself with the needle. She picked at her food, although it looked delicious and smelled heavenly.

Weeks later, as Hagar was braiding her hair for bed, Sarai spoke.

"I have decided I want to tell Pharaoh the truth. But how can I do that? I don't know where he is in this huge palace or how to get an audience."

"You are not thinking Sarai. Pharaoh has absolute power in this land. He is a god. Slavery, banishment in the desert, even death could be the end for both of you. Is this life so terrible?

"Yes. I am a princess from the land of Ur. No one can treat me like this. Not anyone. Not even Abram."

"Reflect on this more tonight. Decide in the morning when you've considered what may happen."

Hagar left and Sarai paced the floor. The moon was high in the sky when she lay on the bed and exhaustion shut her eyes in sleep. As she slept, Sarai dreamed. She saw great hills of sand blowing in the wind. The shapes changed and shifted and moved. Never still. Never the same. The sand had no power over the wind. She awoke with the dream still vivid in her memory.

Hagar entered her room and couldn't grasp what she saw. Sarai was still in yesterday's dress. Her hair was flying in all directions, unbrushed and tangled. Her eyes were red and swollen.

"I don't suppose you want to hear, good morning."

"No. I want you to sit here with me and listen. Don't speak. Just listen while I try to explain to you what I must do."

"I've brought fruit that we can share as you talk and I listen."

"Hagar, last night I dreamed that I was a grain of sand, blown by every wind. There was nothing firm to stand upon. And the dream speaks truth. There is no security for me in this. As a concubine of Pharaoh I will be just another plaything discarded at his whim. To accept this life, will be like trying to hold on to the blowing sand. This life is not what I want, and I will risk everything to regain my place as the wife of Abram, my husband. I will accept the consequences for both of us. What comes from it, I can't control. I want an audience with the Pharaoh."

"You can't go to Pharaoh. Even his queen can't enter his presence unless he calls for her."

"Tell me what I can do. There must be something."

"I can ask for an audience with the queen. She asked me about you. But remember. You are asking to speak to the Pharaoh and tell him Abram has deceived him? The end may be worse than you expect."

"What might happen to us? Slavery? Death? How can that be worse than what I face now? I don't care what happens to me. But Abram?" She stood and paced the length of her room. "He didn't seem to care what happened to me. He looked out for himself. Why should I not take care of myself?"

Hagar opened her mouth to speak but Sarai never stopped for a breath, and Hagar closed it again.

"If mother was here, she would know what to do. She isn't, so the choice is mine. My dreams told me that all is blowing sand and I cannot stop the wind. But I can control this. I will not accept this insult. The truth must be told. But can I bear the consequences?"

She stood frozen to the spot. "Yes. Yes I can and I will. It may be unbearable whatever I do, and I have decided that I want to tell Pharaoh the truth. If he is a god as you say he is, he must be honourable. Take me to the queen."

"You are sure you want to tell Pharaoh the truth, although I can't imagine why. If so, we will go to the queen. Tell her your story of marriage and how you have been betrayed by Abram. She is a good woman. She will understand. But think what might happen to Abram."

"I have decided. Abram had no thought for me. How could he

offer me up to this great god of the Nile? Am I nothing?"

She picked up a fig and took a bite, then threw the rest across the room. "I am Sarai, princess, and I will tell the wife of Pharaoh."

"Remember we do not know what Pharaoh will do. Kill you both. Kill Abram and still take you as a concubine if you please him. If he wishes, he might turn both of you out of the palace and send you away. If you don't want to be one of Pharaoh's women, you need to decide at once. He is asking for a new toy for his bedroom, and you will have to go to him soon."

She stood, trembling, but dry eyed and confident, she told Hagar to take her to the queen. Once she decided, she ate a piece of fruit and bread; then they left the room. Sarai walked, dragging her feet to the room where the women gathered to sew and talk. As she entered, she noticed that the women were crying and talking in hushed tones.

"Hagar, what is happening?"

"A plague has struck the huts of the slaves. They are dying one after another. Pharaoh believes it is a curse from one of the gods and is looking for someone to blame for making the gods angry. I hope it isn't the lie that Abram has told."

That settled the matter for Sarai. Now she was sure she had made the right decision. "Go at once tell the wife of Pharaoh that I want him told the truth. Whatever happens, I will live or die with it. I can do this and be true to myself, but to stand ashamed before Abram, before God and within myself, would not bearable. And whether this plague is Abram's fault, Pharaoh will come to that solution, soon. Better I tell the truth now. We might stay alive this way."

Hagar looked at Sarai, smiled a weak smile and left the room. Sarai picked up her weaving but her heart was not in it. She sat and held it in her hands and waited for Hagar to return.

Much later when Hagar found Sarai sitting alone in the garden, she only said that the Queen listened as she told Sarai's story. Late in the evening a message came from the Pharaoh. Sarai was to come to his grand hall in the morning. The messenger said that Abram had to attend Pharaoh too.

Sarai slept little that night. She paced the room for hours while she wondered how she would re-act to seeing Abram. It broke her heart. Her image of Abram, her wonderful husband shattered and her hopes for the future lay like a broken dish before her. When at last she slept, it was the sleep of a woman possessed. She tossed from side to side, moaning as if in physical pain and she cried copious tears into the sheet with which she covered her heart break.

She dressed with care in the morning. Hagar braided her hair, and she wore a simple robe and cloak, both the colour of sand. Her eyes were red and puffy but she refused to have them painted to hide her agony. She felt sick inside. When it was time, she stood tall and walked with her usual strong strides into the audience room of the great Pharaoh. No mincing steps at a time such as this.

The room took her breath away. Marble floors shone like the moon. Intricate patterns in white, black and shades of brown gleamed in the sun's light. There were great round pillars supporting a ceiling decorated with many paintings, as were the walls. Pictures of stick figures dotted the walls and there were cobras, crocodiles, leopards and many black and gold beetles. Sarai's eyes darted from image to image. A raised dais drew her attention. On it stood two thrones. One was a magnificent golden chair with a smaller one beside it, both empty. Slaves stood on either side with ostrich plume fans to cool Pharaoh.

The sound of trumpets spilt the air and a curtain parted with a swoosh. There stood Pharaoh and his queen. She wore a vivid purple gown with patterns of plum and crimson. The gown was edged in gold thread and on her head she wore a golden circle with a cobra rising from it. Pharaoh was a golden man. His elaborate head dress was gold as was his breastplate hanging from a golden chain and covering his chest. There were wide bands of gold covering his arms and legs. Golden sandals were on his feet and in his hand a staff with a snake of gold at its top.

He looked at her and his eyes were kinder than she expected. He beckoned to her and she walked toward the throne and as she neared the steps, stopped and gracefully bowed. As she bowed low, out of the corner of her eye she caught sight of Abram standing to one side of the throne. The guards led her to the opposite side and withdrew. Silence filled the vast space.

"Sarai and Abram, I have summoned you to hear my verdict on your actions." He looked at them both and all warmth had vanished from his eyes. "Abram, you misled me by not telling me Sarai was your wife. Whatever your motive, you were dishonest and tried to deceive me. For that I can have you whipped, beheaded, hung, imprisoned or fed to the crocodiles."

Abram hung his head. Sarai gasped. Pharaoh glared.

"While in my presence, Abram, you've amused me with your stories, dreams and ambition. I see in you the potential to be a great leader among your people. Learn from this experience

Abram and do not defraud your betters. Because no harm has come from your lie, I have decided that you may leave and return to your home. Take with you only what you brought. I will give you no food, no water, no sustenance of any kind. Be gone at daylight tomorrow morning. Your wife has stood and heard my judgement concerning you; you will stay to hear what I will say to her. Then leave my presence when I am finished speaking. You may not speak. I am showing you mercy, not for anything you've done, but because of the courage and honesty of your wife. As I have spoken, so it will be done."

His words echoed in the marble hall. Abram groaned and dropped to his knees on the cold floor.

Pharaoh then turned his attention to Sarai. She raised her head and looked into his eyes, meeting his gaze without flinching.

"Sarai. You are a beautiful woman, elegant, gentle and accomplished. My queen has spoken of you, and I had been looking forward to welcoming you to my chamber. I have many wives and concubines, but I will not take to my bed another man's wife. I would never profane my perfection by doing that. It took great courage for you to tell the truth, for you did not know the consequences. Your punishment could have been any of the ones I named for Abram, but I will do the same for you. You too will leave at sunrise tomorrow. Sarai, you bear no guilt in any of this and you are a woman of integrity, honesty, charm, and as courageous as you are lovely. I will provide you with one week's supply of grain and three large jars of water. There will be fruit, bread and cheese for you. A wagon and two strong slaves to pull it will be at the city gate at the rise of the sun."

Sarai lowered her head in acknowledgement.

"Also because I admire your character, I give you the opportunity to ask for three favours from me and I will grant them. I cannot change your banishment. Now what will you ask?"

Sarai only thought for a moment, then she dropped to her knees and raised her eyes to meet those of Pharaoh. It surprised her to see kindness in them and what looked to be the hint of a smile on his lips.

"Mighty Pharaoh, I would ask these three things. First, my own clothes and sandals returned to me so I can leave wearing my own garments. Second, in the house of women are many pieces of the golden stone called alabaster. I ask for one small piece of this stunning stone to remind me of the kindness of Pharaoh. Thirdly, if possible I ask that the slave Hagar come with me. She has been a kind and faithful servant and friend while I was imprisoned here. If these things are possible, that is what I ask of your most generous majesty."

Pharaoh stood.

"I grant the wishes of this Hebrew woman. Also, all that she has worn while here is hers to take, the garments and jewels. As I have spoken, so it will be done." He turned, offered his hand to the queen, and with his ministers and slaves left the room.

Abram moved as if he would come to Sarai's side, but she turned her back on him and walked to the women's quarters.

Hagar waited for her at the door and beamed as Sarai approached her. She fell to her knees and with tears on her cheeks breathed, "Thank you mistress. I will go with you. I never dared to hope that I might live among my people again. Thank you." She bent and picking up the hem of Sarai's robe kissed it.

"Are you sure, Hagar? We are nomads; shepherds who wander the earth and live in tents, not even mud huts, and never in palaces of stone. We work hard just to survive. Are you ready for such a life?"

"It was to be my life before my slavery and I will trade all this to be among my people again."

They spent the rest of the day getting everything ready for departure and saying goodbye to the women. Hagar assembled the clothing and the jewellery Sarai had worn. Sarai chose a delicate, filmy, white linen robe, the lavish jewellery she had worn with it, and a soft, silky, sky blue headscarf. She picked out an elaborate golden necklace, some bracelets, an intricate belt, golden headbands and the rings she had worn. The rest she left for the slaves to divide amongst themselves. She looked at alabaster stones and at last chose one shaped like the great tombs she had seen. Its four smooth sides gleamed with a pleasing sheen. A slave came and brought her simple homespun robe and her well-worn sandals. The robe was clean, and the sandals mended and oiled. Sarai slept in her Egyptian bed for the last time. Despite her anger at Abram, she slept. Her last night in the land of the Pharaoh's passed.

Chapter Twenty

The caravan formed in the way Abram had set for the trip south. Rivkah and the servants and guards who had travelled with them stood nervously. Hushed tones expressed gratitude that they were leaving in safety. They understood they were leaving in disgrace, but were not sure why. Abram sullen and quiet, waited, lost in his own misery. He stared at the gate to the women's quarters. The sun was just a thin line of yellow on the horizon when the gate opened. Sarai and an unknown woman walked out and joined the small band.

"We must wait until the cart with my belongings arrives."

Rivkah went to Sarai and stood beside her, staring at her.

"Are you all right? Where have you been? What has happened? Are you leaving with us? Who is this woman with you?" The questions tumbled from her lips.

"Hush. It will become clear. We can leave soon."

Somewhere hinges creaked and the sound of wagon wheels on paving stones rumbled in the morning quiet. Abram walked toward Sarai; she nodded in his direction, then turned and spoke to Rivkah. He stopped. A large cart drawn by four muscular slaves came into view.

"We are free to leave now." Sarai took the first steps on their long journey.

The group fell into line and began the wearying walk to their homeland. Abram moved to the front and Sarai walked at the front of her cart, at the end of the meandering line. Sarai smiled at Rikvan.

"Do you know anything about our homes and our people?"

"We have heard nothing, Sarai."

"They might be dead and we are going back to nothing."

"That may be true, but we cannot stay here and there is nothing else to do."

Rivkah pointed at Hagar, walking alone. "Who is that and why is she with us?"

"She was my servant and friend in the palace. She is Hebrew and a slave in the court of Pharaoh. Hagar is coming with us at my request. You will treat her with kindness, she has had a difficult life."

Rivkah replied with a grunt.

Throughout the long day they walked across the burning sand and there was no singing to cheer them on their way. Occasional muted conversations, and the sounds of the animals, but little else broke the heavy silence. The slaves struggled to pull the litter in the shifting sand, and the drover's voices called encouragement to the sheep and goats to keep them together. Even their urgings sounded quieter than usual. Other than these subdued noises, the caravan moved in silence. When the sun sailed high in the sky, they stopped for a break. They passed the skins of water around, and each drank sparingly. At this rest stop, Sarai sought Abram.

"I will share the food and water I have from Pharaoh. It is for everyone. Drink as you need and when we stop for our evening meal, I will bring your portion to you. When I am ready we will speak of what has happened, for there is much to discuss. The others travelling with us are welcome to the food and to help with the preparations." Sarai spoke in her usual soft, kind voice to Abram.

"Thank you, Sarai. You are kind and generous. I will listen to what you have to say, but I have words that I must speak." He bowed his head to her, something he had never done before and with a weak smile turned to his tasks.

The days dragged by and there was little hope in the faces of the ones who plodded along the trail that led north. They followed the same path through the deep wadi they had used coming south. No one spoke their fears. It was as if saying it aloud might make it come true. Each evening, they stopped at an oasis and prepared for their meal and the night.

A few days later, when Sarai had cooked her portion of lentils, she beckoned Abram to approach. Rivkah and Hagar took bowls of stew and moved away. They sat together and got to know each other and to test each other and try to figure out their relationship to Sarai. Sarai saw them and wondered if they could get along.

Mother would have something to say about this, I am sure. At that thought she laughed a gentle quiet laugh, and it felt good once again to think of her mother, and to laugh.

Abram approached her fire and bowed. It shocked Sarai. Custom said that wives bowed to husbands, not the reverse. Sarai responded with a deep bow and motioned Abram to sit. Once Abram had offered thanks for the food, they ate their meagre meal in silence. As they wiped their bowls clean with the last crusts of bread, Abram asked for permission to speak. He turned away, as if he could not look into her eyes.

"Thank you Sara, this is the best food I've eaten for many days. Dear one, wife of my heart, I have wronged you and I apologize. I need to beg for your forgiveness. I feared for my life, and I allowed my fear to outweigh my love and respect for you. To put you at risk was a grave error, and I ask your forgiveness. I promise I will never again treat you in such a shameful manner. You have been a loyal, kind, devoted wife and for me to repay you by denying you as my wife was a terrible thing."

He shuffled his feet and dropped his gaze to look at the ground. "I am at your mercy, Sarai. I will be your servant until you decide I've paid for my unjust mistake and you can find it in your heart to forgive me. May I also say that this great wrong I did to you is the one thing that brings shame to me? In Pharaoh's court I did nothing that wrongs you, or offends the Almighty One. But that does not diminish the terrible injury I did to you and to our relationship. I wait your judgement, at the mercy of your compassion and the love we remember and cherish."

He turned toward her and looked dejected. The hint of a tear glistened in his eyes, and his voice cracked and broke as he spoke. His hands trembled as he sat hunched over in sorrow. Sarai looked at her husband and her heart ached at the pitiful figure she saw before her. A broken man. He no longer had the bearing of a chief, and the change she saw in Abram scared her.

His words touched Sarai. But she needed to speak her thoughts to him and so controlling her intense feelings in a trembling voice she began.

"Abram, you denied me and hurt me deeply. I could not believe what you had done. At first I was angry, then frightened, and bewildered. And I felt abandoned. As time passed, my emotions settled when I realized I could do nothing to change my situation. As I became calmer, my days in the harem were both pleasant and painful. Slaves cared for me in luxurious and charming rooms. And I learned much from the wise women there. But I did not know what the future held and spent restless days and sleepless nights wondering what was to become of me."

She gathered up the dishes and put them in a basin to clean later. Abram watched her every move.

"The thing I feared the most was that I could become one of Pharaoh's concubines. When that was to become a fact, I acted and told the truth to the Queen of Egypt. I understand it must have been hard for you. You worried for your life and that drove you to lie. I try to understand, but I'm angry and resentful. You showed no concern for my well-being or honour. You treated me as one of your possessions, disposable and of little value."

"Sarai, I—"

She held up her hand to silence him. His mouth closed with a snap.

"However, you are my husband; I am your wife and you are the respected leader of our tribe. You can never be my servant and I would never ask such a thing. We must continue to work as a married couple, as we've always done for the security and well-being of our people. Our troubles are less important than the security of our tribe. It is key to our survival as a nation that we get past this and present a united face to our people."

Sarai paused for a breath, and Abram sighed but did not speak.

"I will cook for you, clean for you, mend and sew for you; nothing has changed in that way. Give me time and I will come to your bed when you light the lamp for me, and I am glad that I can come to you without shame or dishonour. I will learn to forgive you as I think I understand how afraid you were for your life. But I cannot forget this thing that has passed between us."

She sighed and her body trembled. Her eyes overflowed with tears and she wiped them away with her hand. When able to speak she looked at Abram, and in a soft, yet strong voice continued to say what she needed to.

"I still love you Abram, nothing can kill that, but things have shifted. What you have destroyed by your actions is the trust I had in you. Trust is something which you cannot buy and once broken it is not easily mended. It will take time, a long time. We will work together side by side as we always did, and some day, I believe my doubts will ease. My love is still yours, and I will honour my duty, but trust is precious and fragile. Remember and be very careful not to give me any reason to doubt you again."

Sarai stood and took one of Abram's hands and he stood to look at her. They gazed into each other's eyes for a long moment. Then Sarai took a step toward Abram and he enclosed her in the circle of his arms. As the embrace ended, Sarai looked up at Abram, smiled and brushed his cheek with her hand.

The members of the camp stood still, and had held their breath when the conversation began. They pretended to be busy, but were watching and waiting. When these two people whom they loved, respected and followed, broke from their embrace, a sigh went up from the camp as everyone exhaled. With self-conscious grins on their faces, they set to work putting the camp to bed for the night. Tomorrow would be a better day and the future looked to be secure once again. There might be death, famine, pestilence and wars, but the tribe would remain united under the leadership of Abram and Sarai.

In the morning they continued the long walk home. Abram walked in the front in his proper place, and Sarai stayed with the women. Everything seemed the same. The only evidence of the great experience they had been through was the presence of the strangers, the former slaves of Pharaoh. But Sarai was a different woman, and she knew it. She had learned that change could come and pierce the heart to its very core. The old Sarai was trusting and innocent; the new Sarai more knowing. And for a moment she remembered the young girl who felt she had reason to be watchful around this boy she was to marry. *She was wise, but I became too comfortable and forgot. After this, I will remember and I will watch.*

Three nights later, as they camped in the wadi, Sarai and Abram sat together outside of his tent.

"I need to speak with you, Abram. Pharaoh gave these slaves to me. Hebrews captured in a raid. They have been slaves of Pharaoh for many years. I believe they are mine because we spoke the same language and they could be useful on our journey. I do not want to own these men. When we get home, grant them their freedom and offer them a place in our tribe. No doubt they possess much knowledge that we can use, and free men are more likely to share what they know. As slaves they might be unsure of their place and might speak less openly and we do not keep Hebrews as slaves."

"They are yours to do with as you wish. Give them their freedom. And the woman Hagar?"

"She is Hebrew, captured as a young girl and kept as a servant in the Harem, the house of women. She was my companion, teacher and translator while we were in Egypt. I asked for her, as you heard, as one of my three requests granted by Pharaoh. She too must be set free and remain with us as my servant. Eliana needs to be with Reuben, but will remain a friend and companion. Rivkah will still serve me, and she and Hagar are friendly, so I see no tension there."

Abram coughed. "Someday when we are home again, we must share our stories of our time in Egypt."

Sarai was quiet for a long time, and Abram wondered if she had heard what he said. At last she spoke, her voice cold and flat.

"That experience is one I wish to forget as much as is possible. I do not want to talk about it anymore, with you or with anyone. We will refer to it as our time away, and I will offer nothing more. Please respect my wishes in this Abram. We will speak of it only as our time away."

"As you wish Sarai. I do not want to cause you anymore pain and so I agree to lay this time to rest. Only at your invitation will we speak of it again."

As the moon rose over the edges of the hills and Sarai was preparing for bed, she noticed Abram sitting on the ridge looking at the valley that they would enter in the morning. She watched for a few minutes, then walked to the top of the hill. When she approached Abram, he never moved.

What are you thinking as you sit there all alone?

Sarai sat down and leaned her back against him. They leaned into each other, and Abram sighed from somewhere deep inside.

This is how we will survive. Supporting each other. In partnership and in harmony.

She lay down and reached for Abram's arm. He looked at her, then lay beside her. He spread his cloak over her and they snuggled like two spoons in a drawer. Hours later, the warmth of the sun woke them to a new day and whatever it held for this group of nomads.

Return to Caanan

Chapter Twenty-one

The journey to Canaan and to the valley of their village passed uneventfully. By careful rationing, the food and water lasted, supplemented by what they found and hunted. Little conversation, singing or laughter broke the stillness. Each one kept their fears held tightly to themselves. Only Hagar travelled with hope and enthusiasm.

As Abram crested the final hill, he stopped and looked at his homeland. “Come and see. The valley is green, the rains came, water flows in the river. Look Sarai, on the hills there are sheep and goats.”

“The tents are safe and women carry water and are cooking. And oh Abram, the children are playing and laughing.”

In the excitement of the moment they reached out and grabbing hands, danced around in a circle, laughing with joy. Abram stopped and picked Sarai up and spun around in circles until they were both breathless and dizzy.

“Put me down, Abram. Everyone will think we are mad. Put me down before we fall.”

But no one was watching them. The weary travellers stared into the valley. Some were laughing and dancing, while others stood weeping.

Hagar looked at Rivkah. "What is the matter, why is everybody acting so strange?"

"We left because of a terrible drought. The rains never came. We had no food, and that is why we travelled to Egypt. We had no idea what to expect on our return. Everyone might have been dead—people, animals, crops. We might have returned to nothing. But all is well."

Abram raised his arms to the sky and shouted, "Blessed art Thou, maker of heaven and earth. You sent the rains and the sun, and the earth prospers. Blessed be your holy name."

The women in the valley prepared a delicious welcome feast. Sarai and Abram sat and watched the entertainment and the celebration of their return. Life in the valley settled into routine and Sarai and Abram resumed their relationship. As Sarai stipulated, they did not speak of the time in Egypt. They agreed that to heal the rift that separated them. Some things were best not spoken aloud.

One night as they walked beneath the stars, Sarai once more felt at peace with Abram by her side. It was a good time to speak to him about something that concerned her.

"Abram, I want you to sell the necklaces, bracelets, and rings that Pharaoh gave me. I will not wear them here and I would rather have the coins that the gold will bring at the market."

"What will you do with the money, Sarai? Golden pieces from Pharaoh will bring a lot of money at the market. Many traders will want them. You have that papyrus proof of the gift of them to you, I hope."

"I wrapped it with the things I want to sell. I must confess that I have kept one or two pieces that I enjoy wearing."

"They belong to you and that is your right." Sarai heard tension in his voice but ignored it.

"When you get the money, Sarai, you can buy anything you want. It is valuable jewellery, the finest that the traders may ever have seen. They will outbid each other until the price will be more than it is worth. They will all want to own jewels that once belonged to the Pharaoh. Without the proof of the gift they could arrest me for stealing from Pharaoh. You were wise to get it and keep it. When I bring you the money, keep it safe and tell no one. We trust our family, but there will be riches enough to tempt anyone."

Days later, Abram brought her a heavy pouch of money. "Hide it well, Sarai."

She buried it in a large woven chest that held blankets and cloaks. But now Sarai had a new problem. She knew what she wanted to buy, but did not understand how to trade at the market, or how much her coins were worth. Most of them she had never seen before, and she understood they must be valuable. She thought it over for days and then trusted Lot. He was an odd one, but Sarai had never found him untrustworthy. She saw him sitting alone by his tent one day and approached.

"I need to talk to you Lot. Do you have a little while to talk?"

"Sit here beside me. Would you like some dates?"

"Thank you, I am fine. Lot can you keep a secret? One that is very important to me. It harms no one, but I want to tell no one of my plans, and I need your help."

"For you Sarai, I can be as speechless as a dead man."

"This is a serious matter to me Lot. I hope you will treat in as I do. I have money from the sale of jewellery from Pharaoh and I want to buy something at the market that will be expensive and I do not understand about money. Will you help me find what I want, bargain for the price and tell no one?"

"We will go tomorrow to the market. It is a busy day there, with many traders. A new caravan from the East has just arrived and they are setting up their booths. I promise you, I will ask no questions and tell no one."

"Thank you, Lot."

The next day, Sarai took her bag of coins and as they walked to the market, Lot counted it and whistled when he had the total. He looked at Sarai with new respect and admiration.

"I am looking for a stone. I don't know what kind I want, but I will know it when I find it."

Lot took her to a dealer in jewels and rare stones. Sarai looked at the things he had, touching some or lifting them up to the light. She saw many kinds, sizes, shapes and colours. The peddler told her the name of each one as she picked it up: white quartz, purple amethyst, red jasper, bright pink dolomite, black obsidian and the red, yellow and orange bands of travertine enthralled her. Sarai went back and forth testing them, but not one of them was right.

Lot looked at her, and she shook her head. He asked if there were any other types of stone that Sarai could see. "The lady does not want to look at gold or silver. She wants a stone."

"Well, I have one interesting piece, but it is very costly. It came from the Far East and we don't see it often. But it is a lovely specimen if you are interested."

"Please."

The peddler went into the back of his stall and opened a wooden crate. He brought a rounded object wrapped in linen. He placed the bundle on the table and unfolded the fabric. Sarai gasped when she saw it and picked it up.

It was a ball which a talented artist had carved from a lump of stone. He smoothed and polished until it gleamed in the soft light under the awning. She lifted it, and the ball filled both hands. The orb was smooth and cool to her touch, perfectly rounded, but the base remained rough and unfinished. Its rich green colour reminded her of life and growth, the trees and grass, and of a peaceful river. The many hues, dark green to white, swirled and appeared alive. She looked into the shades and patterns and felt very calm. "What is the name of this stone?

"Jade, and and it means wisdom and peace."

Sarai looked at Lot and her eyes told him she wanted this stone. As she stood and held it, touching it to her cheek, rubbing her fingers over its smooth surface, her face shone with happiness.

Lot wished that Sarai didn't look so enamoured by the stone, for her obvious pleasure cut out a measure of his bargaining position. But he loved the challenge and bargained with the peddler. After a great much head–shaking and arm waving, and many words, he took out the pouch and counted out the money. He took Sarai by the arm and led her away from the stall.

"Here is the cloth. Wrap it up, Sarai."

She did as Lot asked and carried her precious bundle pressed to her chest. When they arrived at her tent, Lot spoke.

"Hide this with care Sarai." And he handed her the money bag, much lighter, but Sarai didn't ask about the transaction. She didn't care. She had found the last stone for her circle of stones. It was the one to mark her death.

She turned to Lot, and for the first time in her life, she stood on tip toe and kissed his rough cheek.

"Thank you for your help and thank you for keeping my secret. What will I tell Abram if he asks questions?"

"Tell him the truth. You were looking for something special that you wanted, and it is a secret. You needed someone to bargain for you and someone you trusted to keep quiet about what you purchased. And you chose me. I don't know what this is about, and don't want to, but it is good to see you so happy Sarai, and I am glad to help."

He kissed her cheek and turned and walked to his tent. Sarai took her precious bundle and the coin pouch and went into her tent and hid them at the very bottom of her woven chest, underneath the plain looking, old, worn out tunics. Then she took blankets and folded them and put them on top of the trunk. They looked natural and Sarai smiled at her hiding place. As she turned, she thought she saw a shadow and wondered if she someone watched her, but saw no one.

Sarai had a problem she had to face. She had three serving women, more than she needed, and she decided Rivkah would leave her service. But what to do with her? Sarai didn't want to turn her away, or sell her to someone in a caravan.

I must think of something for her to do. Something that is useful and that she would enjoy.

Sarai had observed that Rivkah often stopped to speak with the two old women who were widows and alone. When she left them, they were always smiling.

Once again Sarai turned to Abram with her idea to solve the dilemma.

"Abram, you know the small tent that is only used to store unwanted things? I want to clean it out for I have a use for it."

"How will you get rid of the stuff piled in there?"

"I'll offer it to anyone here who wants it. If no one here takes it, I'll give it away to anyone in the town who wants it. Whatever is left, we can burn or bury."

"May I ask why? Or is this another secret, or maybe part of the first secret?"

"I don't need three women to care for me. I want the tent so that Rivkah can live in it with the two old women who are alone. She looks after them now, but with a home, and a few coins, they'd be happy together, and Rivkah would have a purpose for her life."

"And where will they get money?" Abram asked with eyes crinkled from his smile.

"Their sons should care for them, but they ignore our laws and their duty. Take a bit of their wages and give it to the women, and you'd pay Rivkah for caring for them. It brings honour to our village if the old ones are loved and looked after."

Abram put his arm around her waist and hugged her. No words were spoken. They both knew that he would not refuse her anything she asked.

For the next few days, Sarai, Hagar and Rivkah worked together. When they had cleared the tent of its bundles and piles of people's cast off items, they cleaned it. That evening, she asked Rivkah to go for a walk with her. They strolled to the river and sat by the gurgling water.

"You have been a faithful companion to me and I am grateful. But I don't need three women to look after me."

The smile disappeared from Rivkah's face. She looked at Sarai, eyes wide and mouth agape.

"Don't worry, everything is fine. I have noticed that you have a gentle way with older women, and I have an idea. The two old widows, who now depend on scraps and random kindness from others, will come to live with you in the tent we have just cleaned. Their sons are herders for Abram, and he will give a portion of their wage to you to care for these old ones. You will get their water, cook their food, clean their clothes and tent, and look after their personal needs. Does this appeal to you Rivkah?"

Rivkah sat for a moment, taking in what Sarai had just proposed. When she could speak, she responded with a catch in her voice.

"Oh Sarai. There is nothing I would rather do. I love those two; they are so wise, so patient and grateful for any little kindness. It will be a pleasure for me to care for them in their final years. This is a wonderful idea, and you are a blessing to me and to Abra and Sachi. Can I tell them, or should you do it?"

"You can invite them to come and live with you in your new home. If you need anything, please come to me and we will work together to make them content."

Rivkah jumped up and ran off, without the formality of being dismissed by her mistress. Sarai smiled and congratulated herself on solving two problems with one happy solution.

Hagar was happier than she ever remembered being. To be among her own people again was a dream come true. She had her own small tent a little ways from Sarai's, and it satisfied her to work for her new mistress. Sarai was a kind woman, and she showed that kindness in the way she treated Hagar. Eliana did not mind sharing the duties of caring for Sarai with Hagar when she heard her story. She remembered losing her parents, and she felt empathy with Hagar.

Soon after the return, Abram realized trouble was brewing with the herders. Lot's men and Abram's challenged each other over who got the best places to feed and water their animals. Nothing had come of it yet, but there might be great animosity before long, and Abram worried it might come between him and Lot. Both men knew that with the great flocks and herds they owned, plus all the people living in the area, the land was being over grazed and the grass would wither and die. Abram and Lot saw the impending danger and recognized they needed to separate and move their holdings farther apart.

Lot expected Abram to choose first, that was his right, and Lot tried not to let any feelings of envy creep into his heart, but he looked at the land and tried to guess what part Abram might give him. Abram showed Lot the land God had promised him, and offered Lot his choice. Lot couldn't hide his surprise.

Lot looked around the valley and saw the rich lands to the south west of where they stood. He pointed to it and said, "That will be my portion." For just one moment he experienced a twinge of guilt because he had taken the best of the valley, and he loved Abram, who had been a father to him since the death of Haran. But he convinced himself that Abram gave him that right when he gave him his choice.

Over the next few days, he gathered his livestock and possession, his slaves, servants and their families. They struck the tents and within a week moved to begin life in the valley. His new home was near to the city of Sodom, for Lot gravitated to the exciting life he saw in the cities. In his eagerness he gave no more thought to the generosity of Abram who was left with the worn out land.

Abram looked at what was now his and noted how depleted it was. They had not moved the tents in a long time and the grass beneath them had died. He needed to choose a new location. This had been the pattern of his nomadic people for generations. As the sheep exhausted the grass, they moved to new pastures. He did not go far, but settled near the grove of sacred trees at Mamre near Hebron. The women and men knew the work involved in moving, but this was a short distance so it would be different. They moved in stages, and that made it manageable. The labourers built pens, and the animals moved to their new grazing land first. They dug a well and marked the locations for the tents. Abram planned a large circle of homes with a common area in the centre. The tents were the last thing dismantled and moved. All settled in just a few weeks. Once again, the first thing Abram did was to find a suitable place for the altar.

Before leaving, Sarai took a last slow walk around. Memories flooded her mind. Good happy memories, births, weddings and the nights with Abram. But there had been sad times too—death, and illness. The most painful memories were the little ones who died before they lived, and mothers dying in the effort to bring forth life.

I always told myself I was not to blame; but I wondered if I should have seen a problem, should have known how to help. I wondered what I had missed? There is so much I do not know, about birth and death and the living in between.

As she walked along the bank of the river, she looked down, and lying in the water was a wonderful stone. It lay there flat and round like the bread she baked in the clay oven. The colour reminded her of the bread, a soft brown, and despite being in the water it rested warm in her hand. The tumbling river had ground it until it was as smooth as the crust on her loaves.

This will be my memory stone from this time of my life. It will remind me that life comprises the common things and the unusual. I too have been shaped by the battering life has given me, but like this stone, while changed, I have survived, and I will continue to endure.

Sarai took her river stone and put it in the bag with the others. Her memory stones had grown in number, and she decided she needed to do something with them. She thought about using them around her fire, but that was not what she wanted. There, they would blacken from smoke and ash, and she wanted them to remain as they were to remind her of her life. She didn't want to leave them hidden in her bag, but neither did she want them visible to anyone. People might ask what they meant, and why she carried them around with her. The story of each stone was too personal to share.

One afternoon she stood on the hill looking south at the stand of trees that grew near the great oak of Mamre. *That sheltered spot barely visible from the camp and close to the sacred tree is the place for my stones.* She hurried to the grove and walked around it, first from one direction, then from the other. The sun made delightful shadows among the trees as she walked from north to south, then east to west.

There is an opening. A natural doorway.

She lifted a branch and squeezed past it. The trees formed a protective circle around a grassy oval. Close to the centre, the small clearing opened to the sky. The grass grew soft and mossy beneath her feet, and lovely flowers dotted the grass. Right at the centre of the open circle lay a mossy hollow. *I do not understand how you came to be here, but I know that you are waiting for my stones.*

She lay on the soft grass and closed her eyes. The sun warmed her face, and she smiled as the tension in her body seeped away into the warm earth.

In the rainy season, flowers can grow here, it will be stunning. This is where I will make a circle of my memory stones. Restored to the earth from which they came. Sheltered by the trees and serenaded by the wind and the bird's song. It will be a sacred space for my prayers to the breasted god of the mountain.

Returning to her tent, she saw Eliana coming toward her, looking as if she had something to tell Sarai. Hugging her close, Eliana whispered, "I am going to have a child. I have not been to the woman's tent to bleed for two moons."

Sarai wept on her shoulder. Tears of joy for Eliana and tears of sadness for her empty womb. She promised herself that she would not let her sadness spoil this time for Eliana, and she,

Sarai, decided to enjoy the pregnancy and anticipate the son she hoped would be born to her dear friend. Time passed and Sarai watched Eliana's belly grow round with the life she carried. When envy filled her heart, she returned to her tent. She sat at her loom weaving a soft colourful blanket for the baby. As she wove, she sang songs to ease her sadness.

"I will be an auntie to this baby, and I'll love him and enjoy him, with none of the worry and demands of an infant."

On a gloomy day a rider came into the camp, panting from exertion, and wild-eyed with fear. Abram met him and offered him water and bread and dates. When he had eaten and caught his breath and could speak, he told Abram that the five southern kings had joined and attacked Sodom. They had ransacked the city, looting and burning and killing. Lot, was taken prisoner. Abram expected a ransom note but decided not to wait. He began preparations for war against the kings.

Abram joined Sarai for the evening meal and they sat in silence while they ate. When all had eaten, he spoke.

"The rider who came into camp brought grave news. The southern kings have attacked Sodom. They burned and robbed the house and killed many. Lot is a captive.

"Why would they do such a thing? Lot has harmed no one."

"The city was the target. Lot just got caught up in the confusion. If he tells them of me, there will be a price to pay to buy his safety."

"What are you going to do?" The tremor in her voice told Abram she knew his answer.

"I must go after the raiders, and rescue him. He is family, and I am obligated by the memory of my brother to free him and bring him home."

"You and the warriors will leave to find these thieves. How long will you stay away?"

"I can't answer that Sarai. We will be away as long as it takes to right this wrong."

"I hate wars and fighting. Many are killed and wounded. This will waste months, carried out to right a wrong. How can killing change the wrong committed? How can making widows and orphans in the village be right? It just makes more wrong for my heart to bear."

"You may not like the world or understand its ways. But you can't change it. El Shaddai sends his fire to teach us we must vanquish evil."

"The breasted one teaches us that life is precious, and each person is to be loved and kept safe from harm."

Abram put his arm around Sarai's shoulders. She rested her head on his chest, and they sat, each deep in their own thoughts.

Chapter Twenty-two

The next three days were a busy, noisy, worrisome time. There were always greedy people who wanted more land or wealth and were not prepared to struggle and work for their goals. At last the warriors understood why Abram made them practise so long and hard. They polished their spears and sharpened their knives. New arrows were made, bows were checked, and the strings oiled to keep them supple. Women prepared food and other provisions and packed them in wooden crates. Three women volunteered to go with the army as cooks, three more to keep things clean, and two healers to look after wounds. The eight women would be company and support for each other and keep each other safe. There was danger from a soldier who afraid of death, might think of wanting a woman and resort to rape before he died.

Abram called Reuben to his tent. “You have not been married a year yet, and your wife is with child. Under our custom and law, you do not have to go to war. You are excused from this battle.”

Reuben paused and then spoke in his quiet firm voice. “Thank you for not expecting me to go and for allowing me to stay here with Eliana. But I know that I am your best archer, and the men look to me to lead them. Eliana is right now busy getting my pack ready. I am going with you. Lot was like a father to me and he saved me from a life of slavery. It is now my chance to rescue him. We will trust in our training, our men, our honourable purpose and the might of El Shaddai. Blessed be the God Almighty."

Abram did not argue or insist that Reuben stay, as he was grateful for his sense of duty and knew that his skill and experience would be a great help in the coming battle. When he had checked everything, Abram went to Sarai's tent to say goodbye.

"Last night we once again knew each other and felt the love we share. It will not be the last time. I promise you I will return when I have freed my brother's child. Take care and do not worry for the mighty arm of El Shaddai will protect us."

Sarai 's eyes filled with tears. "And may the gentle strength of the great mother keep you safe and bring peace to us once more."

They walked in silence to the road where the army waited. Abram took his place at the front and Sarai joined the women, who lined the road to wave their headscarves and wish their men a safe journey. Eliana had said goodbye to her husband and understood why he had to go; but she wished he could be less of a soldier and more of a father waiting for his first born.

The women stood by the road and waved their hands and the colourful headscarves fluttered like a multitude of butterflies. Children ran along the roadside until their mothers called theme back. Sarai and Eliana stood with their hands clasped. With a catch in her voice Sarai spoke. "There will be many cuddles and hugs as these little ones go to bed tonight. It is a blessing that they do not understand what they have just watched."

When the last man disappeared from view and the dust had settled, Sarai went to the grove to pray for their safe keeping to the God who nurtures and protects her children. She prayed to El Shaddai, the breasted one and offered grain and bread, sprinkling it into the circle where her circle of stones would soon be placed. And the wait began

Chapter Twenty-three

Abram and his allies formed an army of four hundred men, and they pursued the kings toward the city of Dan in the north. They travelled long hours, with hard marches over rough terrain, not following the road, as that would have been obvious to any spies, and they would be vulnerable. They walked through fields and forests, scrambled over rocky hills and waded across rivers. When the scouts at last spotted the raiders, Abram's army, tired and foot-sore, made camp and rested for two days and then mounted a surprise attack at night while the soldiers of the raiding army slept.

The kings were so confident in their escape, they hadn't posted a full complement of guards, and Abram's archers killed them with one silent arrow to each guard's neck. He had divided his army into four squads and attacked from each side. The enemy had split into two camps, and many who were in the second camp escaped with their booty and prisoners.

The archers followed Reuben, bows drawn and arrows arcing into the darkness, dimly lit by the embers of many small fires. Abram stood on a rise of ground and watched helpless as Reuben crumpled to the ground, pierced by a sword.

The battle raged until the sun's fire lit the scene. The defeated raiders slunk away, leaving their dead and wounded. Abram stumbled his way to where he had seen Reuben fall. When he reached him, he was taking his last breath. "Look after my son and Eliana."

Abram held him and wept until Lot came and reminded him that there were grave matters needing his direction. The women did what they could for the wounded raiders, and Lot told them to make their way to a village to the north. Abram's army buried the dead where they lay. The heartsick women tended the sons, husbands and father of their friends. Archers carried Reuben to a small cave where they laid him to rest. The army stood in silence and the archers held their bows across their chests in a final farewell. Abram wept as weary soldiers covered the opening with stones.

After burying the dead of both armies, Abram recovered the raider's carts and oxen to carry the wounded and the repossessed treasures. After a rest of two days they broke camp and began the long march home.

They travelled impatiently along the dusty roads. When they came to the road that went to Sodom, it was time to say goodbye to Lot. He and Abram sat in silence and ate a hurried meal. As he said goodbye, Lot tried to thank Abram. Abram shook his head. "Family looks after family. Your loyalty and friendship are enough. I do not need thanks."

During the weeks the men were away, the women tended the flocks besides their other duties. They worked in teams till their backs ached and their hands and feet were raw. The healers waited each evening to treat the bleeding feet and hands with soothing salves and fragrant oils. The bone weary women drank strong, hot teas which eased the pain and beckoned sleep. Each night, exhausted, they slept with no disturbing dreams about the far away battle. Too tired and too worried for singing, they toiled in silence. Sarai spent as much time as she could with Eliana to keep her spirits up. Her belly grew and the baby was very active and all seemed to be well.

After many weeks, a runner came into camp and said that Abram defeated the kings and the army would be home in three days. The women prepared food and drink for a banquet to celebrate the homecoming. Then they rested and bathed and washed their hair to get ready to welcome their fathers, sons, brothers, and husbands home.

On the morning of the expected return of the army, they dressed their hair with flowers and ribbons, put on their finest clothes and lined the road waiting. When the ragged procession came into view, a great cheer rose from those who had stayed behind. Their welcome cry soared around the hills. A louder, deeper cheer from the army echoed back. As the men came closer, Sarai spotted Abram leading the tattered remains of his once gallant forces. She breathed a great sigh and offered a quick prayer of thanks to the Mighty One.

As he drew near, Abram paused and gave Sarai a wave and a huge grin. To him, she looked as beautiful as when she was his bride. To her, he looked dirty and exhausted but a heart-warming sight despite his appearance.

Abram searched the roadside for someone other than Sarai. In a moment his eyes rested on Eliana and he strode toward her. He stopped in front of her and shook his head. Eliana collapsed in his arms. Abram picked her up and carried her to the tent of women. At its door the women took her from him and carried her inside. Abram whispered to Sarai, "I will clean up, rest, and see you when you are free." With a quick kiss, he left and Sara entered the tent.

Four hours later, with no sign she was aware of what was happening, Eliana delivered a still-born girl. For the next two days, Sarai never left her side and held her while she screamed and raged her grief, but seemed unaware of the loss of her child. Late that evening, with no moon in the sky, Eliana joined her husband and daughter. Sarai stole away to the grove of tamarisk trees and wept.

They buried the mother and child together in a cave near the sacred grove and wrapped the tiny body in a tunic that had been Reuben's favourite. Everyone loved and respected the couple and many of the mourners left flowers. They walked back to the village in silence. Sarai stayed by the grave on her knees until the inky sky echoed her pain. Abram stood nearby, and as the stars came out, he gently lifted Sarai in his powerful arms, and carried her back to her tent. No woman was there, and so he took down her hair, removed her clothes, dressed her in a simple clean tunic, and laid her in her bed. She co-operated as he prepared her for sleep, but made no sound. He extinguished the lamp and turned to leave. From the bed Sarai spoke, "Thank you husband. I will sleep now secure in your love and care. Good night."

As the yellow sun smiled on the morning, Abram came to her tent. He fed her broth and freshly baked bread with honey. She ate little and slept many hours for the next two days. Abram nursed her and only left when she slept, and then only to check on his men and look after the affairs of the village. He spent most of his time sitting or lying and sleeping lightly, outside the door of her tent.

When she grew stronger, Hagar looked after Sarai and sang her songs of both lament and hope. She listened while Sarai talked of Eliana and everything she meant to Sarai in her life.

"I can hardly remember life without her. She was my childhood playmate, the confident of my youth, and a friend and sister as I became an adult. Whatever my struggle or joy, she was there."

Hagar sat near Sarai and held her hand, rubbed her back and murmured comforting sounds.

"Eliana never scolded, criticized or mocked. She simply stood by me through all that life brought. She taught me the things I needed to know about being a woman, a wife, and a partner. We laughed, cried and raged together. Now she is gone. No one can take her place. If only the child had lived. I would have raised her as my own and told her stories about her mother. But even that is denied me. I feel alone. Completely alone."

Hagar said nothing, but crooned a gentle song of healing.

Many days later, on a sunny morning, Sarai knew it was time to lay aside her grief and gather the women together in the moon tent.

The women who travelled with the army returned and they needed a place to tell their story. They met in the tent of women at the new moon, and with tears of anger, frustration and sorrow, shared their burden with their friends. As each story unfolded, they poured handfuls of sand on the ground, to symbolize the burying of the sorrow and pain.

Sarai anointed each woman with oil and spoke a blessing as they held hands in a circle. Women brought newly woven shawls for the brave women who had returned. As Sarai spoke the name of each woman, a friend draped a shawl around her shoulders with tender healing love.

"These shawls have been made to remind you we care deeply for your pain and suffering. We will always be ready to listen if you need to talk." The calm, gentle voice of Sarai, speaking from her own place of pain was a soothing salve to their hearts. When they left the tent, they left behind the stories, symbolically buried in the sand.

Later that evening, Sarai went for a walk as the stars came out in the sky. Outside his tent, she noticed Abram's lamp, a soft glow in the dark. She wondered how many nights it burned there unanswered. Slowly she walked to the tent and pulling back the flap entered, not bothering with the ceremony of clapping three times to ask permission to enter.

"Are you sure, Sarai?"

In answer, Sarai slipped out of her robe.

In an instant they were in his bed. He held her with a fierceness she had never known in him. When he was spent, he rolled away, with tears running into his beard. She curled her body around his and held him in her arms. They slept that way until the morning sounds of the camp awakened them.

When Abram went outside to relieve himself, there was a tray with a cover over it. On it was food for the two of them. Hagar sat nearby keeping the dogs away and when she glimpsed Abram, she went to Sarai's tent. He waved that all was well.

Hagar spoke to no one in particular. "Sometimes it takes a greater suffering to heal a smaller one." Singing, she began her chores.

Chapter Twenty-four

The seasons passed, and Sarai was comfortable in the routines of her life in the familiar orderly patterns. Hagar was a satisfying maid and Sarai appreciated her company She sang beautifully, told wonderful stories, and understood that the time in Egypt was not to be discussed. There were times however, when she sensed that Hagar was secretly watching her.

Why does she skulk around and stare at me like that? What is she thinking? Is she really loyal to me or is she planning something? Sometimes I have a feeling that I am being followed. She has done nothing to merit my mistrust, but often I feel uneasy around her. But there is nothing I can complain about or discuss with Abram. I guess I am just getting to be an old suspicious woman.

The work of the women continued as it had since their mother's time. They cooked over their fires and kept the flame alive; a critical task. If it went out, the work of starting a new fire was long and tedious. Abram was the guardian of the pieces of flint, but it was easier to keep a living flame, and so the flame at Sarai's tent was never allowed to go out. Her lamp was kept burning all through every day and night. Abram decreed it was unjust for Sarai and her servants to be expected to provide oil for the whole camp. If the fire was for everyone, everyone had to help with the supply of oil. Sarai was very grateful to Abram, for seeing the need to share this work, and for ordering it to be done.

Sarai awoke one morning to a shocking realization. *It has been a long time since I have bled. More than two moons have come and gone. I am a useless old woman. My life has no meaning.*

She walked to the river and sat on the bank. Tears ran down her cheeks and dripped off her chin as thoughts of the future washed over her. There would be no son, no heir. Sobs wracked her body. When the tears ceased, she dried her eyes and took a deep quivering breathe. As she stood she saw strange stone. She bent and picked it up. In frustration she was about to throw it into the river. She stopped

It looks as if it had once been a tree. I can see what looks like bark and the rings of its life. Now it is hard and dry. Not a tree, a stone. Dried up and lifeless. Like me.

She turned the stone over and over in her hand, staring at it.

My womb is dead and I might as well be. I will never bear a child and my arms will remain empty. The river flows past; it has no beginning and no ending. It just is. But it gives life to all as it passes by. There is no life in me to give. I look at the river and I see the clouds floating free in the sky and the rocks that make the water tumbled in confusion.

She turned as she heard footsteps. Hagar came and stood beside her.

"Look at this stone. It is a picture of my life, a few smooth places but many difficult and rocky times. And just like the river, my life is flowing by. I have many more years behind me than I do ahead of me, how will I live without the hope of a child? But I know I will live, even though the future appears bleak and empty."

"Is this sadness because you no longer have your moon time?"

Sarai stared at the river.

"Life goes on Sarai. A woman's life does not stop when her blood flow stops. Old women carry the wisdom stories, they keep alive our mothers and grandmothers."

Sarai shrugged her shoulders and scowled. "How do I fill all those empty hours, days, years? I cannot join the widows and share their emptiness for my husband lives. I cannot walk into the desert to die and abandon him, for he is not to blame. Somehow I have displeased the gods and my life remains a hollow shell. And just like a shell tumbling around in the sea, I will drift, brittle, fragile, and empty for my remaining days."

"Look beyond the hills, Sarai. A rainbow. It is a rare thing. It must be a sign."

She raised her eyes to the arch of colour. "Perhaps. I suppose it is telling me that beauty still exists. But this moment will fade, the colours will disappear and I will still be dried up and lifeless. This stone tells the truth of my barren existence. I will keep it although I don't need a reminder. But it marks another turning point in my life."

Hagar's hand on her shoulder interrupted her thoughts. "Rivkah is calling. There is food for you. Come."

Sarai followed her meekly, not thinking about food, but about the endless tomorrows that stretched ahead of her. Rivkah stayed with her while she ate, gently urging her to have a bit more wine and some cheese. She rubbed Sarai's shoulders and neck as if she sensed the tension in her body.

Sarai looked at Rivkah and her heart warmed. From somewhere deep within, she realized what could fill the emptiness.

"Rivkah, have you ever thought about learning to be a healer? You are quick and smart, you care about people, you sense when there is something that needs to be looked after. Your hands are gentle and you have some time I am sure with your duties to the widows not being all consuming."

Rivkah grabbed both Sarai's hands, her eyes sparkling and her face a mirror of joy.

"Will you teach me? I would love to be a healer. That is all I really want to do. I have watched you carefully and I try to remember everything you do, but to be taught by you –that would be more than I ever dared to dream."

Sarai smiled. "I have come to realize that I am getting old, my friend, and I need to pass on my knowledge just as Jessica passed on her wisdom to me. I think you will be a wonderful healer. We will begin at the new moon and I will anoint you in the tent of the women, so that all will know you are my pupil and will follow in my steps when I can walk this road no longer."

Rivkah, a slave, did the unthinkable. She grabbed Sarai, hugged her and kissed her on both cheeks. Sarai hugged her back and watched Rivkah walk to her tent.

"Now I will go to bed, and maybe even to sleep."

Despite having settled what she would do with the hours and years that stretched ahead of her, she was still very concerned about her meeting with Abram in the morning, for she had much to tell him. After a near sleepless night, in which she made a momentous decision, she went to Abram's tent. When she clapped at the opening, Eliezar Abram's servant came and said, "He has gone up the mountain to make a sacrifice to his God."

Sarai went to her tent to await her husband's return.

Hours later she saw him coming along the path that led from the mountain. She walked out to meet him. As she came near him, she gasped. *Is that Abram? He is standing tall and straight. He is not bent over as if he was carrying many heavy burdens. His face! He looks youthful, relaxed almost in a different world. There is such a sense of calm about him. What has happened?*

"Abram," Sarai whispered.

He looked up, surprised to see her. "Don't touch me Sarai. El Shaddai has spoken and I must think on the things he has revealed. I will speak with you after I eat."

Without another glance, he walked past her toward his tent.

The day dragged by, and Sarai waited. She ate a simple supper, then tidied herself and sat by the glowing coals of her fire. She had decided something that would change their lives forever and she needed to tell Abram. At last, just as the sun slide behind the hills, he came out of the tent and sat on cushions under his canopy. She walked over and without a word sat beside him.

Sarai watched him. He seemed at peace, and there was a joy is his eyes that was unusual. He stared out into the valley, while Sari sat beside him and waited patiently.

"Sarai, today the Almighty One showed me once again the lands that would be mine. Again he promised we would have an heir and our children would be as great in number as the stars in the sky. To mark this day our names are changed. I will henceforth be called Abraham and you will be Sarah. This is a wonderful day Sarah, mark it well in your memory."

She struggled for breath and a long loud wail of pain and grief escaped from her and flowed out into the valley. The birds stopped singing, the dogs looked up from their sleep and the children ran home to their mothers. It was a cry of agony beyond words.

"Sarah. What is wrong? I bring you wonderful news and you act as if I have wounded you in some way."

Sarah took a deep breath and reached out to take his hand.

"I have not been to the tent of women for my bleeding for months. I am no longer able to bear a child. There will be no son from my womb to fulfill your God's promise. I am barren and our lives will be barren. I can give you no sons. There will be no children to match the stars in the heavens. Is your God playing some cruel joke?"

"Sarah, I only know what he said, and I trust his word. I do not understand the fiery ways of the mountain, and I do not understand the God who lives in the skies. But I trust what I heard."

"Well I don't. I know what my body is telling me. I am not going to bear your son."

They sat in silence for a long time. Sarah broke the silence with a hesitant voice.

"Abraham, you need to have a son; my maid Hagar is young and fruitful. I will send her to your tent and you can lie with her. Her son will be my son, as is the custom with our people. That way the promise of your God will be true. I have thought about it and I am content if you will take her for your concubine. You have been faithful to me and have honoured me as your wife, but I have failed you. In spite of my failure you have loved me and now I show you my love for you by making it possible for you to have the promised heir."

"Sarah I want no one but you. You have been my helper, adviser, and friend. But most of all my wife and I want no other woman. And remember we have the promise of the holy one. I think we need to be patient and wait for God's time."

"God's time! I've waited all my life. I have followed you and your God since I was married to you when I was just a young girl. I have been obedient, faithful and have not bothered you with all the questions that torment me. God has shown me that I am worthless, a barren wife. I am done being patient. You must have an heir. I cannot fulfill my duty and Hagar is the solution. Do not deny me this. It is the custom and law of our people and has been for generations."

Abram opened his mouth to speak, but Sarai held up her hand. "No! This is not a request, it is my demand. There is nothing to discuss."

Sarah leaned toward Abraham and kissed him tenderly. He reached out to her, and taking her arms, he helped her to stand. Then he picked her up and carried her into his tent.

Chapter Twenty-five

Thinking of the days ahead were like a dreadful dream for Sarah. She knew that she had done what she needed to do, but the thought of Abraham lying with Hagar tore at her spirit. Every time she imagined them lying together, bodies wrapped around each other, she shook herself and forced her mind to think of ordinary things. She dusted her dishes, re-arranged her medicines, and spent many hours at her circle of stones, alternately weeping in agony, and cursing the gods in anger. She reminded herself that this was her own doing. Abraham could have taken a second, third or fourth wife years ago and she would have had to learn to live with the pain. That he had not was something for which Sarah felt deep gratitude, but that did not change what had to happen.

On the third day she went through the motions of doing her tasks. But her mind was engaged in trying to find a way to summon Hagar and tell her. After a simple evening meal, she asked Hagar to sit with her by the fire. She took a deep breath and in a voice that sounded like death she spoke to her slave.

"As you pointed out, I am past the time for women to bear children and I no longer go to the moon tent each month. Abraham must have a son to inherit his possessions and to receive the blessing of a father to son and to carry on as leader of this tribe. He has never withheld his love because I am barren. He has not spoken of his longing for a son for many years. The fault is mine and he must not suffer because the gods are angry with me."

Hagar stared at Sarah with her arms crossed. Her face was an icy mask.

Sarah took a breath. "Tonight you will go to him. You will bear a son who will be the heir to Abraham and to me. It is our custom that a child born to a servant by her master will be his heir and the son of his legal wife. This is my plan and Abraham has agreed. Do you understand our custom in this? The son will be the legal heir of Abram and my son by our laws."

For just a moment Sarah thought she saw a glint of triumph pass over Hagar's face. It was there. It was gone.

"You are my mistress and I do your bidding. It shall be as you have commanded."

Hagar's voice was not one of obedience but one of triumph. She stood before Sarah did, and gave the slightest nod to her mistress and walked, head held high, to her tent.

I have done what needed to be done. This will be the hardest time of my life. I thought I suffered before as a barren woman. What will I suffer as a woman who has been replaced in my husband's bed?

Sarah called Rivkah to make a brew of tea and lavender to help her sleep. She sat alone on her stool and watched the stars make holes in the black blanket of night. Even with the drink, sleep eluded her. She could not get comfortable on her mat. In the stillness of the night Sarah heard Hagar singing as she walked by the tent.

She does not need to walk so close to my tent. This is a deliberate taunt, the first of many I suspect. Sarah clambered to her feet. She paced around and around. In frustration she went to her mat and lay down, eyes wide open, and heart sore. Curled in a ball of misery, she lay waiting for something but she didn't know what. The pain within her had no name.

She listened as footsteps shuffled past the tent. A shadow scuttled along the path from Abraham's tent. Not so close this time. It was Hagar returning to her tent.

What does this mean? Did Abraham refuse her? Was he unable to do what needed to be done? But we agreed. Should I ask her? No that would be even more humiliation. I'll go to my mat to try to rest.

Bewildered and dazed, she went back to her pallet and after a time of restless tossing, drifted into a troubled sleep.

Chapter Twenty-six

In the morning, as Sarah sat on a stool at the door of her tent, Hagar came carrying food. While she did so, she stood tall and her smile was one of victory.

"It has begun," muttered Sarah.

"Abraham and I have agreed that I will go to him each week, the day before the Sabbath. You must stay away from him. He needs to protect his seed and not waste it. I will not be here to serve you those days as I need to prepare for my night with Abraham." She turned her back and walked away.

Later, sweeping her tent, which Hagar had not done, she heard Abraham's voice at her door.

"Sarah, may I speak with you?"

Not wanting to face him, she replied that she was resting, but he could come in for a moment. She lay on her mat with her face to the tent wall. Abraham came in and stood by the end of her bed.

"I want to tell you that Hagar came, and I did what I needed to do and sent her back to her tent. Know that I did not lie with her in my arms, but did the deed as the beasts do. Only my wife spends sacred time in my arms. You are welcome there and I will wait for you to come to me. Do not wait for my signal lamp, come when you wish."

"But I can't. Hagar said—"

"What did she say?"

"She told me I was not to come to you. You do not want to waste your seed."

"Since when do you obey her? She is your servant. You are the master. She speaks nonsense. You are my wife and I will wait for you."

And he left. Sarah wept tears of gratitude. This man, who had been her husband these many years, could still surprise and delight her.

He has only one god and only one wife. What a man and how fortunate I am.

Many days passed and Sarah wasn't sure if she delayed going to Abraham because she needed time, or if she wanted to give him time, or if she was unsure of how to approach him. She struggled for many days, and then it came to her.

I will get out of my chest the white linen robe of Egypt, the headscarf that floats as if it was the breeze itself, and the jewellery of gold and lapis. That will make me feel young and like a queen. It should surprise Abraham and give him a reason to smile. It will make him forget that Hagar was ever in his tent. At least I hope it will.

She spent the day brushing and cleaning the white robe. She had forgotten how silky it was and how the fabric fell in soft folds. When she wore it, her shoulders and arms were bare and the dress dipped low in the front and even lower in the back. The large jewelled collar went over her shoulders and covered her bare skin at the front. Made of nuggets of gold strung on metal threads and interwoven with bright blue pieces of lapis lazuli, it glittered in the lamp light. The matching head band and belt gave an exotic aura to the picture she would make.

I had forgotten how comfortable these sandals are. Just straps around my toes and ankles, but so pretty with the sparkling jewels and golden thread. But I remember the headscarf. So light it floats in the slightest wind or movement of my body. It might be made of spider's webs, but I am sure it is the silk from the Far East, woven by worms, or so they say. My hair will fall down my back. In the light of the lamps, the grey will not be noticeable. The shadows will hide the wrinkles in my skin, I hope.

She brushed the dress and polished the jewellery.

When I kept this, I did not understand why. Now I know. It was for this moment. It will surprise him to see me dressed as an Egyptian princess. I have never told him about this. I hope he will be excited by my entrance.

The day dragged on and Sarah tried to keep busy. She walked to the well for water and filled her jars. There were women there who wanted to gossip, but Sarah was in no mood to talk to anyone. She smiled. "I am tired. I won't linger to talk today." Aware that she had given them something to gossip over, she returned to her tent to eat her simple meal.

After her meal she bathed and soaked her feet and hands till they wrinkled. She opened her jar of scented oil, and rubbed it into her feet to soften the hard calluses, and massaged her hands till they were as soft as she could make them. She combed her hair until it shone and brushed it with a cedar branch, scenting it with an air of mystery.

Sarah reached for an undergarment and realized she did not have a shift to suit this dress. It would be visible around her throat. She thought for a moment, shrugged her shoulders and slipped the white softness over her bare skin. She danced around her tent, enjoying the sensuous touch of the fabric on her skin. Breathless, she picked up the belt and clasped it around her waist and slipped the collar over her head.

I wish I dared to go to the quiet pool to see myself in the still water. But that is foolish. How could I explain my clothes to anyone who saw me? And that would be gossip for a long, long time!

Slipping her feet into the sandals, and adding the head band to her forehead, she felt young and alive. Once more she danced around the tent, twirling like a young girl. She stopped.

What if he laughs? Suppose he thinks this is sinful? And it might remind him of Pharaoh and the insults he received in Egypt.

Sarah took off the head band and then paused. "This is what I planned. This is what I will do."

She picked up the blue gossamer scarf and wrapped it around her waist, then draped it over her forearms where it floated like a butterfly's wing. It was the last touch. She thought for a moment and picked up her tambourine.

Sarah stood, slowing her breathing, for she realized she was panting with excitement. It was nearly dark and time to go. She put her cloak over her shoulders and began the brief walk to her husband's tent, her steps slow and graceful.

At the opening flap, she stopped. "Abraham. It is Sarah, may I enter?" Not waiting for a reply, she opened the flap, stepped inside and dropped her cloak.

Abraham looked up from his work; his jaw dropped and his eyes were wide with wonder. He jumped up, spilling the skins in his lap, and with one leap was in front of her. He reached to take her in his arms, then hesitated. His arms dropped to his side. "Sarah. I am afraid to touch you. My rough hands dare not caress such loveliness. Are you real or am I dreaming? My heart is trying to leap out of my body."

He stood mesmerized by the vision in front of him.

Sarah shook the tambourine and danced around him. Cat-like, she circled him, lithe and sensuous; she threw her head back and sang a song of love to him. He followed her every movement, his eyes never leaving her graceful body. As she danced, she removed the scarf, the collar and the belt. Without warning, she leapt into his arms.

He caught her, held her close and lowering his head, kissed her. He kissed her eyes, her cheeks, the tip of her nose. His tongue, teasing her lips open, explored her mouth, moaning as he did. With one motion, he reached the bed and placed her on it. His clothes dropped to the floor and he lay beside her, taking her into his arms. He tenderly removed the white tunic, and they lost themselves in their love for each other. When the candle had burned itself out, just as they had, they fell asleep in each other's embrace.

Chapter Twenty-seven

The sun warmed Sarah's face, and she turned over to find Abraham gone. There was a breakfast tray by the bed, and when she smelled fresh bread, she marvelled at his thoughtfulness. Nibbling on the cheese, she wondered where he was.

He came into the tent and in his arms was a bundle of clothing. "I didn't think you wanted to leave wearing the white robe, so I went to your tent and brought some things. I hope they are all right."

She grinned at him, stretched, arose from the bed, and dressed. Abraham sat and watched her slip on the dress and eat the simple meal. As she stood, he came to her and took her in his arms. They held each other close, looked into each other's eyes and shared a brief kiss.

Sarah gazed at Abraham, as he strode down the hill to the fields to attend the business of the day. As he left, he turned back and waved. She walked to her tent, humming a cheerful tune and sat on a stool to enjoy the morning sun.

"What do you need this morning? Food? Water?"

Sarah startled and looked up. Hagar was standing there, hands on her waist and an expression of disrespect on her face.

Sarah met her gaze. "Abraham made me some food, and he filled the water jars while I was asleep."

Hagar opened her mouth to speak but shut it and stood staring at Sarah.

"Sweep the carpets this morning and the mats. You can do those tasks for me now."

Without a word, Hagar entered the tent. Sarah sat on her stool and shook her head. From the tent she heard a loud thump. *What is she doing?* She stood and pulled aside the tent flap.

"Why are you moving that chest? Put it back. There is nothing in there that concerns you. Sweep the floor mats as I asked."

Hagar glared, but moved the chest back and replaced the things that had been on top of it. Then she picked up the broom and swept listlessly.

"It is difficult to have a servant in my tent that I cannot trust. I hope that I will not have to stay and watch you from now on. If I find you in my tent uninvited, I shall ask Abraham for a guard and that would be most unfortunate. You are still my servant, so be careful, Hagar."

She went back out into the morning sun, and sat at the door of the tent, with her back to Hagar but remained aware of her moving around in the tent.

When Hagar finished, she came out and without a word strode down the hill to the common area in the centre. Sarah sighed and walked to the river. The flowing water always soothed her when she was restless.

Raising her arms in supplication she voiced her distress. "Great mother, El Shaddai. I realize that there is trouble ahead.

But what else could I do? Wait for a miracle? I have waited my entire life for the stirring of a child in my womb. Abraham needed an heir. I did what I felt was the only way to give him a son, and now it seems I will pay the price. I will not speak of this to him. I will take care of it. I started it, and I shall have to finish it. Whenever I go to my stones, I always find peace in that sacred place."

She walked up the hill to the sacred circle, and turned to look back to the camp. It was a comforting sight. Sheep and goats dotted the hills, looking like toys in the distance. Around the tents she caught a glimpse of the activity of the morning. Her friends, sang as they worked and the lilting notes comforted her. Young children ran naked and carefree as lambs on the rolling hills.

She turned her gaze to the grove, and the feathery pink blossoms called her to come and rest.

Chapter Twenty-eight

Many weeks later, Sarah woke as she often did, to the sound of animals and people busy with the day's chores. In her younger days, she was one of the first ones up in the morning. But as the years added aches and pains to her joints, she rested in her bed a little later. She gently stretched and when dressed, went outside. She looked at her fire pit and saw only cold, lifeless ash. Hagar had not started the fire, nor done any of her morning duties. Sarah walked to Hagar's tent and politely asked admittance, although she had every right to enter the tent of her servant. A low moan came from inside and Sarah went in. The tent was dark and in one corner Hagar lay on a crumpled pile of bedding. She glanced at Sarah.

"I have the sickness that comes in the morning. I am going to have Abraham's son. I cannot wait on you and meet your demands. I must protect this child and heir. You will have to look after yourself," and she turned her back to Sarah and faced the tent wall.

Even in the dim light, Sarah could see Hagar's shoulders shaking. It was the movement that comes with laughter not with tears. Without a word Sarah left the tent and went to Abraham. At the tent of her husband, she raged.

"Hagar has refused to work for me. She says she must protect your child and heir. Her shoulders were shaking as she lay with her back to me. She was laughing. Laughing. How can we deal with this?"

"Sarah, we cannot antagonise her. She may have been shaking because she was ill. It would not be helpful to accuse her. We must find another servant for you. The women whom Rivkah was caring for have died, perhaps she can come and help you again. She'll be a good and cheerful companion to you. You certainly do not want to try to live with Hagar as she is behaving. I will see about Rivkah and I will speak to Hagar." He left without another word.

Sarah stamped her foot. Sarah knew Hagar should not be permitted to behave in this way. Most women had sickness in the morning, but they did their best in spite of their discomfort. Sarah realized that Hagar was not her obedient servant anymore. She had become proud and arrogant. She knew she had set this in motion, and she also knew that there was no stopping it. Speaking her worry aloud she grumbled.

"I have to remain calm and not let my feelings show. Hagar will have her day, and when the child is born, things can return to the way they were. This is going to be the longest few months in my life. I hope I can be strong and meet her aggression with understanding and kindness. I must do this for the sake of Abraham's son, who will be my son too. I can and I will do this for his sake."

Rivkah was very happy to come and serve Sarah once again. She was a helpful companion and a cheerful and capable worker.

She had learned much in the time that had passed, including how important Sarah was, and therefore, as her helper Rivkah had status. Sarah thought Hagar might be given to someone else. *Even after her child is born, I will not have her back. Rivkah will stay with me.*

The months passed slowly. Hagar never appeared until the sun was high in the sky and then she strutted about the camp, rubbing her growing belly and talking to anyone who would listen to her. The midwives were tending to her, and they assured Sarah that the baby was growing, that Hagar was eating and resting, and that all was well with the pregnancy.

As Hagar's time drew near, she began to insist that she should be living in Abraham's tent. His strong manly presence would be a good influence on the boy growing inside her. Abraham never heard from her formally and therefore did not have to refuse her. He did, however, assure Sarah that she was still the only one to stay in his tent. Hagar's reaching for ever greater status would remain a dream.

Everything was ready in the tent of women for the delivery. It was a time of waiting for the baby to begin the journey from the womb to the world. Just when Sarah thought all was going to be done properly, Rivkah spoke to her.

"While you were out for a walk, Hagar and Abraham had a loud, long argument."

"What did you hear?"

"Hagar was insisting that she should move into his tent. She said his manly presence would be a good influence on the baby. Abraham firmly said 'No'. Then calmly reminded her of the custom of their people that a slave who gave birth to the master's child was bearing that child for the wife, and the child was considered hers. She kept badgering him and then she started to speak against you. Abraham raised his hand and threatened to strike her. He stated that you were the only woman who would ever stay in his tent."

Sarah sat on the bench and motioned Rivkah to sit beside her.

"Abraham set her straight. He said, 'Sarah will attend you at the birth. She will catch my son, and hers will be the first face he sees. It is Sarah who will bring him to me to be acknowledged. Walk carefully. Sarah and I are the ones with power here. Do not forget she is a princess from the Land of Ur. Think on these things, consider our customs, obey Sarah, and all will be well'."

Sarah let out a long heart-rending sigh.

"Then, without another word Hagar crept away. He stood up for you and sent her away in disgrace. I didn't mean to listen, but it was all so loud and I was walking nearby. What will you do Sarah? You can't let this go unchallenged."

"I did not hear it, and I will not implicate you in this. Abraham defended my position as his wife, and that is enough. I can't upset her anymore, as I have to think of the well-being of the child. But thank you for telling me. I will continue to watch and be careful. Walk with me to my tent."

Rivkah left her with a tender hug and Sarah went inside and lay on her mat.

I am afraid our troubles may just be starting. I hoped that we could live in peace and harmony. I have no intention of taking the pleasure of her son from her, she will nurse him, care for him, teach him to walk and talk, but he will be mine legally, and the law and customs must be followed. But if it should be a daughter, I wonder how that will change the way we feel.

A few days later, Sarah was awakened in the early hours of the morning. Hagar had gone to the women's tent and the midwives were attending her. They sent a girl to tell Sarah that it was nearing Hagar's time and Sarah should come at once.

Abraham was standing outside the tent and Sarah nodded to him, but did not pause. Hagar was on the birthing stones when Sarah arrived. Strain was in her face, and the two helpers on each side were supporting her weary body. The labour had been in progress for many hours, but Hagar was stubbornly silent. When Sarah neared her, Hagar glared.

In her soft voice Sarah said, "Hagar, mother to be, you are tired, but the child needs to be pushed out into the world. Don't be strong and silent. Scream your pain and push with all your strength. Free this son of Abraham into the world."

Hagar looked at Sarah and with a cry that would echo around the valley she gave one last push and Sarah caught the infant. Quickly she cut the cord, tied it off and cleared his mouth and nose. When she saw the first breath she held the baby up for everyone to see that it was a boy. When he opened his tiny mouth and wailed, it was a good strong healthy cry. Hagar was lying on the mat and the midwives were attending to her.

Sarah went and, kneeling beside her, showed Hagar the beautiful son that she had carried. Hagar smiled weakly. "Thank you Sarah." Then Sarah placed him on a clean cloth and carried the baby out for Abraham to see. Abraham placed his large hand on the baby's tiny head and in so doing declared that this was his son. "The name my son is to be Ishmael, and its meaning is, God knows."

Life in the camp went on and in a few weeks, there was a feast to celebrate the new baby, and at the feast, Sarah stayed on the edges of the party. She had decided to let Hagar have this moment. Perhaps it could help to heal the great gulf that had grown up between them. Abraham was congratulated; and Hagar showed Ishmael to everyone, and at the end, she took him to Sarah and asked for a blessing for this their child.

Sarah spoke as she placed her hand on Ishmael's tiny head and looked at Hagar. "I hope that this is the moment when we can begin to respect each other again." Smiling at the infant she prayed. "Welcome, welcome to this world. We have been waiting for you. Waiting to hear the sound of your cry, to kiss you, hold you, rock you. We have prayed for this day, and now it is here. May God watch over you in love and bless you with health. Bless the source of all life."

Hagar made no response, but looked at Sarah with detachment.

Chapter Twenty-nine

The months turned into years and Ishmael grew into a sturdy boy. He was bright and eager and loved to follow Abraham around the camp. His father made a tiny bow and a wooden spear to celebrate his third birthday, and he pretended to be a skilled warrior. Both his mothers watched over him, and the settlement was at peace once more. Hagar was looking after the woman's tent, cleaning and airing it to earn a few coins, and Abraham saw that she wanted for nothing. She outwardly returned to the ways of the past, but Sarah still sensed that she was being watched. There was an uneasy atmosphere between them: hidden, unspoken and yet palpably real.

I wish I could get past this notion of suspicion. She knows I will not have a child. There is no threat to Ishmael and I am no threat to her. Why can she not see that her son's position is secure?

As they did every day, Rivkah and Sarah sat by the stream, dabbling their feet in the sparkling water as it rippled on its way.

"You appear troubled, Sarah. Can I help?"

"There is nothing you can do. Hagar does not trust Abraham. Anyone with eyes can see he dotes on Ishmael. Ishmael spends most of his time with his father and Hagar hovers nearby. I spend little time with him. He does not acknowledge me as his mother. Despite her misgivings, I have no evil intentions. It was my plan, and I take responsibility for my actions. Ishmael is the heir to Abraham, to the birthright, to the cattle, sheep and lands. I need to find a way of not having to wonder and worry over her and her schemes. I don't know what she can do, but I do not trust her."

"Trust Abraham. He will let nothing happen to you."

Like the river, time flowed by and nothing changed. Sarah was ill at ease, but chose not to burden Abraham with her fears.

Late one afternoon Sarah was returning from the river, when she saw three strangers seated with Abraham at his tent. She slipped into the tent and prepared food and drink for the visitors. As she carried it to them, she heard a voice.

"Nine moons from now, we will return and your wife Sarah will have born a son to you." Sarah laughed to think that after all this time she could conceive a child. The visitors chided her for laughing and Sarah was embarrassed and denied her laughter. Laughter to hide her frustrated anger and disbelief.

Where were you when I was young and bleeding each month? Where were you when this promise could have brought joy to my heart? If you had acted then, there would not be this trouble with Hagar and Ishmael. Now your promise only mocks me in my old age.

She spent the day working feverishly, trying to not think about the promise of the visitors or her reaction to it. Working to exhaustion helped to keep the painful feelings suppressed.

That evening, Abraham put his little lamp out at the door of his tent. Sarah answered his summons, and they sat together on soft pillows in the comfortable silence of shared memories. After a while, Abraham spoke.

"Woman, you are to bear the long promised son. That requires action on our part. Come Sarah, lie with me tonight and we will remember and we will hope. Your El Shaddai, the nurturing one, may indeed nurture life within you tonight." The night of tender love left them at peace and they slept securely held in each other's arms.

In a few weeks, Sarah noticed changes in her body. Her breasts grew heavy, and she needed to rest often. Sarah wondered and hoped, and as time passed she knew. She was pregnant with Abraham's promised son. On a quiet afternoon, as they sat in the shade enjoying a rest, she spoke.

"Abraham, I have wonderful news. The promise of the holy one has come true. I carry your son." He sat for a moment, speechless. Then he roared with laughter, borne of his great joy.

"The promises of El Shaddai are trustworthy. The mighty one is faithful to his word. Blessed be the holy one who lives on the mountain."

He stood and helped Sarah to her feet. He held her tenderly in his arms and stroked her belly. "Are you well? How are the mornings? Do you sleep well, eat well, and take enough rest? We are old, and you need to be careful. Pamper yourself. Leave the work to others. Do you need another servant? Just ask, Sarah. Anything you ask, I will do."

"Abraham, I've never felt better, or been happier. I am sorry for any doubts, but I don't think you can blame me for that. We cannot count the time spent waiting. Many rainy seasons have come and gone. We've seen birth and death, many times. The babies we welcomed now have children who are having babies. My deep regret is that we will not live to see our boy grow up. But it is in the hands of El Shaddai and I can change nothing by my worry."

"We will go together and make a thanksgiving offering."

"Women don't attend the sacred rites."

"It has never happened before, but I don't think it is forbidden. And your growing belly is proof the holy one does the unusual. Bring oil and grain and come with me to share in this sacred time."

Astonished, she hurried to prepare herself to go up the mountain with him to the altar. Still, he could surprise her.

Side by side, they climbed the slopes to the holy place. Sarah looked at the pile of stones and was surprised that it looked so ordinary. Common stones held together by common dried clay. The stain of dried blood troubled her for a moment, but she pushed the image away.

"Put the grain on the altar and pour the oil over it. Then I will say prayers and light our thank offering."

Abraham dropped the live coal from the dish he carried and raised his arms and his gaze toward the distant mountain. "Master of the Universe! I thank You for your graciousness to me in granting Sarah, my wife, pregnancy. May your holy name be blessed, lifted up above all blessing and praise. Let your compassion come forth on behalf of my wife, Your maidservant

Sarah, daughter of Binah. Ease the pains of her pregnancy, and when the term of her is complete, may she give birth easily. In Your great, mighty and awesome holy Name we trust."

He dropped dry grass on the fire and the flame grew brighter. Abraham stepped back and motioned for Sarah to approach. She, looked to the mountain and raised her arms.

"May it be your will, El Shaddai, to ease for me the hardship of pregnancy, and increase my strength, and the strength of my child. When my time to give birth arrives, may I give birth easily and let the baby go out into the air of the world without difficulty. Complete my days and years, and I will teach my child to serve You. And guard us, my child and me, that we will not come to harm, but live long, in this peaceful land. Blessed beour Holy Name."

Together, they walked home in silence.

Chapter Thirty

In a few weeks, Sarah's pregnancy became obvious to everyone. There was surprise and disbelief, but also happiness in the tents of the camp of Abraham. The pregnancy filled him with joy and he could not contain his delight. Sarah appeared calm and serene.

Hagar became sullen and withdrawn. She kept to her own tent. For years she had done little but care for her son. Abraham saw that she had everything she needed and she spent her time with Ishmael. He seldom played with the other children, and whenever Abraham was not busy, Hagar was near him, making sure that her son was with his father as much as possible. Sarah knew this was as it should be, but what she couldn't bear was the way Hagar ignored her. She never greeted her, or even appeared to notice her. When she spoke to anyone about Sarah, she called her "that woman".

Hagar approached Sarah at the well one morning. "Good morning, mistress."

Hagar's words stunned her. Hagar had rarely called her mistress, and never in such a pleasing tone. Sarah answered cautiously. "Good morning. I don't often see you at the well this early in the day."

"On such a nice morning, I wanted to get an early start to the day."

"It is a lovely morning. Blue sky, warm sun and just enough breeze to keep it cool, at least until mid-day." Sarah put the heavy water jar on the sand and waited.

"Since Abraham spends so little time with me, I am ready to return and be your maid again. You will need help when your baby is born."

Sarah remained speechless. *What is behind this? What is she thinking? And planning.*

"Thank you, Hagar. But since you left, I have been well taken care of by Rivkah. She has learned what I need and we work well together."

Without a word, Hagar turned her back to Sarah and walked away.

Sarah plopped to the ground. Rivkah had witnessed the exchange and joined her. "I will carry the water jar. You need to be careful now, Sarah. Let me do the heavy chores for you."

"I can scarcely believe what has just happened. Hagar came with honey dripping off her tongue and offered to return to help me. Don't worry, my friend, I said no."

Rivkah picked up the jar, and they walked toward Sarah's tent.

"Does she know that Ishmael will not inherit Abraham's title if you have a son?"

"She has been told, but I can't trust her, can I?"

"I am afraid for you, Sarah. And when your son is born, what witchcraft will she try? You must tell Abraham."

"We have nothing but our suspicions. I will wait and watch before I speak to him."

"Wait and watch if you wish, but be very, very careful."

Sarah tried to control these alarming thoughts, but they were always there, ready to bring down her spirits. She forced herself to be cheerful. In her soft voice, she hummed the songs of her youth and the women songs. As she made garments for her child, knowing that she needed to be at peace for the well-being of her son, she pondered the mysteries of life. When she watched Abraham teaching Ishmael, she often experienced feelings of jealousy and regret. She prayed that he could be as attentive and loving to their son.

Abraham came every day to visit Sarah, and he brought gifts to her—an extra portion of lamb or cheese, or berries he had found. He was very attentive and Sarah was happy and secure in her new status as a mother-to-be. But she wondered about the timing of the gods.

At night, when she couldn't sleep, her mind raced. *Why did the gods wait until she grew old to open her womb? Didn't her child deserve a mother who was young and still full of life? A mother who could laugh and play with him. And a father to run beside him, wrestle and rough-house as fathers did. How would he teach his son the skills needed to oversee the tribe?* But even when sleep finally came, it was calm and untroubled by frightening dreams.

The pregnancy proved to be a wonderful time for her. Sarah had no sickness in the morning, just a sense of being fulfilled. As her belly grew, she seemed to grow younger. Her skin became more delicate and glowing, her eyes shone clear and bright, and she walked with an easy confident step along the paths.

Abraham strode around the settlement with pride and joy and appeared to be young again while he waited for this child of promise. He played with Ishmael with his little bow and sword and taught him about the animals and the ways of the shepherd. Ishmael had his own goat and a lamb, and he and Abraham fed them and brushed them and checked they had no burrs in their coats, or stones in their hooves.

It delighted Hagar to see her son with Abraham. She never said it aloud, but she reminded herself that Ishmael was the first-born son and thus he should be the heir. She told him this every night as she put him to bed, and told him it had to be their secret for now, and he mustn't tell anyone.

The months passed happily. Only occasionally did Sarah sense Hagar watching her. Hagar had reverted to ignoring Sarah and not speaking to her when their paths crossed. But there was nothing that she could report to Abraham.

The primary midwife, Tria, whose name meant earth mother, attentively watched Sarah. She brought fresh milk and cheese, fruit and berries, and looked after her with the tender care of a mother hen. Each evening, she came, and together they walked and talked. They spoke of the time of the birth, and the days and weeks of recovery after the labour. Tria spoke often of the sturdy son Sarah would deliver and how proud and happy Abraham would be.

As the sun slipped behind the hills, Sarah experienced a strong cramp. She walked to the tent of Tria, who saw at once that Sarah was in labour. Tria went to alert the midwives and Sarah walked to the tent of women. The midwives gathered and fussed over Sarah. They sat in their comfortable circle and sang the song of birth.

As the moon sailed across the sky on her journey and the quiet night unfolded. Sarah would soon take her place on the birthing stones, and the work of labour began. Her labour was going well. She walked around in the tent's shelter, enjoying this time for which she had waited so long. She permitted no negative thoughts to enter her mind, and if they tried, she pushed them aside with a prayer of thanks to El Shaddai and a prayer for a safe delivery.

Outside the tent, Abraham sat cross-legged on the ground, his head in his hands. He looked up as someone approached. It was Hagar.

“I've come to attend Sarah.”

Abraham stared at her.

She raised her voice and screeched, “I am here to look after your child when he enters the world.”

“Sarah has Tria to look after her. What could you do? This has nothing to do with you. Go home and care for Ishmael. That is your responsibility.”

Hagar opened her mouth to speak, but the look on Abraham’s face closed it. She stood motionless, her face contorted in rage.

“Go home, woman.”

She turned and fled along the path.

The midwives were prepared. They had a sharp knife to cut the cord, string to tie it, and reeds ready if the nose or mouth needed to be cleared, and the swaddling clothes lay nearby. With a smile that said I am ready, Sarah stood upon the stones to begin the hard work of bringing her child into the world. The labour had gone quickly and Sarah was strong and pushed and panted with an energy borne of longing and hope. With one last push and cry, and a rush of water and blood, a son was born. He cried lustily the moment Sarah freed him from the womb.

"Well done, Sarah. What a healthy cry. Look how he kicks with his strong fat legs."

Tria checked him, washed him and rubbed him with salt to cleanse him and to toughen his skin. She carried him to Sarah, who touched his cheek and smiled through tears of joy. Tria swaddled the infant and carried him outside to Abraham.

Abraham looked exhausted. He had been pacing outside the tent asking, "When will my son be born? Is Sarah well? Why is it taking so long?"

When he saw the tiny bundle, his eyes filled with tears and he stretched out his arms to receive his son. He held him close, then raised him high toward the sky and the sacred mountain, and he called out a prayer of thanksgiving and blessing.

"Blessed are you, King of the Universe. Who bestows good things upon the unworthy and has given me every goodness. You have sent us a perfect blessing. We have prayed for this day, and now it is here. My son is a miracle. A gift from God. Thank You, bless You, Source of all life."

He held him and looked into the face of his promised son. His eyes filled with tears, but his smile belied the tears. He handed the baby back to Tria. "His name is Isaac, laughter, for he brings joy to the house of Abraham." Then he strode through the settlement, sharing his joy and receiving the congratulations of everyone.

Sarah offered her breast to Isaac, and he began at once to suckle. Sarah held him and could hardly contain her joy. When he finished nursing, she carefully unwrapped him and inspected every tiny toe and finger. She stroked his soft ears and caressed his dark black hair. She kissed his fingers and forehead and lay with him in her arms, smiling and content.

When the day came for Sarah to return to her own tent with her baby son, Abraham came to walk with them. Rivkah walked in front and threw flower petals on the path before the little procession. It was a day of celebration.

When Isaac and the camp slept that night, Sarah returned to the tent where she had given birth. She picked up one of the birthing stones, the smallest one that supported the larger ones on which she stood. Quietly, not wanting to be seen, she returned to her tent with her stone to celebrate the birth of her son. A common brick, made of mud and straw. On it were a few brown stains, the blood of her delivery of her son, Isaac. But it was as precious as a jewel.

In days following the birth, Sarah remained in her tent with Isaac. Abraham came to see them, bringing Sarah a small gift. One day a flower, another a honey cake, a new comb for her hair. Each day there was something for her from Abraham.

Hagar watched from the shadows. *I received no gifts, no daily visits. But this is not over. No one will push Ishmael aside for this puny infant. My son is the first-born son of Abraham. He is the rightful heir. I have been planning since his birth and I have been teaching him. He will lead this tribe of nomads and together we will build a city that will be the envy of even the Pharaohs in faraway Egypt.*

Sarah had not spoken to Abraham concerning Hagar, but he had been watching. After the incident at the birthing house, he felt ill at ease and wondered what Hagar might be thinking. Everyone in the camp noticed that a trusted servant of Abraham stayed near the tent of Sarah, day or night. He slept just outside the entrance, and no one could enter the tent unnoticed. Sarah and Isaac were constantly guarded.

Three years passed and Isaac grew strong, and when it was time for him to be weaned, Abraham prepared a splendid feast of celebration. Sarah sat in the seat of honour and everyone remarked on her beauty and the growth of the boy Isaac. They proclaimed that he was a fitting heir for birthright and assured the proud parents that the Holy One of the mountain favoured them. As the day ended, Ishmael, now a strapping youth, and Isaac were standing together. They were close to Sarah, and she overheard Ishmael.

"All this show does not matter. I am the first-born son of Abraham. I am the rightful heir to his blessing and to all he possesses. You will be my slave when I come into what is rightfully mine."

Isaac looked puzzled, and as Ishmael continued his taunt, he began to cry.

"Baby, cry baby. Wah wah wah. You will never be the head of this clan. It is my birthright. You will see me make this a great nation. It will be a golden city, not a group of tents and mud."

Ishmael mocked Isaac until he ran to Sarah for comfort. That night Sarai told Abraham what she had seen and heard.

Abraham pulled at his beard. "I have been afraid of this. We have watched Hagar skulk around and withdraw from our lives. No doubt she has been filling the boy's mind with her poison. I will talk to him and see just how dangerous this is."

In the morning he summoned Ishmael to him and talked with him at length. Abraham was gentle and patient. Ishmael repeated what his mother had been teaching him since he was at her breast and would not retract one word.

"Father, I am your first-born son. That you cannot deny. I am the heir to your blessing. That you cannot deny. That puny son of your old age is too weak to follow in your steps. He is only good to be a slave. Do not deny me my birthright. I will make a great nation of this scruffy, rag-tag group of shepherds. Our fame will spread even to the lands of the great Pharaoh and he will envy the tribe of Ishmael."

Abraham was grief stricken. He knew that he had to do something before disaster descended on his house. He called Sarah to him and with great sadness spoke.

"You heard correctly. I have talked to the boy, and his mother has taught him falsely but thoroughly. We cannot trust her. She is your servant; you decide what you will do with her and Ishmael. He is my son and I cannot do what needs to be done. It is in your hands to do as you see the need. It is your son who was foreshadowed by the visitors so long ago to be the heir to the promise of a great nation. Lying with Hagar was a mistake. We tried to take control of something that was in the hands of El Shaddai. This is our punishment. Dissension. Ambition. Greed. I will go up the mountain now, to make a sacrifice."

Sarah's voice trembled as she spoke. "Abraham. How can you just walk away from this danger? It is your son who is causing the trouble, making threats against Isaac. Why do you run and hide Abraham? Are you afraid of this woman?"

"I have given you power over her. Do what you must."

He turned and walked away. Sarah ran to the sacred grove she had created. She touched her stones, one by one, and remembered. As she recounted her life, she drew strength and courage from her spirit stones, and she became calm. Her anger at Abraham softened, and she felt it replaced by a firm resolve.

This began with me. I brought this on us with my impatience. It isn't right that I blame Abraham. He wanted no woman but me, and I talked him into this. I started it and I shall have to finish it. But what should I do? I could have them killed, but the breasted one is a god of mercy. In my heart I cannot order someone else to commit murder, and I cannot do it myself. She is a mother, and she loves her son and wants him to be important. This is not a crime worthy of death. What shall I do?

Sarah stayed and struggled with her decision until thirst drove her back to her tent. When she had decided, she summoned Eliezar and gave him instructions. Later she saw Hagar strutting to the common area and called her to the tent. Eliezar stood at the door and two slaves stood with him. At their feet were skins of water and a large bundle.

"Hagar, you knew from the beginning that by our laws Ishmael was my son too. Our ancient custom acknowledged him the heir of Abraham. But once Isaac was born, my son, the son of Abraham's one and only wife, became the heir, and Ishmael the second son. Ishmael could have had an enjoyable life here and grown to a position of responsibility. Abraham loves him and would not have seen him disgraced or forgotten. And I bear him no ill will."

Hagar's eyes blazed. "You useless, dried up—"

Sarah held up her hand as if to strike Hagar. She fell silent.

"You knew the truth. You chose to mislead Ishmael and fill his young mind with lies. He and you must both bear the consequences. Here is water and food. Pack what you can carry, and leave. You have proven that we cannot trust you and we banish you and Ishmael. Forever. These are two slaves who will go with you for two or three days journey and then you will be on your own. I regret that this is the way it is, but you have chosen your path. Abraham has put this into my hands, so there is no appeal to him. I expect you will return to Egypt and so I give you this bracelet of gold that I received from Pharaoh. Return it to him to prove your right to be at his court. Abraham has made his mark on this skin to prove you have not stolen the gold. May El Shaddai save and protect you."

Hagar glowered at Sarah, put the golden circle on her wrist in silence. Sarah had never seen such hate, and she trembled at its depth. At that moment, she knew she did what had to be done. The two slaves picked up the bundles and led Hagar to her tent. When she had gathered her things, they accompanied her and Ishmael out into the desert, heading south as she chose. Egypt had been her home, and that was where there she planned to live and raise her son.

Days later when the slaves returned, they reported that they had found a small caravan that took Hagar and Ishmael with them. Hagar was to work as a cook on the journey to pay their way. Sarah thanked the slaves, gave them a small reward, and praised them for doing their task well. Abraham heaved a sigh of relief it was over when Sarah related what had happened.

As she walked back to her tent, she noticed a stone shaped like a tear. She stooped and picked it up.

Chapter Thirty-one

Each year the seasons changed as they had since time began. It was the wet season and rain pelted down, driven by fiendish winds. Tents dripped water. Paths became slippery, and on occasion someone fell in the cold wet mud. Cooking fires sputtered and died. Dark clouds hung on the mountains hiding the peaks. The weeks dragged endlessly. Each morning Sarah watched for the first signs of the sun. When the clouds were tinged with pink and gold, the rains would vanish back to where they lived. The first day the sun shone high in a blue sky, everyone spilled out into the clean, fresh air. Soon the mud would dry and planting could begin.

In the women's tent a celebration lasted for many hours. Grain and oil were offered in thanksgiving for the pleasant days ahead. Crops were planted and tended with care and hope was high for a bountiful harvest.

The seasons rolled by and years passed. Isaac was nearing his tenth birthday. Sarah had been planning a celebration to mark the day. It was to be a wonderful family day by the river. They would go, just the three of them, and enjoy a day to rest and play with their son. They planned to swim in the river, fish along its banks, and walk together in the meadows that sloped away from the water's edge. In the evening, by a fire, they would once again tell

Isaac the stories of his ancestors and the journeys his parents had made. They would recount the story of his miraculous birth and the birthright which was his. They seldom mentioned the names of Hagar and Ishmael. For a time, after they left, Isaac sometimes asked for his brother, and he was told Hagar returned to the land of Egypt where she had lived for most of her life. Satisfied with the answer he spoke of them less and less as time passed.

When Sarah awoke the morning of Isaac's birthday, she rose from her bed and looked at the eastern sky. The sun, just peaking over the hills, touched the day with warmth. The blue sky stretched cloudless from horizon to horizon. A perfect day for Isaac's birthday. She dressed, brushed her hair, braided it and left her tent to start the morning meal. Rivkah was still sleeping, and Sarah was glad to have this time alone. The fire lay grey, and the ashes were cold and lifeless. Not an ember glowed as Sarah blew on the cinders. She thought it strange that Isaac had not started her fire as he did every morning.

She looked up the hill where Abraham's fire glowed, and she took a dry reed and went to get a spark. The water was low in the jars, and Sarah needed to find Isaac to get more from the well. Sarah had to admit that the days when she could easily fill the water jars were in the past. She started cooking barley in the water and it would be ready later to enjoy. She ate some cheese, dates, and the bread Rivkah had made yesterday.

Around camp, people began stirring and stretching in the warming sun and fires burned by the tents. Sarah glanced up the hill, Eliezar was poking at Abraham's fire, but nothing seemed to be cooking and she saw no sign of her husband.

"It is time to find that boy." She walked the scant distance to his tent and gently called his name. After three tries, she pulled aside the flap and looked in. His sleeping mat had been rolled up and lay at the edge of the tent. His cloak and sandals were gone. And so was Isaac.

"He must be with his father. They often are together in the early morning." She went back to her tent and tidied it up for the day and as she went back outside saw Rivkah walking toward her.

"You are up early, Sarah. It must be a special day," she teased. "I will finish the barley and get the other foods ready for the rest of the day. I'll make the bread, and honey cakes, and get the fruit and cheese ready. You will need oil and lemon for the fish, plates and spoons, cups and some wine. I will get it ready and packed for you."

Sarah thanked her. But Rivkah was not finished talking. "What do you have for the boy to mark this day? He is growing so fast, soon he will be a man."

"Abraham has a young donkey colt that he is giving to Isaac. It will be his to look after and care for. It is time he began to learn about responsibility, and this is a good way to do that. When the colt is grown, Isaac will learn to ride him and train him to carry and pull loads. He loves animals so this will not be difficult for him. He has a wonderful teacher in his father as well. It will be a wonderful day, and when we are gone, you can have the day to do as you please. What will you do?"

"I will wash my hair, and braid it in those small braids that take so long to do. I'll do my mending and sewing, but mostly I'm going to go for a long walk in the hills and sleep by a tree and dream wonderful dreams."

It was time to find Isaac. Sarah went to the tent at the top of the knoll and looked for the boy and his father. She clapped at the tent flap, but no one answered. She tried three more times. Then she called, "Abraham, have you seen Isaac?" Still no one replied. She shrugged her shoulders and breathing a deep sigh, opened the tent flap and walked in.

The tent was neat and tidy. The bed roll lay in its usual place. There were no dishes or food lying about and no sign of either of the two—father and son. Eliezar had left. Wondering where everyone was and why they weren't excited about the day, she walked to the tent of Eliezar. He was sitting outside, and when he saw her coming, he hurried away.

"Eliezar. Stop. I need to speak with you." He stopped but did not turn around. "Where are Abraham and Isaac? I can't find them anywhere?"

He did not turn to face her, but said, "I am not sure exactly where they are."

"Do not play games with me. Answer me."

He would not meet Sarah's gaze, but looked over her head into the distance.

"What is happening? Eliezar, I demand that you tell me what you know. No more avoiding me. Answer my question. Where is Abraham and is Isaac with him?"

Eliezar shuffled his feet.

"Speak now." Sarah demanded.

"Very early Abraham woke Isaac and took a donkey with wood tied on it, and they climbed up to the Holy Mountain. That is all I know."

"Didn't he take a ram?"

“Only the donkey and the wood. I did not see a ram or a sheep.”

Sarah screamed. She ran back to her tent and kept running to the path that led to the mountain, howling like a wounded animal. She ran gasping for breath, scratching her legs and arms on the bushes as she stumbled along the path. When she could run no more, she collapsed into a heap, sobbing huge, dry, heaving breaths. There were no tears, only anguish in her heart and disbelieve in her mind.

There was only one reason that Abraham would have taken Isaac. Boys did not go to make a sacrifice. Her mind recoiled. *He has gone to make a sacrifice to the angry god of the mountain. He did not take a goat or a ram. The people who lived here before we came worshipped the god Moloch, who demanded the first-born child. I know some still follow these old ways, but not Abraham. What has happened to make him even think of such an abomination?*

Images swirled in Sarah’s brain. Sarah had seen idols of their god, the head of a bull with horns and a human torso with hands. There were still those who followed this god and sacrificed children to him, throwing them alive into the fires that burned on the altar. Sarah had not been to such a sacrifice, but other women had. She learned that the women were expected to stand silently, not wailing or crying, but honouring the custom with their silence. Musicians played flutes to make the scene feel normal, and drum beats muffled the other sounds. Sarah could not be sure if any children of their tribe had disappeared, but the number of people was very large, and it was possible that some still worshipped Moloch in secret. She wailed her anguish to the empty rocky crags.

"No, no, no. Abraham only worships the god of our people, El Shaddai, who does not demand human sacrifice. But there was no animal taken for the offering. What can it mean?" She wailed her anguish to the empty rocky crags.

"Today, why pick today? Had he forgotten our plan for the boy's birthday? Or did he simply not care? How could he be so cruel? Has he forgotten how long we waited for this child? Does he not realize there would be no other born to us?" The mountain winds carried her voice away into nothingness.

Sarah knew she could never find them. There were many, many altars on the mountain and many paths. She had no way to know which one Abraham would use. Getting lost on that vast mountain could not help. Even if she found them, she'd never be in time. They had left hours ago. She stood and, with unsteady steps, started the walk back to her tent. As she turned to go back, she saw a stone in her path. It had three straight sides and sharp points where they met. Across the centre of the stone was a deep crack. *This is my stone of pain. Each of us is here, a side of the stone for Abraham, for Isaac and for me, separated by a great gulf of sorrow.*

As she walked home, she was glad that Rivkah would not be there. There would be no need of an explanation. Back at the tent she entered, lay down and pounded the ground with her fists.

"Why have you forsaken me, El Shaddai, god of flame and thunder? Your angry noise and flashing light, the dust that covered the sky and the earth when you roared, always frightened me, and I know now that it was proper to be afraid. I worship El Shaddai, the mother god I know, the one who nurtures us. But where is her protection today for my son?"

Sarah lay exhausted from her exertion and drifted into an agitated sleep. When she awoke, she got up and went outside. In the next few hours, she ate nothing and drank only a little water. She decided hard work would pass the long day, and she trudged to the well and struggled to fill the water jars. Without stopping to rest, she gathered dung for the fires and added it to the box kept a short distance from her tent. She grabbed her broom and swept the tent until the dust inside choked her and she had to go out to get her breath. She took the combs and brushes and cleaned the milk animals pastured on the hillside. When she could not move another muscle, she took the small bench from inside the tent and put it where she could watch the trail. There she sat without moving. Waiting—just waiting.

When the sun was beginning to set, she saw movement on the trail. She sat straighter and strained, trying to make out the shadowy shapes in the distance. Her eyes burned from the glare of the sun as she tried to focus on the blurred movement she saw. As it came nearer, she saw Abraham and then the donkey came into focus. But where was Isaac! Where was he? As they came closer, she saw he was riding the donkey, lying with his head against the neck of the beast. He was alive.

She jumped to her feet and blew on the dying embers of the fire. She willed it to come to alive. When the flame licked at the coals, she set the barley pot to heat, cut come bread to heat with the fruit Rivkah had prepared.

When they came near the tent, she ran to them and pulled Isaac from the donkey.

She hugged him close; so close he cried out. Sarah knew he didn't like to be hugged or carried, but she didn't care. She carried him to the fire, sat him on a bench and began to feed him as if he were a small child. When he had eaten, she washed his face and hands and led him into her tent. She settled him on her pallet and began to sing to him. He was asleep in just a few minutes. She sat with him, holding his hand until she heard Abraham whisper her name outside the tent.

Looking for one long moment at her son, she brushed a damp curl from his forehead. Stealing herself, she went outside to face her husband. He looked at her and said, "Sarah, you are cut and scraped. What has happened to you? Are you alright?"

"Am I alright? Am I alright? No. I am not alright. I am exhausted and heart sore. I am confused and angry. Very, very angry. What were you going to do? Why were you doing it? And why especially today?"

Abraham reached toward her to take her in his arms, but she jerked away saying, "I need an explanation."

"I have not heard the voice of the holy one for many moons. I have prayed that he speak to me again. Last night I had a troubling dream. I heard a voice telling me to take Isaac to the altar. It was an answer to my plea."

Sarah stood, frozen, numb.

"The voice said that I was to offer him to the mighty one as a show of my trust and loyalty. I tried to ignore the voice, but it gave me no peace. It was the voice of the Almighty One. You know I have always been obedient even when I did not understand."

He reached for the flask and took a long drink of water.

Sarah never moved.

"At dawn I gathered wood and Eliezar brought the donkey. I woke Isaac, and we climbed the path up the mountain."

She shuddered.

"We climbed to the high altar, and I arranged the wood. I tied the boy's hands and was ready to place him on the altar. But I paused. In that moment the voice spoke and said, 'Do not harm the boy.' I heard a noise, and I saw a ram caught in a thicket. I untied Isaac and offered the beast instead. The Holy One has no reason to doubt my complete loyalty and devotion now, and all will be well for us in the future."

Sarah remained silent for a long time, and Abraham pulled at his beard. Without meeting his gaze, she took a sip of water. Her voice was harsh when she spoke. "I do not understand your God. I cannot worship your God. He seems to be no different from Moloch and all the other brass and wooden idols. I shall continue to worship the one who only asks for grain and wine to prove our devotion to her. Do not ask me to revere such a cruel God."

She became silent again, and Abraham wondered if she had finished. He was about to ask when she spoke again.

"All day as I worked myself to exhaustion to pass the time, I hated what you were doing. What has happened to you that you could do such a thing behind my back and then come back and try to take me into your embrace as if it was of little importance? I am trying not to hate you, Abraham. We have shared too much of pain and happiness for hatred. But this is a terrible day. I know that someday, the pain will grow less and because of everything we have shared and for our son Isaac, I will lay this aside." She exhaled, sighing deeply.

Abraham waited. When she spoke once more, her voice was flat, measured, and as cold as the winter winds. "After you lied to save your life in Egypt, I forgave you as you asked, and you promised that you would protect me and keep me safe from harm. Now today, of all days, you cause me the worst pain I have suffered in my entire life. I spoke of trust after Egypt, and I speak of it again. It will be a long, long time before I can trust again. I will not forget, Abraham, I cannot forget. But in time, the memory of this time of terror will fade. Now, I need to sleep. We will speak of this no more tonight."

She rose and walked into her tent without looking back.

Abraham staggered up the hill to his tent, weeping.

Chapter Thirty two

The days that followed crawled for Sarah and Abraham. Each was dealing with their pain, isolation, and deep sorrow differently. Sarah kept busy. She worked from dawn to dark hoping that physical labour would help her sleep. However, when she slept she had terrible visions of Isaac, flames, knives, and blood. She drank wine each night and into it she put the herbal powder that helped induce sleep. It did help her to sleep, and the rest helped her to think during the day.

Abraham withdrew. He seldom left his tent, never bothered to check his flocks or the herders and did not seem to care about the responsibilities that were his and his alone. Eliezar prepared food which he hardly touched, and he rarely spoke to his trusted servant and friend. When Isaac came to him, he made an effort to talk to his son, but he stayed with the boy in the tent. He no longer shot arrows or whittled with the knife as he had. Isaac began to come and sit with his father in silence. He did not know what else to do.

Rivkah spoke to Isaac as he sat glumly on a log. “Why don’t you go and spend some time with your mother? She is not very busy today.”

“I don’t like it. She wants me to sit on her lap. I am not a baby. When we do something she doesn’t sing anymore, she never stops to get a drink or a treat. We just work. I hate it. I am just waiting for my friends."

"The ones you get into mischief with?"

"It was fun to let the goats loose. They ran all over the place and knocked things down. We sure laughed.?

"Did you laugh when you saw your mother and others trying to round up the goats and get them back in their pen? Was it funny to see her picking broken jars? Was it funny when she tripped and fell?"

"No. But we didn't mean for that to happen."

"Did you ever tell her you were sorry for the trouble you caused?"

Isaac sat, downcast until he heard Jacob call.

"I have to go now. Bye."

Rivkah watched him run to meet Jacob and frowned. That boy needs his mother and his father. I need to do something."

That evening as the village was settling for the night, Rivkah walked to Sarah's tent. She was sitting motionless by her fire. The moon was high in the sky and it was time for everyone to be at rest. Rivkah sat on the ground across the fire from Sarah and spoke from her heart.

"I do not know what trouble there is between you and Abraham, Sarah, and I don't need to know. But I have to speak up. This camp is a place that has lost its way. No longer do the women chatter and gossip at the well. They come with sad faces, get their water and return to their tents. The men no longer joke and tease each other. They don't rough house any more, they only do their work and then hang around the camp. Many of them are drinking too much beer and that causes a lot of other problems.

Sarah shifted her weight. She stared intently at the far horizon.

"Isaac does not know what to do with himself and you and Abraham are like dead people walking. Something has happened, and whatever it is, it needs to be made right. And you need to do it now."

Sarah met her gaze for a moment, then without speaking stood up and walked into her tent closed the flap. Rivkah's words echoed in her head and she knew they were true.

I have to come to terms with what has happened, leave it in the past, and find a way to reconcile with Abraham.

The next morning Rivkah came to help with the fires and the meal. Sarah said, "I want you to go to Abraham and ask him to come to my tent this day for the evening meal."

Rivkah was shocked. Men did not come to a woman when summoned. Astonished, she was glad that Sarah was doing something, and hurried to Abraham's tent with the message. Eliazer stopped her. "Abraham is not talking to anyone. You'll have to leave."

"I have a message from Sarah and I am to give it to Abraham and no one else." Eliezer started to speak when Abraham rushed out of the tent. "Tell me. Tell me. What did Sarah say?"

Rivkah passed on the message, and Abraham dropped to his knees. He covered his face with his hands and appeared to be either sobbing or laughing. He made no sound so Rivkah could not tell. Not wishing to embarrass him, she left. A noise made her turn and she saw Abraham grab Eliezer's hands and dance around in a circle, dragging the old man with him. Eliezar pulled away as soon as he could. They exchanged some words and Abraham sat down and began to eat the food that was before him as if he was starving.

From the door of her tent, Sarah watched as well, and she smiled and wiped a tear from her cheek.

"It will be a long day Rivkah, filled with excitement and anxiety. I will make Abraham's favourite lentil stew to pass the time. I also need to bathe and wash my hair and sweep my tent to get ready for this evening."

Chapter Thirty-three

From the moment she was awake, Sarah was panicky. *What will I say to Abraham? What if I make things worse? But I have to mend this horrible rift between us. We've spent years as husband and wife building a life together, and today we need to settle this turmoil and reach a place where we can grow old together in harmony. Not just for us, but for everyone touched by our estrangement.*

She tied her hair with a ribbon and walked to the river to calm her churning belly. She had not eaten as she was too troubled. *I have to do this today. In a few days I will anoint Rivkah as a healer. I cannot come to such a sacred act with an unforgiving heart. I must be at peace within myself and until Abraham and I are at peace, my heart cannot be at peace.*

At Sarah's tent, Rivkah was stirring the fire to heat water for their meal. Sarah approached. "Today is important for me, Rivkah. I need you to be patient with me, but I cannot tell you my plans."

"It is fine, Sarah. I need to say I am sorry for my outburst, and I suspect that your worry has to do with the message I carried to Abraham. I will do whatever you ask."

They worked together preparing for the evening. Sarah insisted on making the stew by herself, but she let Rivkah bake the bread. For the first time since that tragic day, she hummed as she worked. When Isaac came by, she gave him a smile and asked what he was doing. The sadness left his eyes, and he smiled and chattered away with his mother as they had always done.

After the meal was ready, and Rivkah had gone, Sarah sat for a moment to collect her thoughts. The sun disappeared over the hill, and she sat and watched as it set. A few small streaks of clouds dotted the sky, and as the sun slipped beneath the horizon, they bloomed with colour. Pink and gold ribbons across the arch of the heavens waved and swirled in the darkening sky. She watched them until they faded into the velvet night sky. As she sat and watched the sky, its beauty gave her hope. *This is a sign from the holy one. She is offering a blessing on the day. I have to believe it will be all right. I have to believe it.*

Sarah looked to the moon for its blessing and went into her tent to dress. She put on a clean, sand coloured tunic, and picked out a cobalt blue cord to wrap around her waist. Then she moved to her trunk and drew out the diaphanous sky blue scarf. Draping it over her hair, she tossed one end under her chin to the back and slipped the other under the corded belt. She had braided her hair into one long braid and fastened it with a bit of blue ribbon. Satisfied, she walked outside, and carried two stools to place by the fire.

Bowls, cups and spoons were ready for their supper. She glanced up the hill and saw Abraham walking toward her. His beard was washed and combed, and he wore a brightly coloured red robe that floated around him as he strode toward her fire. She looked at him and her heart swelled with hope as she saw that he was coming to her with a warm and tender look on his face.

"Sarah." He reached out both his hands.

"Abraham." And she offered him her hands.

He gently raised them to his lips and kissed them, while looking into her eyes.

"We will eat together and then we will talk." She gestured for him to sit and served him, filling his bowl and giving him bread and wine. Picking up her own bowl and cup, she sat beside him.

Abraham raised his for the prayer before a meal. "Blessed are you, God of the universe who gives the sun and rain to nourish the land."

After he said the blessing, Abraham devoured his meal with many smiles and murmured words of praise to Sarah.

When the meal was over Sarah cleared away the remains and they sat side by side in silence, watching the stars come out and the moon tracing an arc across the darkening sky. It wasn't the uncomfortable silence of anger and blame, but the silence of two people who had spent a life-time in each other's company.

Abraham cleared his throat. "Sarah. I am deeply sorry for the pain and sorrow I caused you. I can only imagine what you suffered that day, and I wish I could change the past, but I cannot. You had every right to be angry, and I am surprised and gratified that you are ready to talk to me. Ask what you will of me in the way of repentance and I will do whatever you think is right."

In her quiet, tender voice, Sarah spoke. "I had many emotions that day: anger, fear, uncertainty, disappointment, betrayal. My mind and heart were torn, broken, shattered. I reacted out of my pain and exhaustion. And I do not apologize for that. As I have struggled with it, I've come to realize you did not do what you did with any intent to hurt me; you just never gave me a thought. I have always known that your God came first; Isaac and I came second. Not that you don't love us, but you've always loved God more."

Abraham sat motionless. His gaze never left her face.

"When you heard the voice, you had to obey. You didn't stop to consider anything. You obeyed, as you have always done. Since it was not a deliberate act to hurt me, I need to try to understand your actions. It is hard for me to be second in your life, especially when it could bring harm to our son. But I need to consider the eventual outcome. What you spoiled was our family day by the river and my trust in our relationship. Isaac has not been affected, so you must have explained it to him in a way he understood and accepted. The signs are there that he will someday love this mountain God as you do."

Sarah shifted on her stool and took Abraham's gnarled hand in hers. She smiled uncertainly.

"I've struggled to understand why you were asked to do this. I will never totally understand the command you heard. But I believe that El Shaddai, the nurturing one, has spoken to me through this ordeal. After much deep thought, I have confidence it tells me that human sacrifice is wrong and evil. Children should be loved and cherished, taught and nurtured, not burned alive in fires to appease a vindictive god. When I was just a girl, I sensed you were a determined person, and you could only see your way of looking at things. Sometimes I was afraid, because I saw ruthlessness in how you got your way. I had forgotten I told myself I would be careful and protect myself from this side of you. And that young girl was right. I need to remember her wisdom. Egypt can never be forgotten and I will never forget this. I can forgive, but I cannot forget."

Abraham put his arm around her shoulders and she relaxed under his touch.

"In the future I need you take me and my feelings into consideration. If only you had awakened me and explained. I would have raged against your God and you with all the fury of a mother when her child is in danger. We both know that I could not have stopped you, but at least I would not have been ignored and dismissed. Nothing could have changed the anguish of that day, but at least you would have acknowledged my existence in your world. I need to feel I am of some small value to you."

Abraham spoke and his voice broke. "Sarah, my wife, the mother of our promised son, my love. I never dared to hope that you would understand so fully and with so much compassion. Your life with me has been difficult, and I am responsible for most or your trials. I struggle with many regrets, but I can't change the past, only live with hope for the future. I will try, really try, to stop and think before I act. Not just in the big things such as this, but in the smaller things of our daily life."

Sarah leaned in close and laid her head on his shoulder.

"Sarah, I've learned from this too. Isaac is a wonderful boy, wise beyond his years, and whenever I see patience, gentleness, and wisdom in his actions, I see you in him. I know that the one destined to follow me had to be your son, not the son of another. He needs to learn from both of us, and to have qualities of each of us as part of who he is. I will begin anew, for all our sakes. For your sake first of all, then for Isaac, and for the future. But mostly for me, for my past folly, for my impetuous actions and my arrogance, I apologize. Sarah, I pledge myself anew to you and to our future.

They sat listening to the night sounds and watching the arc of the moon glide across the sky. Sarah cleared her throat.

“There is one thing I ask—no, demand," said Sarah in a firm voice. “Take to heart the lesson you can learn from this. El Shaddai does not want the sacrifice of our children. Children are our gift and a blessing. They must be loved, cherished, taught, and nurtured. As our leader, you must make our people understand that never again will a child be sacrificed on an altar to any god. Promise me, Abraham. That is what I need to close this painful episode.”

“Sarah, I vow to you, never again will anyone sacrifice a child in our tribe. Punishment for such an act will be banishment from the circle of our tents forever. To show you I am sincere and grateful that you opened my eyes to see the lesson that the Holy One gave me; I brought a gift to seal that pledge.”

He handed Sarah a small bundle, wrapped in the purest white cotton and tied with a blue ribbon. Sarah unwrapped it and smiled. It was a necklace made of pearls, separated by tiny golden beads. She held it and looked at it, her heart beating in wonder, and her eyes shining with affection. She shivered.

“You are cold. Can we go into your tent? I will put the necklace on you if you like.”

They stood and walked hand in hand into the tent. Abraham gently took the blue scarf away, lifted Sarah’s braid and slipped the necklace around her neck, kissing her where her hair touched her neck.

Sarah turned and said, "Let's have a glass of wine to seal our pledge to begin anew."

They sat on cushions and sipped the wine. Sarah had one more question. "How did Isaac like the colt when you gave it to him?"

"I did not give it to him. It is from both of us, and I waited. We will do it tomorrow, so we can share his joy. The camp has been suffering with this trouble and a celebration would be in order, Sarah. Something simple, but including everyone."

Sarah clapped her hands. "We will build a fire, and dance and sing in its warmth and light. Before it is dark, we will plan races and contests. Everyone can bring something to the feast and share it. And we can give Isaac the colt then. When we tire of dancing we can sit around the fire and tell stories and ask riddles. It will be wonderful Abraham. The people shared our sadness and they need to laugh and sing once again."

They sat in silence for a while, enjoying each other's warmth and company.

His voice husky, Abraham spoke. "Sarah will you put the scarf on again and dance for me, as you did once. But before you do, may I spend the night here with you? I know that is not done, but we have already thrown tradition to the winds many times, so why not this custom too?"

Sarah recovered her scarf and with trembling hands placed it on her hair and wound it around her neck. She found her tambourine, and knowing exactly where this would lead, danced for Abraham.

Chapter Thirty-four

Sarah awoke when the sun was well up in the sky. Stretching her limbs, she felt at peace, and she began another day but now filled with harmony and hope.

There were just a few days until the time of the new moon and Sarah had much to plan. She went to her wicker box and lifted its lid. It was full of items placed for safe keeping. She took each item out and placed it on the rug. *I need to get rid of some of this.* Sarah dug right to the bottom and there, as she knew it would be, lay a small parcel, carefully wrapped in linen and tied with a piece of cord. She took it out, put it in her lap and replaced the other items.

Sarah stood and held the small bundle close to her heart and a tear made its way down her cheek. She wiped it away, and a smile grew on her face, softening the lines the years had etched in her once flawless skin. Tenderly, she opened the package. Knowing what she would see, she still felt great emotion. Sarah held a necklace in her hands, for the first time in many years.

Jessica made this for me with her own hands. She was my teacher, my mentor, but best of all, my friend. She must be at rest with the grandmothers by now. I wonder who has taken her place back home in Ur. Sarah turned and gazed out the doorway. *I have not thought of Ur as my home for many years. Mother must be at rest now too. I hope the years of decline were bearable for her. She was a woman of great courage and strength. The women's place would have given her the support she needed as she faced her death.*

Sarah folded the cloth that had protected this cherished symbol for so many years. The face of her mother, young and beautiful, formed before her eyes. It faded away and in its place came the strong, cheerful image of Jessica. She held the emblem of her profession up to the light and breathed deeply.

Two wonderful women who made me who I am today: a strong, independent woman, who loves deeply and is loved. I love Isaac, but often wonder how different life would have been if I had a daughter to pass on my knowledge and thoughts. But Rivkah has helped to fill that empty place in my life, and tonight I pass this necklace on to her.

The simple leather cord was still pliable and the light sandy colour seemed to glow. At its centre was a striking, irregularly shaped piece of polished black onyx. Jessica had explained to Sarah that the stone stood for inner strength, spiritual wisdom, compassion, discipline, and reason. It was the emblem of a healer and too valuable to wear every day. In its place, the woman wore a leather bracelet with a simple black bead at the centre; an echo of the necklace. Sarah looked at hers, old and well-worn. But it carried its years with dignity, just as Sarah hoped she did.

In the time since she had been instructing Rivkah, Sarah had woven a bracelet for her. It was ready and tonight she would add the bead and tie the bracelet to Rivkah's wrist at the ceremony. Sarah had finished all the preparations: food and wine, flowers and candles, the sacred fire and a basin of water. Now she could rest and anticipate the sacred moment when she placed the necklace on Rivkah's young shoulders.

As she settled for sleep, she thought what a perfect idea it had been to ask Rivkah to be her successor. *She was a wonderful student, eager and attentive. Nothing escaped her notice and she remembered everything I showed her.*

You are ready to take my place, my child. My years as the healer have been filled with joyful times and sad times. But age is making it too difficult for me to continue. It is time to recognize and honour you with your ceremony, naming you as our healer, as I step aside.

Sleep came, and when she drifted into that mysterious realm, her dreams were peaceful and filled with contentment.

Chapter Thirty-five

As the sun made golden streaks of light in her tent Sarah woke from a restful sleep, and watched as specks of dust danced in the light. She dressed in a blue tunic, then ate cheese and dates to break the night's fast. During the morning she kept busy near her tent, trying to hurry the sun across the expanse of azure blue sky. Just after her rest in the heat of the day, Abraham came to her tent.

"I have sent Isaac to bring Rivkah here. I need to speak with both of you. Ah, here they are now."

Sarah felt her throat tighten. He used that stern voice that he always used when there was something wrong.

What can he possibly want to say on this day? What displeases him now?

Abraham dismissed Isaac and asked the two women to stand before him. "Sarah, I know that you have been teaching Rivkah the ways of a healer. I understand that you need to train someone for the day when you can no longer do this strenuous task. But there is a great impediment to your plan. Rivkah is a slave. A slave can only treat other slaves, not free men and women. Have you thought of that?"

Rivkah looked stricken, and Sarah's heart sank. In her eagerness she had forgotten. She almost fell with the weight of his words, but Rivkah put her arm around her and supported her. They stood, wooden-like, unable to speak or move.

Abraham stroked his beard. "As I see this problem, there is only one solution

Sarah lifted her eyes to look at him, and she saw in his deep, brown eyes the twinkle he had when he was up to something.

What is he going to do? What is his solution? Look at his eyes and that hint of a smile. He is teasing me again. When will I learn that he enjoys these dramas? Worry turned to curiosity as she wondered what Abraham was planning. He reached into his sleeve and pulled out a small piece of rolled up skin.

"On this skin I have written the symbols that declare you to be a free woman, Rivkah. I shall announce it to everyone at the evening meal. Guard this well, it is your proof of freedom from this day onward."

Both women gasped, hugged one another and danced in a circle of joy. When they stopped, Rivkah went to Abraham and started to kneel.

"Do not kneel to me. Stand tall, for you are not a slave. You are free." Abraham reached out his hands, and taking one of Rivkah's in his, he placed his other hand on her head.

"May El Shaddai protect you and keep you. May he shed his light upon you and give you peace." He smiled at them both, gave Sarah a broad grin, and went to his tent, leaving them to finish the preparations for the evening.

"What does it mean, Sarah? Am I really a free woman?

"Yes, my dearest friend. It will change nothing between us. I have always felt you were my friend, not my slave."

"But to everyone else? How should I act now?"

"All you need to remember is that you are now a free woman, equal to me and all the other free women. But you are still who you have always been. Honest, kind, generous and patient. And that won't change. Relax Rivkah, your life will be what you make it. And that has always been so."

"I think I understand. This changes nothing, and yet it changes everything."

With another hug they parted.

The people of the clan gathered around the communal fire after the evening meal. Abraham once again stood on a cart and everyone stopped to listen.

"Hear my words. Today, I granted freedom to Rivkah. She is no longer a slave, but is ready to be set apart as a healer. She will assist Sarah and everyone will respect her and her wisdom. Tonight there will be a ceremony in the woman's tent to honour her."

A cheer rose from the gathering, and men raised Rivkah to their shoulders. They carried her around the circle and friends cheered and clapped. When the celebration quieted down, the women left to prepare for the ceremony. Sarah and Abraham stood arm in arm.

Sarah and Rivkah dressed with care to honour the ceremony that was to take place. The last thing Sarah did was to slip the necklace over her own head. She touched the cherished healer's emblem she had received so long ago from Jessica. It rested comfortably on her shoulders. When they were ready, a young girl, wearing the yellow sash of a music maker came to the tent to lead them to the tent of women with the beat of her small drum.

As they neared the place, Sarah could hear the rich voice of Debra, the best singer in the entire community. She was crooning a wordless melody, and the women sang it back to her. As they entered the tent, the singing stopped, and an expectant silence filled the space.

Debra moved to the centre and led the women in a song of welcome. They sang and the music makers played their drums and flutes and tambourines. As the songs grew more spirited, women swayed and danced their joy and happiness and the small bells or beads they wore around their ankles added a magical quality to the song. As the music faded, the women returned to their places and sat on the rugs that covered the outer ring of the dirt floor. Sarah moved to the raised place by the fire, and Rivkah joined her. Since she could not remember the words that Jessica had used, she had planned her own.

Sarah nodded to the flame bearer, who walked gracefully around the outer edge of the circle of women and lit the lamps that had been placed in spaces between them. Soon the flames were dancing and giving life and energy to the moment. Then the sacred fire, which had been carefully laid in the central pit, was brought to life. This ceremonial fire was made of wood, not dung, and as the flames caught, cedar branches were added and the rich woodsy aroma filled the air with hope and promise.

"During this sacred ceremony, I ask each of you to hold Rivkah in your thoughts as she receives these symbols of her new role as our healer. Rivkah, it is time for you to go to the basin and wash your hands as a symbol of your purification. When ready, come to me for the anointing."

A soft, warm hush filled the room. The only sounds were the gentle wind that made the trees sing, and the birds twittering their last evening notes.

"Rivkah you have been learning from me for many months. You have studied well. Your questions showed wisdom and knowledge. You have helped many with your potions, salves, and herbs. It is time for you to receive the symbol of a healer. Jessica, my teacher, gave me this necklace many years ago, and now I pass it on to you. Wear it in both pride and humility. Keep it safe and in time pass it on to the one who will follow you in this holy calling."

Sarai lifted the necklace over her head and placed it on Rivkah's shoulders and kissed her in blessing. She turned her to face the women and Rivkah turned in a circle so that all could see her. When she faced Sarah again, the women joined in a silent salute. They raised their hands and fluttered them in blessing.

"You will wear the necklace only at special times, and so I give you a bracelet to wear every day as the symbol of your place among us as our healer and midwife."

She tied the leather cord with its bright black bead around Rivkah's wrist and once again hands fluttered to recognize Rivka's new status. Sarah handed her a cup and a plate of bread.

Rivkah took a piece of bread and dipped it into the wine. As she ate the bread, the women sang a healing song. Sarah anointed her with oil and gave her a sprig of mint. Again the hands fluttered in the candles' glowing light

"I have given you the badge of your work and anointed you with oil. This sets you apart for the task of healing the hurts and illnesses of those who come to you. Remember that you are a daughter of El Shaddai and return often to her for strength and wisdom."

Sarah placed her hand on Rivkah's head and prayed.

"Blessed is the one who brings grain from the earth.

Blessed is the one who creates the olives for healing oil.

Blessed is the one who causes herbs to grow, flowers and seeds for potions and salves.

Bread and oil and plants of the earth.

Gifts from El Shaddai.

Thanks be to the mother god who lives on the holy mountain."

There was a moment of complete silence. The birds hushed their song, and even the wind held its breath.

"What is your spirit symbol, and what does it mean to you?"

"My symbol is the cedar tree. It is rooted in the earth, and it points to the sky, connecting all things. To me it means shelter and security, cleansing and purifying, growth and life."

Sarah took a small piece of cedar and placed in it Rivkah's hand. Once again hands fluttered in blessing and celebration around the circle.

"And now," said Sarah, "It is time for us to enjoy food and wine."

The celebration lasted long into the night. One by one, as they tired, the women came to Rivkah and welcomed her as both a free woman and a healer and midwife. At last, only she and Sarah remained in the tent.

"You will stay here alone tonight, Rivkah. It is a time for you to consider your life and what it will be like to live as a healer among us. I know you will consider the responsibility, the honour, the joy, and pleasure. But also reflect upon the sorrow that you will be asked to bear, the grief that you will share and give deep thought to ways you will keep your spirit alive and well. Create rituals and symbols you will use to heal yourself from the burdens that you will bear with others and for others. You are strong and wise. You will be a healer who will be loved and remembered long after you have drawn your last breath. Think on these things. And now I offer you a blessing."

Sarah placed her hand on Rivkah's head and said the words she had planned.

"May you be filled with love. May you walk in light. May you serve with strength and patience. And may there always be health and happiness within you."

Sarah walked out of the tent, into the gentle night. Rivkah sat and looked through the openings in the roof of the tent at the night, watching the stars spin their path across the sky.

In her tent as Sarah prepared for sleep, a glorious wave of happiness filled her heart. She would still help anyone who needed her, but the great responsibility was now passed to Rivkah. As she thought about Rivkah, Sarah realized that she loved her as a daughter.

She walked to her prayer mat and standing there with arms outstretched, she sang a song of thanksgiving for each blessing life had brought to her. Sarah felt grateful for the women who had taught her and helped her to grow into a powerful woman such as they had been. She thought of Abraham and Isaac, the two men she loved as she loved no other. The pain and sorrow that had been hers through her life, was what had helped to make her strong and wise, and she was grateful for those struggles. But mostly she was glad that so much of her life had been one of joy and happiness.

With those warm and pleasant thoughts, she lay on her mat, and knowing her dreams would be pleasant, she was asleep almost at once.

The Sacred Grove

Chapter Thirty-six

Sarah sat by the river on the bench Isaac had made. She watched as he swam in the river. His eyes were the eyes of Abraham, warm, soft brown, kind and wise. But his smile and laugh were hers, and the thought warmed her heart.

Can he be the infant I birthed so long ago? Strong and confident, wise and capable, gentle and kind.

She marvelled at her son, born of her old age. He was tall and well-muscled from his work . He could run like the wind and he often did when he went to the fields to check the herds. His black hair curled when it was damp, and it shone like the midnight sky. The dark beard was trimmed, quite short compared to many of the men, but it added to his look of intelligence and wisdom. Memories of an infant, a young boy, and the man crowded her thoughts.

What a beautiful baby you were, so easy to care for, and you were never sick a day in your life. You chafed at the lessons we made you study, you would rather be in the fields tending the sheep and goats. I wonder how much you remember of your birthday, and the events of that day. I hope you have forgotten it completely. You handle your weapons as well as Reuben did, winning all the contests with the bow and arrow. I have not thought of him or Eliana in a long time. Memories may fade, but the friendships never do.

Isaac waved at her from the river and she waved back.

The troubles that came to Abraham and me seem not to have affected you, and for that I am grateful. You are so full of life and energy. But you are also wise and gentle and kind. You listen for the voice of the mountain god and you obey him just as your father does. But you have learned respect for women from us as well and that is hopeful for the future when you lead this great band of shepherds and craftsmen. I hope the woman you marry will love and honour you, be a good wife to you, but one who will keep you attentive to her and your children. I pray to god that you will have many sons and daughters.

As he came up from the river, wearing only a loin cloth she felt her heart would burst with love and pride.

He leaned toward his mother. "Are you ready to go back to your tent? I'll help you up the hill just to be safe. I know you can do it alone, but a strong arm never hurts."

Sarah was grateful that Isaac pretended she could climb the hill on her own. Her lack of strength and energy annoyed her, and she accepted his help without any hesitation. Her once beautiful dark brown hair was now completely gray and her back, so strong and straight was now bent with the years. Part way up the hill, they stopped and looked toward the crest at Abraham's tent. He sat there watching them and smiled.

As Abraham watched, his heart was filled with love for them. His wife of so many years he couldn't count them and the son of their old age. *He does all the heavy work now and I can rest. I must think about finding a wife for him. And as Sarah and I agreed a woman from Ur, our homeland. A woman who knowns the God of the mountain.*

Abraham waved, but they didn't notice as they continued up the hill.

Sarah, out of breath from the walk in spite of Isaac's help, sank into the cushions in her tent. She spent much of her time resting. But her hands were not idle, she could still weave on the small loom, and she could mend torn and tattered garments. Rivkah who still cared for Sarah often asked her for advice. They both knew it was a kindness to honour Sarah, as Rivkah could do the work as well as Sarah did. She had been a quick and enthusiastic pupil and Sarah was at ease knowing that Rivkah had taken her place as the healer in the tribe.

In the evenings, Sarah and Abraham sat and talked, and they spoke of family. They remembered their mothers and their father Terah. Telling stories of their goodness but not forgetting their mistakes. Lot was often the subject of their conversation.

Sarah shifted to look at Abraham. "The shaking of the earth and the fire that destroyed Sodom was a terrible thing. I was happy to hear Lot escaped the wrath of your angry god."

"The news has not been good since they left. He is alone now that Ado died as they fled. He and his daughters live in a cave near Zoar."

"Do you think he lost his reason when she died?"

"It is possible. Grief can do terrible things to the mind."

"How different it all might have been if he had stayed with us."

They spoke of the traders who came and talked to them about Egypt. They knew Hagar was dead but Ishmael was an important man and had many sons and daughters.

"Do you know Sarah, that Isaac sent a message to Ishmael? I have wondered why and what it said."

"Yes. He told me. I think he must have told him that we are nearing the end of our days. The passing years have eased the hurt of Hagar's ambition, and maybe it is time for Ishmael to visit his family."

"It would be good to see my son, before my eyes are too dim to recognize him."

Abraham stood and stirred the fire. The embers blurred before his eyes. He sat again beside Sarah and she took his gnarled hand in hers to get him to look at her.

"Abraham, there is something have never told you, but it is the time now. Over the years I have gathered stones that mark for me significant events in my life. In the tamarisk grove I have made a circle of those stones, and I used to go there often to pray to El Shaddai. It is a beautiful and peaceful spot and I would like to go once more before I die. Could you take me there tomorrow?"

Without hesitation Abraham replied, "Of course we can go tomorrow. I will get a gentle mule for you to ride and we will take some food and wine. We can stay as long as you wish."

"Thank you dear one. You have always humoured me when I had these strange notions. You never questioned me. Not when I wore Egyptian clothes to your tent, or when I invited you to come to my tent to spend a night with me."

"Why would I question a woman who knew her own mind and planned such delightful surprises for me? Do you remember Sara, all those nights so long ago? You were beautiful, and I was young and filled with desire. We had some good times." Abraham cupped Sarah's chin in his hand. "You are still beautiful but I am no longer young; the same desire is there but not the youthful responses to your loveliness."

"The eyes dim, the ears fail, our limbs grow stiff and tired, but love does not die. You are still my handsome young groom, the love of my life. You and I will be together, somehow, in death as we have been in life."

Sarah patted his hand and quietly said, "I have one more request Abraham and it is important. After we see where I have made a circle of stones I will give a stone to you to keep safe somewhere. It is in a bag and please do not open the bag until the right time. And that will be when I die. When I have been laid to rest, put it in the circle in the space I have left. Then my circle of stones will be complete as will my life. When we go there in the morning, I will explain it to you."

Abraham nodded and gently squeezed her hand. "Sarah, I would like to lie with you again tonight. To hold you in my arms, smell your hair, feel your body close to mine. To sleep with our arms wrapped around each other will be the perfect beginning for the journey tomorrow. I promise nothing more, but to be with you will be all I need."

"It will be all I need too, Abraham. But one never knows. Miracles have happened before when we bedded together."

They stood and shared a kiss under the tender gaze of a full moon. And hand in hand entered Sarah's tent.

Chapter Thirty-seven

Sarah stood and rubbed her back. She stretched her arms out and shrugged her shoulders. With care she removed her night tunic and pulled a soft sand coloured dress over her shoulders. Abraham's voice came from the edge of the tent.

"Good morning, Sarah."

She walked out to greet him. "It is a good morning. It is good that we have plenty of time these days. It takes so much longer to do anything."

Abraham smiled in agreement. After they had eaten some fruit and cheese, and before the sun was high in the sky, Abraham brought the donkey to Sarah. She would ride up the hill to the grove of trees. Neither could carry much, so a second donkey was brought. A simple meal, some wine, a small rug and some cushions were fastened to its back. Sarah handed Abraham a small, heavy, linen bag and he tied it to the donkey.

Abraham tied the donkeys together, the pack animal behind the first one. Sarah stroked the donkey's neck and settled herself on the blanket. Abraham picked up the reins in one hand and a stout walking staff in the other, and they set out to climb to the sacred grove.

It was farther than Sarah remembered and the path appeared steeper and more difficult. The donkey seemed to know how precious his burden was, for he walked very carefully, taking dainty protective steps. Abraham leaned heavily on his staff, and they stopped often.

"Look back to your tent Sarah. How small it looks from this distance."

"It does, but it is a comforting sight."

Along the way, he pointed out an unusual tree, or a pretty flower, or a strange cloud formation. Sarah understood he was stopping to rest, and she played her part with thoughtful enthusiasm.

They reached the grove and Abraham looked for the stones; he could see nothing. He lifted Sarah from the donkey onto the soft grass. He held her a little longer than necessary and she smiled up at him. Abraham unloaded the donkeys and tied them near some tender shoots of grass. Working slowly, for bending was difficult; they laid out the rug and put the pillows down to make a back rest in the shade of the tamarisk trees. Abraham handed Sarah the basket. From it she took a loaf of bread, new cheese, grapes and two honey cakes. They sat and ate. The cool goat's milk from the skin refreshed them and they rested together, watching the far horizon covered in a beautiful lacy mist.

Sarah said, "It is time." They stood and Abraham leaned on his staff. Sarah held his arm as she led the way into the grove to the circle of stones.

Abraham saw them at once. His jaw dropped and he looked on them in wonder. As he looked at the stones his eyes filled with tears. He was able to see what some of them represented. He marvelled that she had collected them over the years, had carried them with her on her journeys, brought them to this sacred place, and made this circle. He looked at her with new insight. This was a woman of great intelligence and deep emotion, whose life had meaning and which she had marked its stages in this unique way.

He helped her to sit with her back against a tree where she could see the circle. "If you can Sarah, I would like you to tell me what they mean to you."

She spoke so softly that Abraham had to sit very close to hear her words. "The old plain one at the top in the direction of the East is from my mother's cooking fire." Her hand trembled as she pointed to it. "The alabaster one on the south side is from Egypt, but you could tell that. The northern one comes from Mamre, as it reminds me of the smoking mountain. It is black as if it had burned in the flames. The one on the south side is the stone of our wedding night—white for our innocence and the streak is the blood I shed."

Abraham squeezed her hand and smiled.

"The small rough looking one has the image of a leaf in it. It is to mark the day my flow of blood dried and I knew I was old and dried up like the leaf." Her voice broke and she wiped a tear from her check. "The mud and straw brick is part of a birthing stone from the time Isaac was born. That one, nearest to us shows the tears of sadness that came and went with Hagar. I had never seen a tear shaped stone before."

Abraham reached out and brushed some dirt and leaves away from the stone.

"The light sandy coloured one is a reminder of all our travels over the sand dunes, and also the desert places in my life. The three-sided pointed one marks the day of misunderstanding, one side for each of us, you, Isaac and me, and the deep crack in it speaks to me of the rift that was between us at that time."

Abraham put his arm around her and she laid her head on his shoulder.

In silence they looked at the stones, each one holding in its core the story of Sarah's life.

Abraham pointed. "There is an empty space, Sarah."

"It is for the one that is in the bag I gave you. That space is for the last one which you now have. You will put it there after I am gone."

Abraham felt his chest tighten and his eyes filled with tears. He knew that Sarah was frail, but he didn't want to face a future without her.

They sat in silence, each deep in remembrance. When Sarah spoke, her quiet voice sounded content. "They do not make me sad, Abraham, for they are the stones of my life. My memories—some good, some sad, some painful, some joyous. They are all noted here and these stones are the markers of my living and my dying. When the last one is added in that open space it will be complete."

Abraham brushed his hand across his eyes, and put an arm around her shoulders.

She leaned against him. "When I have come here, they have brought me peace. It was important for me to have this memorial to my life and my being. You are the only person who knows of this place unless someone has found it by accident. I leave it to you what happens to it after you add the last stone."

The silence was heavy between them, broken only by the whisper of the wind in the trees and the call of a bird flying above them.

Sarah squeezed his hand. “I have another favour to ask of you. Go back to the rug and bring us each a cup of wine.”

He did and sat again beside her. “Are we going to raise a glass in honour of our day?”

“This day and all our days. We can’t kneel very well so help me to stand.”

They stood and held their arms high in the air and drained their cups. Together they shouted, “l’chaim.”

A flock of doves rose from the trees. With misty eyes, their faces creased with the joys and sorrows of a lifetime they embraced.

\

Chapter Thirty-eight

The wet season came, and endless grey rain fell from an ominous sky. During the entire time of the rains, Sarah never went outside her tent. Abraham left her when necessary and then Isaac stayed with her. Rivkah hovered nearby, ready to respond to the slightest cough or moan. Women came to the door, wet and shivering, bearing steaming bowls of nourishing broth for their dying friend and mentor. The sombre mood of the sky, and the moaning sound of the wind, added to the misery that enveloped the camp. In the valley the river ran black and cold and people left their tents only when necessary. Silence hung like a shroud over the camp. Fires sputtered and died under the continuous, pelting rain.

After many dreary weeks, the weather showed signs of change. Glimmers of light kissed the early morning sky, and ribbons of pink tinged the evening clouds. One morning dawned with pale streaks of gold on the hills, and the camp's spirits lifted. Isaac kept a careful watch and when the rain stopped, he and Rivkah carried mats and pillows to the top of the rise, and made a soft bed for Sarah. When the sun warmed the air and the ground, Abraham carried her out, supported her with pillows, and settled her on the bed, in the warm sunshine.

"Thank you. It is wonderful to see blue sky and the clouds and to feel the warm touch of the breeze again. The air is so fresh." She pointed to the river. "Look at the rushing water. The river is bursting its banks and flowing out into the meadows. I have never seen it like this." She cupped a bony hand around her ears. "Listen. I can hear many wonderful sounds; birds, sheep, goats, the tumbling river, the wind in the trees. And I can breathe in the scent of the flowers, the grass and even the mud. It makes me feel alive after these tedious weeks."

People walked by and smiled and waved, but did not come close. No one wanted to intrude. Sarah stayed all morning, taking in every sight, sound, and smell, all the while chatting with those closest to her.

When she dozed, Isaac carried her back inside, and they began their vigil once more. Rivkah tried to coax Sarah to eat and drink but she could swallow only a little broth. Day by day she grew weaker. Abraham remained by her side, ready if she needed him. She slept uneasily, and Abraham got little sleep, as he listened for every sound. Isaac tried to get him to go to his tent to rest, but he stayed and held Sarah's hand and waited.

On a moonlit night, she spoke. "It is time Abraham. Take me to the women's tent. And you will stay with me. Rules are made to be broken, and I will break one more before I die."

Women had created a soft, comfortable bed close enough to the sacred fire so Sarah would feel its warmth. They muttered as Isaac carried his mother to the tent but said nothing. He knelt as he laid her on the bed. Rivkah covered her with the blue cloak Sarah loved. The three devotedly kept their watch. Isaac sat on the floor and cradled her head in his lap. Abraham held her hand

and stroked her, murmuring words of love and comfort. The long night passed slowly.

As the day dawned, Sarah drank in the sunrise through the opening in the roof. Rivkah, always present in the background hummed songs of blessing. Women brought food and drink to the tent.

At the moment the sun blazed a ball of red fire on the hill top, Sarah drew her last breath. Rivkah walked outside and left the family alone. They sat, holding their memories tenderly in their minds. Sarai, the curious girl, always asking why or why not. Sarah, the loving wife, strong and courageous, testing limits with every new thought. And finally, in her old age, the devoted mother, loving her only child passionately with every breath.

Abraham gave a deep shuddering moan, and stood. Isaac closed her eyes and straightened her cloak. They held each other in their shared grief. Silently, they walked out of the tent and raised their weary eyes to the hill of Moreh, where a dry cave was to be her tomb.

The women, waiting outside, entered the sacred space in silence. They placed their mats and cushions in a circle around the edge of the tent. A song of lament began and was sung over and over, rising and falling, filling the tent. During its singing, Rivkah dressed Sarah in the white and gold robe that she had requested. She cut the anklet of her womanhood from her leg and her healer's bracelet from her wrist. She stared at them for a moment, and placed them in the cold, folded hands as tears ran down her cheeks. Tria, the head midwife, came to stand beside Rivkah. Stooped with age, with trembling hands she cut the leather thong that held the worn and threadbare bag that was around Sarah's neck. It had hung there since the day of her first bleeding. It held Sarah's spirit stone. Tria held it against her cheek for a moment, then placed it over Sarah's heart. The two women arranged myrrh and aloe around Sarah's body and covered her with the well-worn blue shawl for a shroud. The singing stopped and quiet sobbing filled the room.

Rivkah and Tria carried cedar twigs to the fire and dropped them into the flames. They crackled as they burned and the woodsy scent floated in the air. The women rose to their feet and joined hands in a circle around the fire. Rivkah's voice filled the silence.

"We say good-bye to Sarah. Daughter of Binah and Terah. Wife of Abraham. Mother of Isaac. Friend to all. She has been our sister, our teacher, leader and healer. A wise counsellor and as strong and dependable as her spirit stone. It is time for you to rest old friend. Join the grandmothers who have gone before. Watch over us and guide us. Your story will be told for generations. Gone but never forgotten."

Silently the women left the tent.

Chapter Thirty-nine

Eliezar brought a cart to the sacred tent as the golden rays of the sun warmed the sand. A straw bed had been prepared in it, covered with a soft blanket. The women placed Sarah in the cart. Isaac noticed some things along one side, and wondered about them, but said nothing. They started up the hill to the grove of trees. Many people followed, women, men and children. Some were weeping quietly, others moaning softly, but most were silent.

They passed the grove and continued to the field which Abraham had purchased in Machpelah, east of Mamre. At its edge was a large dry cave. They travelled slowly and the short distance took most of an hour for all the people to gather. Abraham sat on the grass and waited until everyone was present. Isaac laid Sarah to rest in the cave and prayers were offered to ease her journey and the pain of those who mourned.

Women left flowers, bread and spices and slowly returned to their homes; walking in silent grief and devotion. Men stayed and closed the opening with many large stones to protect the one they called Mother.

Abraham and Isaac stood alone. "Father, let me help you into the cart for the journey down the hill." Abraham climbed into the cart and Isaac led the ox down the well -worn path. When the cart neared the grove of trees, Abraham spoke.

"Leave the trail and follow that path to the trees."

Isaac did as his father asked.

"Stop here," said Abraham and he climbed down from the cart. "Tether the ox. We will be here for a while. I have something to show you and much to tell you." He handed a shovel and the embroidered bag to Isaac and asked him to carry them.

He picked up his staff, and trudged to the opening and lifted the branch that hid the entrance. Isaac followed his father into the grove. He stopped, stared and gasped in wonder. Abraham sat down at the edge of the circle and beckoned Isaac to sit beside him. "These stones tell the story of your mother's life; happy times, and times of anger, despair and grief."

"What do they mean? Do you know?"

Abraham pointed to the one at his feet and indicated Isaac might want to hold it. Isaac picked up the piece of alabaster. In an unsteady voice, Abraham told Isaac the story behind the stone from Egypt. Isaac replaced it in the circle as he listened to his father.

"Mother told me stories of Ur, Haran and journeys you made together. I knew nothing of Egypt except Hagar was from that land."

Abraham pointed to the next one and explained its meaning. They sat together deep in thought after each story.

Isaac pointed to the stone at his feet. "That one looks very ordinary, father."

Abraham heaved a great sigh.

"It signifies the day we went to the mountain to make a sacrifice. Your tenth birthday."

Isaac rubbed his temples. "My memory of the mountain sacrifice is very unclear and I did not know it was my birthday. Why would mother keep a reminder of that day?"

"Your mother did not know until we returned that a ram had been sacrificed. She thought she would never see you again."

"Why would she think that?"

"I cannot speak of it now. Maybe someday. Just know, that I did your mother a terrible wrong that day. She forgave me, and it was not the only time I needed her understanding and compassion."

Isaac put his arm around his father's shoulders.

Abraham continued to tell the stories of the stones, speaking gently and pausing often to wipe a tear.

Isaac whispered, his voice, hoarse with emotion. "I have always loved mother, but now I understand her better. So much I didn't know. Did you know about these stones?"

"Not until recently. Your mother brought me here and told me about them. This was a sacred place for Sarah and she came here often to remember and to pray."

They sat together deep in thought. Each lost in memories of the wife and mother now gone from them.

Isaac broke the silence. "There is an empty space father."

Abraham shook himself as if coming back from far, far away. He took the linen bag and for the first time noticed that it had a tamarisk tree embroidered on it. The tree was covered with the long, lacy pink flowers that made it so beautiful in the spring. From the bag, he took the stone, which he had not seen until this moment. It was a piece of jade. Part of it was round and polished, and that orb sat on an unfinished base of rough stone.

"What can it mean?" asked the old man. "Each stone means something, what does this one mean?"

After a long pause, in a voice breaking with emotion, Isaac replied. "The traders of stones and jewels say it means many things. When I think of mother and the meanings of this stone, I believe she wanted us to remember her wisdom and her friendship and love. It is also a healing stone and one of protection. Mother wants us to be well and to live, healed of our grief and pain."

Abraham gave the stone to Isaac and he held it in his strong rough hands. He stroked the stone and after a long pause he spoke. "I think it is her wish for us to remember her and her life, but to leave the past here, with her stones. The rough part at the bottom remains unpolished or finished. That is like life and mother wants us to carry on and finish what we have begun."

"Please put the stone in its place, Isaac. I cannot do it."

With great respect, Isaac settled the remarkable green stone in the circle with the others. The two men sat, locked in an embrace. Tears ran down their cheeks. After a long time Abraham nodded. "It is good. This time is an ending and a beginning. Just like evening and morning."

The mournful song of a lone dove broke the silence.

"Sarah said that I could do what I wanted with this place and these stones. I do not want them stolen, dishonoured or profaned. That is why I brought the shovel. They will lie in their circle in this little hollow forever. Please, bring earth and cover them, smoothing it out so no one will ever know, and then we will seed it with grass. We will return them to the earth from which they came."

Without a word, Isaac started to work. Before long, the stones had vanished, the ground was smooth and seeds were scattered on the earth. When Isaac finished, Abraham spoke.

"From the earth they came, to the earth we return them. These stones will sleep here for eternity, but as long as we live, we will remember. This is a sacred place, Isaac, never forget that your mother made this circle of stones. She named it a sacred place, and we will remember her and the story stones of her life, and you will tell the story to your sons and daughters."

Isaac patted the earth once more. He looked around the grove that had meant so much to his mother, and he felt her strength and love.

"I am tired son, let us go home."

With a last poignant look they walked to the cart. The old man climbed in and Isaac took up the reins. As they descended to the valley, the clouds behind them turned gold and silver and pink. Ribbons of colour furled across the sapphire sky. The sun broke through a cloud that hung low over the sacred mountain, and a beam shone straight into the grove.

It was El Shaddai setting her seal and blessing on Sarah's life, on her circle of stones.

List of Characters

A Circle of Stones

An Ancient Foremother's Journey
Sarah's Story

From the Hebrew Writings, the book of Genesis

Sarai/Sarah
Terah … father of Sarah
Abram/Abraham … son of Terah, husband of Sarah
Haron … son of Terah
Nahor … son of Terah
Milcah … daughter of Haran
Lot … son of Haran
Eliezar … servant to Abraham
Hagar … servant to Sarah
Isaac … son of Sarah and Abraham
Ishmael … son of Hagar and Abraham

Fictional Characters

Binah … mother of Sarai
Eliana … companion to Sarai
Moriya … leader of women in Ur
Jessica … healer in Ur
Reuben … servant to Lot, husband of Eliana
Pharaoh … ruler in Egypt
Rivkah … slave of Sarah

Questions

1. From what you may know about Sarah in the book of Genesis, how would you describe her?
2. How would you describe her as told in *A Circle of Stones*?
3. How does Sarah deal with the different understandings of El Shaddai?
4. Consider the different attitudes toward a woman's body in that society and the world of the women who gather in the house of women.
5. Are there influences of this difference still affecting relationships today?
6. Is it possible for modern women to identify with the reality of being childless that existed in Sarah's world?
7. Talk about the relationship of Hagar and Sarah.
8. What were the agents of change in Sarah's life?
9. How would you describe Abraham in this story?
10. Speak to the challenges and struggles that faced Sarah in her relationship with Abraham.
11. Do you keep mementoes or markers for the times of change in your life?
12. Is there any space in your spiritual journey for a feminine understanding of the mystery we call God?

Acknowledgements

There are many who made this book possible.

To the women who read the first draft and shared their responses: Bessie, Jackie, Kathryn, and Lois. Thank you for your support.

To my daughter's, Deb and Kathy whose encouragement kept me going when I was ready to give up.

To the readers who read the nearly finished book: Larry Pat, Shelley, and Stacey. My thanks for your comments and affirmations.

And to my editor, Gloria Nye for your wisdom and patience, skill and knowledge. I am grateful beyond words..

About the Author

Betty Turcott is a teacher, workshop leader, and story teller. She has studied the history of women throughout the ages, including formal recorded history, as well as stories passed on from woman to woman, and letters and poetry written by women.

Widely travelled, she treasures the memories from women of varied ages from many countries and diverse backgrounds.

Stories of the women of the Biblical era have been a passion since Betty's youth. Her vivid imagination enables her to tell their stories in a way that brings the ancient journeys to life for the modern reader.

Sara's story, told in *A circle of Stones,* is the first in this new Series, *Woman From the Bible*. Watch for Rebekah's coming next.

Manufactured by Amazon.ca
Bolton, ON

21769248R00171